White Collar Slavery

White Collar Slavery

Based on a Bit of Truth and a Few White Lies

LAURANCE RASSIN

TRACY MEMOLI

iUniverse

White Collar Slavery
Based on a Bit of Truth and a Few White Lies

Copyright © 2014, 2015 by Laurance Rassin, Tracy Memoli.

All rights reserved. No part of this book may be used or reproduced by any means, graphic, electronic, or mechanical, including photocopying, recording, taping or by any information storage retrieval system without the written permission of the publisher except in the case of brief quotations embodied in critical articles and reviews.

This is a work of fiction. All of the characters, names, incidents, organizations, and dialogue in this novel are either the products of the author's imagination or are used fictitiously.

iUniverse books may be ordered through booksellers or by contacting:

iUniverse
1663 Liberty Drive
Bloomington, IN 47403
www.iuniverse.com
1-800-Authors (1-800-288-4677)

Because of the dynamic nature of the Internet, any web addresses or links contained in this book may have changed since publication and may no longer be valid. The views expressed in this work are solely those of the author and do not necessarily reflect the views of the publisher, and the publisher hereby disclaims any responsibility for them.

Any people depicted in stock imagery provided by Thinkstock are models, and such images are being used for illustrative purposes only.
Certain stock imagery © Thinkstock.

ISBN: 978-1-4917-0047-1 (sc)
ISBN: 978-1-4917-0048-8 (hc)
ISBN: 978-1-4917-0049-5 (e)

Library of Congress Control Number: 2013913631

Printed in the United States of America

iUniverse rev. date: 12/29/2014

CONTENTS

Visiting Hours 1
Whistle-Blown 12
Barnes & IgNoble 27
Dante's Hatchery 37
Dilettante Interrupted 45
Millionaire Matchup 63
Purple Raincoat and a Pink Thong 70
Don't or Da Silvano 76
Occupy "Maul" Street 87
Velveteen Meltdown 94
Paranormal Paranoia 111
Assorted Nuts 133
Do Not Pass Go 165
The Fantastic Voyage 191
Two Months Later 212

Visiting Hours

"Square Jane, you wanna li'l action on this? It's from Colorado," whispered Zeela Matta, a zaftig Haitian woman in her early forties. Her kind eyes and soft smile exuded an air of confidence and congeniality.

"*Ki sa se bon, pomee-sha,*" Zeela continued in her thick accent, extending her arm and offering a half-smoked joint to Lulu Norris.

"No thanks, I just had some Thai stick with my Chinese buffet," Lulu muttered sarcastically, green eyes sparkling despite her depressive tone.

"Oh, Square Jane, you gettin' funny," Zeela mused on in her broken Haitian Creole accent.

"In here, anything sounds funny," Lulu said as she looked past the cold concrete walls of what she dubbed the "Grey Bar Hotel."

Lulu was longing to get back to her seemingly normal life. She was beginning to lose all faith in her mouthpiece, who had sworn six ways to Sunday on his gray crocodile Armani attaché that he would waltz through the door at exactly the right moment and save her ass. Lulu, wearing a neon-tangerine cotton jumper, certainly didn't miss the mornings and the hours spent obsessing over which respectable suit to wear. The orange jumpsuit played against Lulu's long, thick, auburn hair and fair complexion as she sat in the elevated salon chair.

"You ain't a fish no mo', but you definitely still fresh meat in here; ain't she *sha?*" Zeela asked, eyeing Lulu up and down, holding a pair of pink and silver thinning shears in her large right hand and the joint in the other, motioning for Lulu to grab it.

Zeela had a comfortable and carefree manner about herself. In the short amount of time Lulu had known her, she had grown to admire and respect Zeela's honest ways.

Sharing memories of her family back home in Haiti, Zeela's stories always began with family gathered around a pot of vegetable stew, or *legim*, how Zeela referred to it, and always ended with someone having too much sugarcane spiced rum to drink. Then there were the devastatingly sad stories of the earthquake that had destroyed everything save for the clothes on her family's backs. Zeela would tell these stories a lot, because deep down she still felt a sense of remorse that at the time of the earthquake she wasn't by her family's side. Instead, she was vacationing in New Orleans with her cousin. It was her first time in the United States and a trip she had planned for what seemed like a lifetime. Zeela had never felt so far away and helpless.

And it was on that trip that Zeela had met an oh-so-charming Haitian man who, unbeknownst to her, was in trouble with the law, and had stashed an obscene amount of cocaine in her hotel room. When the cops finally found him there, they arrested both Zeela and her new love.

The past five years had been tortuous for Zeela in the Grey Bar, unable to be there for her loved ones in the critical rebuilding of their decimated homes and neighborhoods of Port-au-Prince.

Zeela's smooth, ebony skin glowed against the fluorescent lights that were hung cockeyed throughout the makeshift salon. Her hair, loosely gathered in a bun at the nape of her neck, was held together only by a pencil.

"With all your book fans you need your own talk show, apparently," said Ingrid Kokono, sporting a freshly cut, ruby red bob and speaking in a wiser-than-thou, broken Russian accent.

Ingrid was known as the *Kapayna*, Russian for *commander*, a moniker she was quite fond of ever since she was brought to the facility in the early nineties.

In her former life, Ingrid had been involved in one of the largest white-collar cases in Wall Street history. She easily might have been a breakout Internet mogul along the lines of Meg Whitman from eBay if it hadn't been for her greed and the mystique of illegal activities that drew her toward a life of crime.

Ingrid found solace in the underground world through her interconnected web of Muscovite nightclub contacts. It wasn't until after she earned her degree from a university in St. Petersburg that she turned to a life of automated crime. She eventually turned herself in out of fear of a KGB reprisal, and had been running the salon efficiently ever since.

Davio Spinoza burst through the heavy aluminum double doors. Looking like he came out of an audition for *Glee*, he was decked out in a preppy argyle sweater with a purple collared shirt underneath, neatly tucked into his khaki pants. Davio was Lulu's hired gun and longtime gal pal.

"Girl, we gonna get you out of here. There is a sample sale at Barney's next week," he sang, plopping down on the salon chair next to Lulu and slowly opening his infamous Armani attaché. "We are getting you out of here this week."

"I'll settle for my thirtieth birthday," joked Lulu.

"They didn't tell me two," Ingrid interrupted, addressing Davio. "Princess, are we cutting your hair also?"

"No thanks, honey, I gave at the office," Davio chirped.

"Lulu, your hair look like auburn waterfall. We should cut for Locks of Love," Ingrid demanded in her Russian rapid-fire.

"Yeah, just give me a Miley Cyrus, cut it all off," said Lulu. "Girlfriend, have you lost your fucking mind?" shrieked Davio, snapping a tiny pair of pinking shears in Lulu's direction.

"Clearly. I'm locked up, with no end to this nightmare in sight," said Lulu, as she turned toward Zeela.

"Girl, I know this ain't what you're used to; this gonna take a while. I got a seventy-two Conair, 850 watts, but more than half of them don't work, so we workin' wit' 410 watts of mystifying, stupefying, hair-drying love," mused Zeela.

If Zeela had one thing, it was a sense of humor, a trait that Lulu truly adored. In her book, anyone that could make her laugh under such duress deserved her respect and equally earned her trust.

Humming a Zydeco tune, Zeela began cutting a four-inch swath off of Lulu's soft curls. "Your book fans are going to set you free, Square Jane. They love your pretty, little white ass."

"No. No. I am going to get you out of here," exclaimed Davio, pushing back his gingersnap red highlights.

"I've heard that before," Lulu replied.

"Mm-hmm, ain't that the truth," Zeela chimed in.

"I may not be the best lawyer in town, but I certainly sleep with the best. And I have something that will settle the score, wherever that bitch is hiding."

* * *

"If you don't mind me saying, you seem a little too egotistical to kill yourself, lady," said the paramedic, Jimmy, as he monitored his patient from inside the crowded ambulance.

"You would think," Lizette Hansen muttered under her breath. Her mousy brown coif had seen better days, but in her own subjective opinion, she thought she looked pretty damn good for a post-menopausal, fifty-six-year-old woman who had just been twisting in the wind over the East River. After all, she was Lizette "Screwzette" Hansen, the epicenter of spin, and somehow she would fix this mess.

"I mean, twenty freakin' minutes ago, you offered me a gold watch to leave ya dangling off the side of the Queensboro," said Jimmy, his thick Brooklyn accent making it hard to understand him.

"It's a diamond-encrusted Cartier tank, you provincial fuck! You should have left me there. It's worth more than your whole year's salary."

"Ma'am, I don't do this for the money,"he replied. "C-clearly," shot Lizette, choking on her own ego.

"I'd drop you off right here on Third Avenue, right in front of this fucking Korean deli, but I am bound by certain moral codes and obligations,"he continued.

"Fuck the moral codes; are you gonna take me to Lennox Hill or not? I don't think you know who I am," Lizette impatiently blasted. "You'll know who I am when you read tomorrow's paper! You dickless dolt!"

"I know who you are," Jimmy replied. "You're the lady that was dangling wit' a nosebleed, like a fucking Magic Tree air freshener that I just rescued off the Fifty-Ninth Street Bridge. And if it weren't for your bloody jacket, you would have fallen to your certain death."

"That'll teach me to buy hand-sewn clothes," retorted Lizette. "Yeah, next time buy some cheap Chinese shit, it would have split right in half," said Jimmy. "I suggest you grow up today, lady."

"Got any ideas? Who should I call, handsome?"

Clad in a tattered khaki Burberry trench coat and reeking of booze and children's Benadryl, Lizette Hansen was not the picture-perfect corporate commander of one of the most powerful public relations firms on the planet. No, rather the thought of her looking like a Magic Tree swinging from the Fifty-Ninth Street Bridge above the hordes of onlookers, journalists, and news crews taunting her to jump was more than she could handle, and she began welling up with tears. Her pale Irish complexion was flushed with fear, not for almost plunging to her certain death, but for the ignominious reprisal that was occurring daily in the media about the fall of Kline Allen & Robbins Public Relations. She needed more than a raincoat. In fact, she needed to wear her Chanel leisure suit in court to look calm and collected.

* * *

Lulu's stint in jail began to feel more like *Brokedown Palace* than *The Shawshank Redemption*. Surprisingly, her sleep had improved, and her apnea had nearly vanished.

Lulu had a rare gift to be able to drown out sounds. Unfortunately, this gift couldn't make her any money, but it gave her solitude, particularly valuable over the past few months. It seemed as if she had been training her whole life for this jail sentence. Without that gift, she surely would have gone mad within the first twenty-four hours with all the "cell soldiers" screaming at their hired guns.

It was high noon in the yard. The scores of women were going about their daily routine on the compound, exercising their version of nation building between the different factions of roving gangs that ran the yard of the Metropolitan Detention Center. The yard looked the same as the ones Lulu saw in the movies. It was made up of dirt, with two basketball hoops at either end.

"Get your butcher's hook into this, Square Jane," said a gaunt-looking young Latina wearing curlers covered over by a yellow cotton kerchief, waving a copy of the latest *New York Post*. Missy Alvarez was Lulu's cellmate and confidant. As far as Lulu could tell, Missy was yet another decent girl who got caught up with a bad guy, getting into some trouble with an abusive boyfriend after college. What started as a petty campus scam running credit cards turned into a global identity theft ring, leaving Missy with a ten-year stint in the Metropolitan Detention Center, located near Gowanus Bay on Twenty-Ninth Street between Second and Third Avenue in Brooklyn. It housed close to three thousand inmates on a busy day. Reviews of the facility varied, but a top liberal blog claimed the facility to be "a decent room with no view."

Missy smoothly palmed off the *New York Post* to Lulu, who snapped open the folded newspaper to find the salacious headline:

"Leap of Fate: Ex-KAR Exec Hangs by Thread"

"Your nemesis made the front page! No tellin' how much longer you're gonna be in here for," Missy interrupted, as Lulu read on carefully.

> The alleged architect behind the white collar crimes involving one of the largest, most powerful public relations firms, now being investigated by the SEC, attempted suicide last night atop the Queensboro Bridge.
>
> KAR PR executive Lizette Hansen was found hanging by a thread from the Fifty-Ninth Street Bridge around 10 pm last night in a failed attempt to drown out the public scorn surrounding her impending court case.
>
> "At first, I thought it was just an adventurer. Then as I got closer, I realized it was a high concentration of craziness," said Jimmy Sullivan, the EMT who found Ms. Hansen. "She reeked of booze and cigarettes and was hysterical after I saved her life."
>
> Once one of the most respected and successful PR firms in the US, KAR PR is now embroiled in a lawsuit and smear campaign that has brought down some of the firm's top clients, and their stock prices, and has decimated the firm's reputation.
>
> In recent months, the firm, a target of a series of SEC investigations focusing on allegations of criminal activities and corporate wrongdoing against their employees, clients, and national news media. Suspected to be initiated by a

competitor or whistle-blower employee, the firm has been under close surveillance by New York's Attorney General by order of Mayor Michael Bloomberg.

Lulu Norris, a former vice president of KAR PR, remains detained at the Metropolitan Detention Center. Her novel is due out next week, while Ms. Hansen has been released on bail.

"Oh, Miss Mo is comin' for you now," Missy sang.

As the burly female guard approached Missy and Lulu, Miss Mo said, "Lulu, your not-so-gentleman caller has arrived."

Lulu was escorted to a visitor's booth in the main building of the detention facility where Davio was waiting for her across the thick, bulletproof glass. It resembled a giant bank teller's window, except with a chartreuse-colored phone receiver on either side of the window that was drenched in sweat and whatever other petri dish of misanthropic germs one could muster to imagine.

Before Lulu could take a seat, Davio pulled out a copy of the *New York Post* and plastered it flush against the glass window, motioning for Lulu to pick up the phone receiver.

"Girlfriend, this will all be over soon. In the meantime . . ." He held up a small paperback titled *Prison Slang for Dummies*.

"Fuck off. Where are we with the senator?" Lulu questioned, growing impatient.

"Well, you'll be happy to know that we are going on a cruise this weekend to the Bahamas," Davio replied. "And honey, if it doesn't work out with him, it's going to be raining men on the lido deck."

"Listen, Julie McCoy, you better not fuck this up. I have to get out of here. My book signing is next week. That bitch is a mess. She even fucked up killing herself," said Lulu, hastily slamming down the receiver.

* * *

On Manhattan's Upper East Side, Lenox Hill is a five-star, six-hundred-bed hospital and one of the most prestigious facilities in New York.

Choking on her own ego and catatonically staring out of the hospital window, looking past the blossoming dogwoods that perfectly lined Seventy-Seventh Street, a forlorn Lizette fumbled for the nurse call box that was intertwined with her IV drip.

"Yes?"

"What's taking so long? I should have been discharged hours ago. I am not staying here overnight!" Lizette screamed into the receiver, her mouth moving sideways like an evil cartoon crab.

"Please, Ms. Hansen, like I told you ten minutes ago, the doctor is on his way in to see you." The nurse replied

"I don't need a doctor, I need to see the fucking hospital administrator in my room, now!"

Lizette threw the call box across the room, only to find it had a longer cord than she thought. She nearly hit Marni Zhuk as she opened the door, carrying enough copies of the *New York Post* to choke a news kiosk.

Marni, a first generation Romanian immigrant, spoke textbook English and kept Lizette out of hot water with the firm's partners, and in their minds, out of jail. Until now.

Marni was one of KAR's "well-meaners." Her long, jet-black hair fell gently against her milky white visage. Still, Marni's English was a bit too perfect and Lulu thought perhaps she was a spy for another PR firm, or at least the Cartoon Network. The way Marni interrogated people reminded her of Natasha in the *Rocky and Bullwinkle Show*.

As Marni slowly glanced around the room, resentment bubbled within her. She stared at Lizette, who looked less like she tried to commit suicide six hours ago and more like she had just euthanized her childhood puppy.

Lizette was an evil person at heart; cruelty is the Devil's own trademark.

She knew how to treat people nicely to get what she wanted. Marni, like the guy that lived with the family of bears, feared the reality that eating with them and grooming with them would in the end lead to her becoming breakfast for them. One day Lizette, the bear that she once had a respectful fondness for, might turn on her, claws bared, ready to tear her torso to sheds.

"At least your room is nice, really nice," Marni awkwardly stuttered. "Um, I hate to ask, but are you gonna do any of these interviews?" She busied herself stacking the newspapers neatly in the corner of the room by the love seat.

"Geraldo's people showed up at the office this morning. They really want to talk to you," Marni continued. "They spoke to Kline . . ."

"F-u-u-c-k Kline. Fuck Geraldo. Fuck the *Post*. Fuck them all—no, make that fuck this hospital!" Lizette screamed as she pulled out a copy of the *New York Post* and flung it against the TV, knocking over her breakfast tray and spilling its contents onto the floor.

"I want the hospital administrator now or this is going to get ugly," Lizette barked into the nurse call box that Marni had neurotically picked up and neatly tucked back into Lizette's bed.

"Fuck the firm. They're the ones that got us into this situation!" Lizette adjusted herself in bed, turning toward Marni.

"I'm worried I'm going to lose my house," muttered Marni.

"Your house? Your fucking house? I was almost fucking Pepperidge Farm goldfish food and you're worried about your house? You need to pull yourself together."

"I can't keep doing this," exclaimed Marni.

"We are telling everyone absolutely nothing! Do you hear me?" Lizette's eyes suddenly widened and she sheepishly smiled, straightening her hair, "So, do you think I should do Geraldo? Was that cute producer asking for me?"

"He wasn't there," replied Marni. "Fuck Geraldo," Lizette snapped.

Marni had witnessed a ton of erratic, insane, illegal, and even paranormal behavior from Lizette over the past decade, but these past few days took the cake.

"I gave the medic five hundred dollars, a Tiffany tennis bracelet, and a bottle of Percocet," said Lizette.

"Wait a minute. Putting aside the cash and diamonds and the fact that you were gonna leave your only son without a mother . . ." Marni trailed off, more confused than ever. For the first time in over three years, tiny, fine wrinkles started to appear on Marni's pale forehead. After all, she'd been seeing Dr. Lunawich religiously every three months, ever since Lizette gifted her an exclusive membership to his office for her twenty-sixth birthday.

"You mean to tell me he actually took the bloody bottle of Percocet to bring you . . ." Marni continued.

"Damn right. I wasn't gonna have him take me to Bellevue. Those sharks have enough chum on this story with that whistle-blowing bitch's book coming out next week. I hope that 'C U Next Tuesday' rots in jail. We were all culpable. Do you hear me? And besides, he needed them. He said something about Obamacare and budget cuts…"

Whistle-Blown

It was an unusually blustery day in April. Lulu remembered it well, as she waited for her arraignment. The afternoon sun broke through the cloudy expanse that lingered over the jail yard.

Since being courted by numerous publishers nearly a year ago about her days at KAR PR, Lulu had waited with anticipation — undergoing a federal investigation and exposing the wrongdoings orchestrated by Sergeant Screwzette and her minions. None of this mess was at Lulu's behest. However, she was the one taking the fall.

Lulu's book signing at Barnes & Noble in Union Square would be her new beginning. Like all great thinkers, her day would not come easy. Struggle was the watchword, along with the worse-tasting film in her mouth left by the Queen Bitch — worse than any bite, worse than any jilted heart, for it was of the betrayal from her beloved mentor.

In the yard, Zeela and Missy were arguing over the last cancer stick; a small group of ladies were playing a game of horse, gambling for Parliaments, Marlboros, and joints. Several others were divided in pairs, parked at picnic tables playing gin rummy. Lulu sat listlessly on a rusty steel bench, graffiti scrawled into its metal presumably with a yard shank, slang words such as *Agani* and *Elephant*, decoded only by the gangs who ran the guard and the yard. As Lulu slowly surveyed the grounds, reflecting on the fiasco that led her to Club Fed, her eyes began to well up with tears, but not for the fact that she was locked up and surrounded by dangerous criminals. She found solace in the confinement and in the women whom she had met that seemed to possess more honesty than a lot of the women she knew on the outside with designer bags and bad BOTOX jobs to match. She chuckled to herself as she dried her eyes, realizing there was literal meaning in the sayings "There is honor among thieves" and "Prison food really sucks ass."

* * *

Lizette's office had been a ghastly nightmare of epic proportions. On any given Friday it could very well resemble a low-budget horror film: PowerPoint pitch presentations, press releases, and quarterly reports strewn around the room in a vortex of corporate sorcery.

It was so rare for Lizette to come into the office that Lulu had a sneaking suspicion something had gone awry. Being there simply interfered and usually slowed Lizette down. She believed she was more effective conducting business basically anywhere else than in that office. Lucky for Lizette, most clients were peppered around the globe, which meant meetings took place virtually anywhere. Taxi cabs. Saks. Barneys. Jimmy Choo. Frédéric Fekkai. And Lizette's absolute favorite, over a few bottles of white wine at whatever restaurant she read about on Page Six that week.

But for appearances, when Lizette first started with the firm, she hired the most celebrated interior designer in Manhattan: designer to the stars Cici LaRoche. Lizette once said, "If she's good enough for Gwyneth, she's good enough for me." So one weekend Cici went to work, transforming her office into a tranquil sanctuary. It was ironic Lizette didn't spend more time in it. The walls were painted a deep blue, which Cici said, "Promotes productivity and curbs appetite." That didn't change the fact that Lizette hated it, and that it did not live up to Cici's promise to curb her appetite.

Lulu could still hear Cici explaining, as if her life depended on it (and it did), "It's a proven fact that people are more productive in blue-colored rooms. And study after study shows . . ." as she was escorted out of the double doors of KAR PR.

Lizette's office could go from HGTV to a toxic dump all in the matter of a few minutes.

Marni and Lizette were wrapping up yet another crisis within the confines of the blue sanctuary. Lulu waited patiently as she listened to the conference call that sounded more and more like a geek team devising a liftoff plan at NASA. As she gazed out of the narrow double windows that overlooked Sixth Avenue, she noticed a sea of yellow taxicabs. The tiny yellow specks stood still. Lulu couldn't hear the symphony of horns honking; the office was too high up. But she knew it was there. It was a sound she fell in love with when she had visited Manhattan for the first time as a little girl. But now the sound hurt her eardrums and just left her feeling anxious, like she'd had one too many cups of coffee.

"Just make sure you deliver this before 5:00 p.m. today, so that blogger has what he needs," demanded Lizette as she handed Lulu a nondescript manila envelope, as Marni sat by and swore her witness.

"Got it," replied Lulu as she took the envelope and headed back to her office.

Lizette, zoomed out on a self-prescribed dirty cocktail of Adderall, children's Benadryl, and Xanax and had spent the previous night in full-blown psycho-soccer-mom-mode, concocting the elaborate plan she dubbed "Operation Blue April."

As Lulu left the office to meet Theo Zirko, Lizette tossed over her coveted Burberry raincoat, as if to say, "Someone out there is watching over you." The raincoat was a true talisman, a gift from her St. Stephen, which would ironically later save her life on the ledge of the Fifty-Ninth Street Bridge.

Theo was a young, hotshot Turk trader turned quasi journalist who spent his post-college years making millions in the European market with his predictions on ZipStreet.com, the blog he created out of his college dorm while attending the London School of Economics. Theo was known for his irascible, outspoken spin on the markets and had a chummy reoccurring spot on one of the top EU business networks, which would later give way to his Gordon Gecko–like greed.

Looking too much like his Greek countrymen Telly Savalas than he cared to, Theo's shaved head, piercing green eyes, and Cheshire grin made him a smooth television favorite. Lulu had never met him; she only recognized him from his bio on ZipStreet.com. Dressed in a gray Marc Jacobs trench coat and black leather Cole Haan shoes, Theo stood impatiently on the corner of Forty-Forth Street and Fifth

Avenue, talking on his cell phone. It drove Lulu nuts that he held a tilted umbrella, allowing half of his body to get drenched. Sure, everyone she passed by on the street gave her dirty looks and made snide comments for carrying an obnoxious Fairway umbrella, but it played the perfect cover, shrouding her face from passersby, and from anyone else who might be on the make. She had a gut feeling that something was amiss. For Lizette never loaned her clothes to anyone, let alone her post-menopausal, provocative, prized possession: her Burberry raincoat. The way Lizette haphazardly tossed the trench coat led Lulu to believe something was rotten in Denmark. She couldn't quite put her finger on it. It was just the way Lizette averted her eyes when tasking her with this delivery to Zirko. It bothered her that this might be yet another attempt by Lizette to unwittingly bring her into some caper that she was not privy to. KAR PR was not for the faint of heart.

"Hey, my three-wood broke; could I borrow yours?" Theo snidely remarked. "You're Lulu, right?"

His face in plain sight, never lifting her umbrella to meet his shark eyes, Lulu nervously replied, "I don't loan my clubs, but you could play through."

Lulu had no clear idea about the true meaning of her retort. She despised golf and especially loathed watching it on TV. There was nothing more utterly insipid to her than watching a white dimpled ball flying through the wind. She had heard enough golf innuendoes over the years from the firm's partner Kline, ad nauseam on conference calls to one marshmallow headed client or another, saying things like "Do you mind if we play through?" or "Let me hold the flag for you here, bud." One thing was certain: something stunk here, she felt it. Every waking hour, Lulu and Marni were given do-or-die tasks, proffered up by the lizard's lair in the form of an encrypted e-mail, or worse, face-to-face fire-breathing assignments. Screwzette would grab their attention with a toxic combination of children's Benadryl, sauvignon blanc, and Nabisco Snackwells wafting from her breath, jamming the tasks down their throats, always giving them the *malocchio*, the evil eye.

Lulu discreetly palmed Zirko the envelope under the dry side of his cockeyed umbrella. She quickly scurried off, never looking back, as if she were fleeing the town of Sodom, and quickly shot off a text to the lizard: *Done.*

Making her way into the office the next morning, after a predawn personal errand for Screwzette to acquire nude-colored Spanx and codeine, Lulu made a beeline from the N train that let her out at Fiftieth Street and Seventh Avenue.

She quickened her step as she headed east on Fiftieth Street, passing the hordes of street vendors that were out and ready for the flocks of tourists. Lulu could smell the sweet roasted cashews as her heart began to race. She had a strange feeling in the pit of her stomach. It was a familiar feeling she would often get or think she would get when something was off. That morning, her feeling directed her toward the ticker on the FOX News building. As she squinted her eyes from across the street, she could see the news tick through the crimson glare of the morning sun, scrolling across with the headline: "NASDAQ down more than 600 points."

"Fuck," Lulu muttered under her breath. The market had only been open for nine minutes. She had an eerie hunch that she'd had a hand in this.

These premonitions would float in and out of Lulu's consciousness faster than an insomniac flipping through late-night cable. It was not clear when these feelings would occur, or how, but they would arrive in perfect sets of southeasterly swells crashing into the sand. The sand was her psyche, one hunch leading to another. She would painstakingly look for signs that would point toward answers, sometimes inventing them to thread the tangents and create a framework with which to hang and display these hunches on.

Growing up halfway between the Magic Kingdom and Cassadaga, the "psychic capital of the world," forged an idyllic spiritual childhood that perpetuated her self-proclaimed clairvoyance; she considered herself, among other things, a seer of spiritualism.

White Collar Slavery

Lulu was a textbook Gemini. She was cursed with the constant inner struggle, moody feelings, and fits of indecisiveness that incessantly plagued her professional life, personal shopping habits, and regifting prowess. She never knew what to buy, wear, give, or regive. It was this odd duality, coupled with heated, opinionated mantras, which in her mind formed the empirical absolute to any situation that she weighed in on. Lulu had stronger-than-thou opinions on most matters and waxed on about them, often overconfident that she knew the tact to take on any subject, which propelled her into the position of vice president before the age of twenty-seven. Being so cocksure yet so indecisive at the same time played on her corporate psyche.

She got these feelings mainly when she found herself stuck smack dab in the middle between passion and apathy. Unfortunately for her, she was never able to capitalize on her hunches monetarily in the form of gambling or the stock market. Like any true New Yorker, she relegated her feelings to heated emotion and self-preservation.

Littered across the conference room table on the forty-seventh floor, hordes of news clippings pulled for Client #10 nearly covered the antique mahogany table. As Lizette, in a panic-driven crisis mode over Grangeway Trucking's possible bankruptcy, glanced out the office window overlooking Rockefeller Center, she noticed a set of unseasonable storm clouds moving in from the east. Dulcet gray tones slowly enveloped the amber rays of the midmorning's warm sun. In an apologetic tone, Lizette attempted to backpedal her way through the morning headlines, with a litany of excuses, reassuring Roger Sloane, the company's CEO, that she would immediately demand a retraction. More importantly, Lizette would make sure the rogue reporter was deported, and assured Mr. Sloane that Martinez's next story would surely be penned from a South American prison.

Lulu burst into the front part of the conference room. "I went to four Duane Reades and could find only two bottles," Lulu said as she emptied out the contents of the white plastic bag onto the table.

"What the fuck?" Screwzette blasted. "I have an important fucking conference call in fifteen minutes. Next time, I'm sending Sasha to New Jersey; she'll get it done."

Screwzette clearly prescribed to the Leona Helmsley/Tony Montana way of doing things. Ruling with an iron fist and a verbal machine gun, her rapid-fire New York, holier-than-thou, bitch attitude enabled her to rise to the top of the flack game as executive vice president of one of the most respected and powerful public relations firms in the world.

"Don't fucking lay this on Marni. This story in the *Wall Street Journal* has your name all over it! You really fucked this thing up. How did the release go out like that? This stunt is really gonna help you in your review next week. I will make sure the partners hear about this."

Marni barged through the frosted glass door of the conference room dressed in a Ralph Lauren Parisian sailor suit, circa 1998, that was buttoned way too tight around her gut, making her look more like an ultramarine lava lamp than a savvy dresser.

"You pulled me off of it and gave it to Sasha," declared Lulu.

"I remember telling you to make sure the release went out correctly," Screwzette continued. "It was fucking crucial!"

"Last Tuesday you told me to concentrate on that other thing for Client #9, so I'm not even sure what you're talking about."

"W-h-h-a-a-a-a-t? Are you serious?" Screwzette shrieked as she grabbed the tiny bottle of cough syrup, and took an assembly line of swigs, downing the soothing, cherry-flavored children's elixir until the bottle was nearly empty.

"I don't have this kind of time; I have to get on this conference call," Screwzette began dialing, hitting the speakerphone button.

"Stock market's down over six hundred points, hope that's not related to Zirko," Lulu muttered under her breath but loud enough for Screwzette and Marni to hear.

Fuming over yet another bullshit fire due to Screwzette's gross corporate incompetence, Lulu marched back to her desk and began rummaging through her office, a futile exercise that she would submit to weekly in a "take this job and shove it up your Pucci fat ass."

First she would begin by saving her client files and her extensive contact list of journalists, editors, producers, and VIP clients, stealthily downloading them to a flash drive, as if she were part of some crack counterterrorism unit. Next, she would throw away everything and anything that wasn't nailed down, tossing files and gathering up her things as if it were her last holy hour at KAR PR. This cathartic ritual, despite being in vain, served to quell her nerves. But with the Dow dropping well over six hundred points, she felt that day might come sooner rather than later, because she had a hunch that Screwzette and wunderkind Zirko were behind this.

Come Friday, Lulu's anxieties had come to a head, as IJM, a direct competitor to Grangeway Trucking, dominated the headlines: "IJM Transport Trades Off in Huge Volumes." Lulu's fear was substantiated when IJM's stock price lost more than seventy percent of its value in three days, adding to the empirical evidence she had found: an annual report linking Zirko's consulting firm to IJM Transport. Screwzette had undoubtedly forced Lulu's hand, making her a pawn in this stock Ponzi.

Lulu waited for a weak moment in the conversation, pursuant to some idle chitchat about Screwzette's affair with Stephen "Raincoat" Walker and his fondness for Le Cirque. She attempted to interrupt, but before she could get a word in, she knew what was coming—a diversionary tactic in the form of some pathetic designer trinket, clearly regifted.

Right on cue, Lizette pulled out from under her glossy west elm walnut desk a rather large Henri Bendel signature brown-and-white-striped bag. Over the years, Lulu had received a number of "slush items." However, this was the biggest swag to date. Usually gifted was the cheaper-than-thou costume jewelry or the occasional ill-fitting second-hand dress that either couldn't be returned or wouldn't fit over Lizette's supersized thighs anymore.

Lulu's heart sank all the way down to her Sam Edelmans as she realized she had been majorly duped. In that split second, her whole career at KAR PR flashed before her eyes. Hired as an entry-level well-meaner account executive, now seven years later she had been used in a Ponzi scheme of disinformation. Whatever she handed off to Zirko that day in the rain must have conveyed contorted credence to someone somewhere; this misguided information could have very well been the catalyst to collapse the already fragile market in a complete economic downturn, due to the failed policies of the last several administrations.

Urging Lulu to open the present, Lizette untied the loose, brown, monogrammed Bendel ribbon and revealed an anticlimactic, coal black, nylon Burberry satchel.

Lulu thought to herself that this bitch had some New Jersey trailer-park nerve, sending her down the East River with a fucking free gift with purchase.

I mean, kiss me off with a leather Louis Vuitton or at least a Marc Jacobs, so I have something to look forward to, Lulu thought to herself, staring at Lizette, who appeared to be nothing more than a striking Komodo dragon.

Remembering yet another one of Kline's southern ole boy sayings, "You can catch more flies with sugar than shit," she decided to graciously accept the bag as if it were the holy chalice of handbags and come at Lizette from a different way—in a whistle-blown way.

* * *

Across town and later that evening, at the trendy La Piscine on the rooftop of the Hotel Americano in Chelsea, Lulu, poolside, surrounded by chic cabanas and cozy daybeds divulged every ugly detail of the Zirko situation to Lars, her compassionate, artistic boyfriend.

Lars fancied himself as the next great American expressionist, but couldn't exactly figure out how to get there fast enough. His motto was: "I intend to live forever; so far so good," and even found an obnoxious T-shirt to say so. Lars' auburn curls offset his big brown eyes and captivating smile. His inexhaustible energy always left Lulu feeling motivated and inspired. What she loved and admired most about Lars was his honesty.

"How exactly does this Burberry bag mean that we're in a fuckload of trouble?" Lars asked, looking confused.

"*We're* not—*I* am," replied Lulu.

"Lulu dear, if you're in trouble, I'm in trouble," Lars lovingly maintained. Lars was a good guy—an eccentric, New York artisan who adored Lulu and his work so much that he rarely left his live/work loft, where the two had been living together for the past six months, along with their Havanese puppy Kingsley.

"You don't understand," Lulu replied as she motioned to the waitron, a dead ringer for k.d. lang to bring over another dirty martini. "Look, a reporter we know may or may not have made a trade based on some information I gave him. I have a feeling . . ."

"Calm down," Lars interrupted. "The last feeling you were sure of was that the CIA was behind the valuation of the yen, which I don't actually doubt, considering it now. But baby, you gotta stop. I can't take much more of this. Your job is driving me crazy."

"You? What about me?"

"You're getting paid for it. I'm subjected to this because I love you, but c'mon, this is too much," Lars said, growing slightly impatient over yet another ridiculously twisted story as he chomped on baguette and sipped his green tea.

"And that's what collapsed the market this week," Lulu continued as she took a bite of her tuna tartare.

"That's ridiculous; that didn't happen. Baby, I don't think you need another drink," said Lars.

"That's why I need another drink," replied Lulu. "I think I need to go to the police."

"Police? That doesn't sound like something that is going to be exactly good for either one of us. Maybe you need to take acting classes . . . at Bellevue," Lars muttered.

"Fuck you," replied Lulu. "I'm going to call Chloe. She'll listen to me."

"She's a freelance ne'er-do-well aerobics instructor who lives in Arizona. They're not even in a legitimate time zone," Lars said. "I'm telling you . . . let it go."

Lars was constantly at odds with Lulu, challenging her hunches. He was every bit of a Sagittarius, complete with narcissistic tendencies coupled with a messiah complex. But he cared for Lulu deeply and tried to indulge her fits of quirky cosmopolitanism, despite feeling most of it was a Greek lady with black stockings strung by a rubber band reading tea leaves kind of thing. It concerned him greatly that she would occupy her time with these social conspiracy theories.

Walking north on Tenth Avenue, the two strolled arm in arm, passing by a few galleries on their way home. It was a pathetic display of artistic expression, according to Lars, who was always miffed over the work that made it into the marquee galleries. The West Chelsea art district was an odd sandbox made up of club goers, hipsters, and creative executives that went full tilt 24-7. With the recent gentrification of the High Line, West Chelsea was buzzing as the "it" neighborhood in New York.

"It's such a nice night, why don't we walk on the High Line and get your mind off of this Burberry-induced nightmare," Lars said jokingly. "That plaid drives me crazy anyway. I don't blame you for going ballistic," he added as the two ascended the staircase on Twenty-Sixth Street to the elevated park in the sky.

"We're almost home; what is three blocks going to do?" Lulu asked, now irritated over Lars taking her news lightly.

"You need a little assault of the senses, look at how pretty the moon is," continued Lars.

"Okaaay, you're right," Lulu agreed, trying not to be overcome by the sweet scent of the honeysuckle vines.

"Mmmmm," he pulled her closer and passionately kissed her.

She despised it more than anything when Lars dismissed her hunches as little more than *National Enquirer* headlines but went with the moment, for the moon was particularly inviting. As they walked toward their loft on Thirtieth Street, they made their way through the evening crowd mixed with New York families and tourists.

Stuck behind some bridge-and-tunnel kids dressed in ComicCon garb, Lars seriously wondered, "Now, if I were that age, would I really walk around New York wearing that stupid shit? I was never into video games, so probably not."

"You do stupid shit all day long; what's the difference?" questioned Lulu.

"Maybe it's cool, I don't know." "It certainly is expensive."

"Of course you would see it that way." "What way?"

"Monetarily."

"You know I don't like to waste money. Anyway, what was the name of that guy in *The Matrix* that followed Keanu Reeves around, trying to kill him?"

"Uh, Agent Smith?"

"Yeah, well, I think I have one of those. Look back at that guy wearing the gray suit and the skinny black tie . . ."

"Baby, you need help. He's carrying a saxophone; he's probably going to play at Americano. Didn't we see that guy last week at their jazz brunch? C'mon, you've completely lost it."

"Noooo. But I swear I saw him the other morning when I was at Duane Reade getting children's Benadryl."

"Wait, what? I am fucking telling you, I can't take your job anymore."
"Me neither."

"Do something about it. Stop driving me and your mother crazy."

Hands down, Lars was the greatest guy Lulu had ever met. To her, "He was the most handsome man she'd ever seen, dead, alive, or in a coma."

It was love at first sight. She immediately fell for his erotic, neurotic, offbeat behavior and sense of humor when they both attended a friend's Fourth of July party in Southampton five summers ago.

She found his quirky charisma magnetic, and she was instantly drawn to his charming personality and affectionate demeanor. His sense of humor was contagious, and his comedic timing was tolerable. Lars proclaimed he had a FedEx sense of comedic timing: you might not laugh or get the joke right away, but you certainly would crack up the next morning before nine thirty, guaranteed every time. He was a cross between Larry David and Jim Morrison. Under his disheveled hair, paint-stained jeans, and torn cotton T-shirt was a brilliant man-child that Lulu completely adored. They were so similar that they were constantly at odds with each other.

Sure, she knew she could be difficult at times, neurotic, and a bit demanding, but Lars was the only person that could handle her, and in turn Lulu was the only person that could handle Lars' semiadorable, nutty outbursts of his perverted TV jingles like "Love BOTOX . . . we'll be injecting another run. Love BOTOX . . . we'll be plumping everyone."

His Frank Sinatra impersonation got under her skin, but it was his impersonation of Robert Francis "Bobcat" Goldthwait singing Sinatra that really irked her. It was painful to hear, and even more painful to watch. Then there were his incessant chants of fictitious African calls, "*Ya la we a mon a yay,*" "*tu tu naaa yaaa,*" or "*Oooh na yal.*" Or his humming, an obnoxious mix of medleys that he would blurt out in between his show tunes and African chants while painting, sculpting, or meddling in the kitchen while Lulu was preparing basically any meal. Lars' sister Vicky had warned Lulu years ago that he was the most annoying human being on the face of the earth.

Lars had an idea a minute. It was probably due to the fact that he never took Ritalin as a child. He was an insomniac's insomniac, working twenty-plus hours a day, trying, as he dubbed it, to "paint his way to freedom," selling his oil paintings and bronze sculptures to the Palm Beach and New York social set. The vice president of Bonhams & Butterfield auction house in New York observed that his work "continues along the historical lines of fine art painters working in figurative studies in ceramics and bronze set forth in the tradition of artists such as Bouthaud, Raoul Dufy, and Picasso."

Despite all of his shortcomings, Lulu considered him the most passionate and loving man she had ever met and couldn't live without him. His offbeat sense of Woody Allen wannabe humor kept her forever in stitches.

And Lars loved Lulu passionately. Lars was an inventor, a poet, a playwright, a musician, a designer—a complete artist, a true Renaissance man, which comprised clear, definable reasons why she could put up with his asinine antics and his never-ending lineup of assorted New York characters that he would befriend until they proved otherwise. He was a trusting, sometimes *over*trusting soul that always saw the good in people. Like the time when he found $135,000 stuffed in a duffle bag at a sports bar in DC and returned it.

Channeling his Jim Morrison complex, Lars fronted a rock band called Clusterfunk that occasionally would play around town, in a vain attempt to rekindle his youth, from his twenty-something years.

In the late nineties, his ensemble held dominion at the now defunct Club Felix on Eighteenth Street and Adams Mill Road, nestled amidst the cultured playground of the nation's capital in Adams Morgan, where he played and recorded with jazz greats such as the legendary Blue Note recording star, Butch Warren on bass, Ricky "Sugarfoot" Wellman on drums, sax-man Ron Holloway, trumpet sensation Donald Tillery, and Mikey "Bossalingo" Harris on jam guitar.

In New York, it was a different set of jivers, with Joe Berger on guitar, Thomas "Hutch" Hutchins on saxophone, and Eric "D-Key" Oster on rhythm guitar.

It was Lars' honest approach to every artistic endeavor that Lulu admired most and found so endearing. His creativity and passion for life were inspiring. The sheer fact that Lars created a fashion line and sold it to Saks Fifth Avenue and Lord & Taylor with no formal retail or fashion experience was astonishing to Lulu.

Lars was an artrepreneur in every sense of the word, developing everything from his own reality show to reinventing garment labels that would soon revolutionize the fashion industry.

His bootstrapped methodology toward creating something from nothing would serve as the inspiration for Lulu to have the chutzpah to finally pen her first novel.

Barnes & IgNoble

The sun broke through a dewy expanse of green leaves, muddied by the hard rains of late April that covered the center of historic Union Square. The organic farmers' market along the perimeter of the square bristled with greenmarket shoppers and a bounty of fresh local produce. That day was to be Lulu's breakthrough moment. Instead, it served to further incarcerate her, both mentally and physically. Lulu's book signing at Barnes & Noble on Seventeenth Street between Park Avenue and Broadway would have to go on without her, for she was stuck on an extended stay at the Grey Bar Hotel, otherwise known as Club Fed.

The scattered clouds gave way just before noon as the streets surrounding the bookstore began filling up with hordes of international and domestic journalists, reporters, and TV news crews that had been closely following Lulu's plight over the past year. A small encampment of well-wishers started filing into the area in front of the bookstore, carrying picket signs that read *White Collar Slavery*, *Free Lulu*, and *NY Loves Lulu*. Lulu's supporters came to the square in droves that day, restlessly awaiting her tell-all book. All secretly hoping to hear the behind-the-scenes, sleazy skinny on her exposé focusing on a designer set of mean girls embroiled in one of the largest scandals since Bernie Madoff's grand Ponzi scheme, bilking hundreds of millions of dollars in their own insider trading ring.

This quasi bit of nonfiction, exposing the underbelly of one of the world's most successful PR firms, had the right salacious mix of sex, scandals, sci-fi, suicide, celebrities, politics, conspiracy theories, and drugs to be a *New York Times* best seller.

Lulu, incensed over her inability to enjoy the fruits of her memoirs, was hoping that her beloved Lars, whom she sent in her place, would be able to handle the media attention. Although charming, she wasn't quite sure if he would act more like Kramer from *Seinfeld* or McDeere in *The Firm*.

* * *

A line producer from FOX, whom Davio, Lulu's Latin mouthpiece, had been introduced to by his handsome southern senator, walked into the makeshift beauty salon and over to Zeela. "We're gonna go in fifteen minutes."

"Square Jane, you really popped your lid off on this one, darlin'," said Zeela while continuing to run the hair straightener through Lulu's long locks. "Now, am I gonna see your pretty little white ass on TMZ? Where's Harvey Levin and his posse of Benetton dwarfs? They gonna be there? Right?"

Lulu was fuming, doing everything she could to make it through this interview. Why on earth was she the one incarcerated for the crimes committed by her employer? Sure, she was guilty of some petty, off-color crimes of the heart, but clearly not enough to be the focal point of an SEC investigation. The fact that she was rotting away in a twelve by eight for the past four freaking months with a single toilet was beyond any sense of injustice she could have ever conceived while studying poly-sci at the University of Miami. This was a case study in the psychosis of her superior and her misguided sexual and corporate malfeasance. This exclusive interview from Club Fed coupled with her book release would surely put a holy dent in the revenge cupcake she was going to cram down that ghastly bitch's piehole. With this exposé, Lizette might try to kill herself again.

"Three minutes, Lulu," warned the line producer, donning a silver-and-black headset. He was followed by Lulu's Miami-born gal pal attorney. Spinoza was Lulu's old marathon shopping partner from their days at the University of Miami. He turned out to be one of the top criminal attorneys along the East Coast, but there was only so much that even he could do, after sleeping with a very influential Southern senator.

It still wouldn't be enough to spring his dear Lulu from her extended stay at the Discomfort Inn.

"How can we get autograph copy so I can sell on eBay? Ha!" joked Ingrid in her thick Russian accent. "Now that you like movie star..."

"Girlfriend, you gonna get Brangelina to play you in the movie?" Zeela interrupted.

"Wouldn't it be just fabulous if we could get Ellen Barkin? And maybe Jennifer Lawrence to play you, Lulu," Spinoza had a dead-on Barcelona lisp despite maintaining he was a distant relative to the great Baruch Spinoza, who was actually Dutch.

The former Spinoza reigned as one of the most important and certainly the most radical philosophers of the early modern period. Of all the philosophers of the seventeenth century, perhaps none have more relevance today than Spinoza. Lulu could only think of how worried Lars must be and how much she missed him as the din of the voices droned on in the background of the jailhouse salon.

Lulu couldn't stand to be in the bloody Grey Bar another day. She yearned to be beside Lars in his arms. She even missed his African chants and his freaky impersonations, like Louis "Satchmo" Armstrong doing Led Zeppelin: "and she's buying a stairway to heaven." She longed for his lovable, asinine drivel over the catcalls from the cell soldierettes at 4:00 a.m.; the weird looks from the butch guards, and all the holy, heart-stopping, defiling charm that the federal penitentiary system had to offer. The only thing that was keeping her halfway alive in the stony lonesome was her love for Lars and her adorable pooch Kingsley, not to mention spending the last year and a half penning her nightmare—which was completely unraveling her plans to donate the proceeds to charity, her future with Lars, and most importantly, her revenge on the firm.

> There is no hope unmingled with fear, and no fear unmingled with hope.
>
> —Baruch Spinoza

The golden light of the afternoon sun cast long shadows over the yard. In the distance, female inmates dressed in neon-orange jumpsuits congregated in pockets of activity, looking like a sea of mop-topped Motrin pills, curious over the Hollywood hullabaloo, rare for the beleaguered yardbirds doing serious time for their societal crimes.

As the line producer escorted Lulu and Davio to the makeshift set in a discreet corner of the yard, Davio turned toward Zeela and Ingrid, who were each flashing Lulu a proud parent smile. Davio, mustering up his best jailhouse for dummies lingo, mused, "Shank you very much for shaping up her locks, ladies. She looks dope."

"You're quite welcome, Ricky Martin," Zeela playfully teased, admittedly never having seen a man as flamboyant in all her years in the hair industry.

"I'm afraid Geraldo is detained in the studio on a story breaking in the Middle East," said the British-born reporter, Ben Wheatley, as he introduced himself.

"Of course he is," Lulu said.

"Oh, no he didn't . . . That fucking war has been going on for centuries. This here, girlfriend, is *breaking* news . . ." Davio mused.

"Oooh, I was looking forward to cutting Geraldo's coif and his freaky fucking Frito Bandito mustache. That's *too* bad," Ingrid smugly chimed in.

"Wait, give us a minute," Davio said, pulling Lulu aside to an alcove in the yard. "This may be to our benefit," he whispered to Lulu.

"Really? How?"

"It will kill that bitch to see your interview. And it will really send her over the edge when she sees that Ben Wheatley is the reporter that got the exclusive interview with you. So, you see, we really couldn't have planned it better!"

"Yes, I suppose you're right," Lulu agreed.

"Girlfriend, you know that bitch is boozin' it up somewhere, waiting with bated breath for this thing to air. Wherever she is, she is waiting and watching, trust me," Davio declared with a devilish grin.

* * *

The legendary Waldorf Astoria on fabled Park Avenue stands as a beacon of five-star hospitality, hosting royalty, celebrities, and tourists for well over a century.

The clubbiest of the hotel bars is the celebrated Bear and Bull Steakhouse, keeping investment bankers and financial types cushy with a stock market ticker and tables the color of cold, hard cash—mint money green. A favorite haunt of the city's financial elite, it earned its name from the bronze bull and bear—symbolizing Wall Street's boom and bust—proudly set against the gleaming polished mahogany bar. Teeming with lavish comfort since 1931, market movers trade tales over the city's best martinis. Sucking down four of these indulgent cocktails is a cosmopolitan feat—even for a well-trained liver. Anything beyond that is considered quite murky territory.

Lizette, posing a seemingly small flight risk, poured herself into her nude-colored Spanx, slapped on her Bobbi Brown war paint and grabbed her Lana Marks aqua-bitch-blue sport bag along with her chubby arm-candy, Marni, who by a stroke of fabricated luck managed to evade any criminal wrongdoing from Operation Blue April. Living in an Eastern Bloc country for the majority of her childhood taught her a few basic things. One, how to thwart the system and work in mysterious, underground ways. Two, a love for anything shiny, gold, platinum, or sparkly like diamonds or Swarovski crystals. Three, the need to be around money and power.

Car #48 was waiting for Lizette and Marni on the northeast corner of Fiftieth Street. There was a love triangle between car #48, the firm, and one dickhead dispatcher, Singh Raditi. Over the years,

Singh purposely wed Lizette and her minions with some of New York's smelliest, most inept, tackiest, non-driving newbie, PhD, card-carrying lunatics that the streets of the naked city had ever known. It was only car #48 that could tolerate the maniacal nonsense every few nanoseconds from the queen bee herself, Lizette Hansen, and her hatchery of well-meaning working drones. There was one such occasion in which a driver named Lopez in car #33, after being bitch-slapped around both verbally and physically, stuck up for his rights, dropped the ladies off in the middle of the Fifty-Ninth Street Bridge, and said in his best Tijuana tongue, "Bambinas, Barneys is that way." He had raised his bejeweled, tattooed finger and pointed in the direction of Manhattan before speeding off in his black town car, blasting a Carlos Santana tune on his way back to the city. Come Monday morning, Lopez, his wife, his three children, his sister, two cousins, his grandmother, and his Guatemalan babysitter were magically deported through the Mexican authorities. Lizette would stop at nothing, like a science experiment puppeting lives, loves, and anything she could sink her teeth into. No, she wasn't the self-proclaimed corporate dragon slayer; no, in fact she was the dragon herself. Very few were privy to her true ways—and even fewer could outthink her, outdrink her, or outmink her. This bitch was a poster child for PETA, ASPCA, and even the EPA. She relished wearing dead animals, and rarely dined on anything but flesh. She threw trash in the city streets, a public nuisance dressed in Pucci.

By 3:30 p.m., Lizette was three sheets, trying to outmuscle a few money manager jerkoffs busy brokering a dirty martini challenge.

"I can't wait to hear what fucking lies that ungrateful bitch will try to unleash," slurred Lizette, turning toward her cohort Marni, as she ravenously gulped her fourth Belvedere martini, spiked with three sodden Spanish olives.

Marni, stuffed into her usual Roy Orbison, lamp-black, ill-fitting pantsuit, decided to lay back a bit in case her now defunct boss went cage-fighter crazy, opening a can of whoop ass on anyone that may get in her way, after witnessing the FOX interview with her whistle-blowing corporate nemesis nightmare, whom she now deemed unworthy, unfit, culpable, and criminal.

"Are you worried?" asked Marni.

Biting into a Fred Flintstone–sized piece of Pittsburgh rare, oak-plank-grilled filet mignon reduced in a warm, bloody Béarnaise sauce, Lizette looked more like a pit bull at a luau than a corporate commander. With her fangs bared, she was glued to the flatscreen TV that hung straight above the bar. Lizette snidely awaited what surely would be unmitigated, unsubstantiated claims against her charity and good nature, that surely only promoted the little bitch's agenda.

"Worry? I'm going to crucify that little bitch and put her in a wooden kimono."

* * *

Ben Wheatley, an award-winning reporter, formerly of the BBC, was as adept in corporate matters as in international affairs. For the past ten years, he had been a great friend to Kline Allen & Robbins Public Relations, respectfully delaying and killing an unusual number of stories by closed-door requests from the firm.

Lulu sat uneasily for the ghoulish makeup girl that in her opinion had applied way too much powder to her face. Lulu had arranged many TV interviews at all of the major networks, and she despised seeing interviews where the subject looked like a reject from Madame Tussauds, a drippy, surreal nightmare.

"Listen, Spectra, can you cut me some slack on the powder?" Lulu sardonically asked. "I'm not doing an interview for *Monster High* here."

"They couldn't get the HMIs through security, so we're on old-school tungsten, thirty-two hundred degrees here, kid. They are *hot* and we don't want you sweating out there, Abbey," retorted Jessie the make-up girl, in a Hollywood, all-knowing, "we can stop traffic if we want to—we're TV folk" haughty smile.

"Abbey?"

"Yea, Abbey Bominable," replied Jessie.

Lulu shook her head, she could only focus on tearing Screwzette apart, tissue by tissue, cell by cell, during this tell-some interview. A house arrest bracelet in hell would be too good for this bitch, who had altered Lulu's life in such immeasurable ways that she was ready to go *Kill Bill* crazy on her ex-boss in the next few minutes for this illogical, farce of an incarceration.

"Honey, this book is going to put her on the streets," Davio said as he checked out Lulu's caked complexion. "When we're through with her, she'll be ringing the bell for the Salvation Army, and that's if she's lucky. Sister, phytoplankton have more brains than this bitch."

Davio turned toward Jessie, who was now chatting with Ben and the cameraman on a raised platform with two black director chairs placed opposite one another. Center stage were two Mole-Richardson 5K Fresnel lights and a 1200 soft box. An egg crate and blue gels were clipped to the lights to match the daylight.

"Doll, what's with the Goth look?" Davio quipped sarcastically. "Hello? She's not going to ComicCon. Baby, give my girl some color."

From the FOX headquarters on Sixth Avenue, Craig Rivera came back from commercial break with a teaser for the next segment: "Up next, a woman wrongfully accused, now serving time, breaks her silence in her latest book, *White Collar Slavery*, which has turned into an overnight sensation and a *New York Times* best seller. Ben Wheatley sits down with the author at the Metropolitan Detention Center for an exclusive interview."

"Lulu, thank you for joining us today. I had the pleasure of reading your book, and I've got to hand it to you, it reminded me a tad of Ayn Rand's *Atlas Shrugged*, with a bit of Upton Sinclair's *The Jungle*. I mean, your plight must have been pretty incredible, from vice president to federal inmate all in the same year. Well—what has this journey been like for you?" questioned Ben.

"Well, Ben, it's been a bit like *127 Hours* times four months. Instead, my livelihood, my love, and my family have all been severed by this horrific injustice."

"According to our sources here at FOX News, you are the only one currently incarcerated for the alleged insider trading; is that correct?"

"That's correct, to my knowledge and chagrin." Ben broke a smile and let out a chuckle.

"I think it was the British politician William Gladstone who once said, 'Justice delayed is justice denied,'" Lulu continued.

"Yes, yes. In the book, you explain how you are incarcerated for insider trading, yet you yourself have not profited a dime. Is that correct?"

"Absolutely. The people that have profited from this mess, well—they are walking free."

"That sounds like a travesty of the legal system."

"Clearly."

"Do you have any idea how many men and women can identify with your plight? This book has sparked a huge controversy over the employer-employee paradigm. When you were writing this book, did you have any idea of the impact you could have on young men and women in the workplace?"

"I wrote this book for all of the nameless faces who dream of making a difference. They are the people working seventy hours or more a week or working two or more jobs just to provide for their family. I dedicated the book to a young, homeless mother whom I met at an Occupy Wall Street rally, a young attorney who lost her job and then her home due to the foreclosure crisis, like so many other Americans. She represents not only the millions of people that have lost their jobs, falling through the cracks of society, but also the millions of employees that are still employed but continue to endure a form of slavery out of the fear of becoming unemployed—most stopping at nothing to keep their jobs."

"Could you elaborate further on your former employer? As I understand, she's out on bail, while you remain locked up in here."

"Well, the work environment was literally like something straight out of *Lord of the Flies*. Instead of the conch, we had smartphones. The management behaved like savages. My direct superior was constantly in blood-lust mode, basically like a canine with no cerebral cortex."

* * *

"Marni, get that fucking senator on the phone right now. That is it. This bitch is going down!" screamed Lizette as she choked on her filet.

In shock, Marni turned toward her mentor. Marni's face was flushed - she was about to toss up her lunch. "Ohmigod! Ohmigod!" she said, her hands shaking, barely able to dial.

Lulu's voice was audible from the flatscreen as Lizette and Marni stared intently at the monitor. The bronze bull beside the TV set stared Lizette down, as if to say, "You can't outrun these horns."

"I mean, I had no grand illusions that this woman was my friend. She acted friendly, but on a daily basis she would mentally and physically abuse her staff," Lulu continued.

"Physical abuse? Did you ever go to HR?" questioned Ben.

"Yes, of course. We went to HR many times, and we were made to look like we were the troublemakers."

Dante's Hatchery

Lizette Hanson attended Our Lady of Hit and Run, a private parochial school for wayward juveniles nestled in the backwoods of New Jersey. For a long stint she was a favorite among the hierarchy of the nunnery for her "take no prisoners" attitude. She spent the majority of her scholastic life trying to turn the nunnery into a cannery, with her *Gidget Goes Berserk* antics. It wasn't until she discovered martinis one spring night after blurting out "You first!" in a holy confessional, with the archbishop wearing nothing but a mod, red pleather raincoat and reeking of Tanqueray and Marlboros that she clearly exhausted her welcome at the strict Catholic center of higher learning.

She went on to attend St. Johns College in hopes of getting a Mrs. degree. However, after a string of doltish law school suitors, Lizette decided aspiring golf pros had more distinction, not to mention a greater upswing. Countless invitations to open bars at posh country clubs and a leather bag larger than hers aroused her psyche to no end. Eventually, she burned through the entire tri-state area country club set with a less than stellar reputation.

Coming from a repressed, corned beef and cabbage, Irish Catholic home, her mother a psychologist and her father a city worker, Lizette was one of seven children, with three older sisters and three younger brothers. Lizette was a true case study of middle-child malaise. She had it so severe that on her seventh birthday, when her mother asked her to watch her baby brother, young Lizette tied the rope from the window blinds around her brother's neck, wishing him to stay put for her tea party picture. She never realized the severity of what she had done to her baby brother, or so she maintained, until her mother came into the living room seconds later, yelling and screaming, to find the baby at the open window gallows. Lizette was even banned from playing hangman, a favorite childhood word game, with younger siblings and was forced to play with her mother's collection of Camelot memorabilia and secondhand, broken-down dollies.

Dating pro golfers in her youth was amusing, but in her early 30s when her figure started to drop, Lizette finally admitted to herself, after a long night facing her reflection in a wine-colored toilet bowl, that she must settle down or face her own conceited and deliberate demise. So, when Lizette met a dashing, successful doctor twenty years her senior, recently divorced with four children, it was a match made in tri-state heaven. And after only two short years of dating, she and Curt decided to make it official in the eyes of the hospital board of directors and marry in a June civil ceremony in Cherry Hill, New Jersey. An unseasonable hailstorm kept a handful of her heinous bridesmaids and even her own mother from attending the wedding due to fallen trees and power lines. In the midst of getting ready for her daughter's wedding that morning, after catching the morning weather report, she stopped getting dressed and decided she would fix her daughter's wagon for marrying a Southern Baptist. This resentment would follow Lizette throughout her adult life, manifesting itself as pure and distilled forms of calculated mistrust in the workplace.

The revolving door of the hatchery saw its countless share of hopeless well-meaners—that either weren't tough enough, didn't have the right moral compass, or didn't hold a master's degree in bullshit. In the seven years Lulu was employed at KAR PR, she saw more than one hundred well-meaners come and go in an endless assembly line, each awaiting the demise of the next, getting their turn to fail miserably for Sergeant "Screwzette" Hansen.

The smarter half of the unglimmer twins, Marni Zhuk, married for the past five years, was already pregnant with her second child before her firstborn turned one. In hatchery speak, it meant she was out for blood, for the rest of the girls knew that she couldn't stand the heat in Sergeant Screwzette's kitchen with her self-involved daily nerve grindings and hourly berating. In order to collect her Upper East Side, socially acceptable paycheck and maintain her sanity, she started pumping out Zhuks, knowing they would never terminate her employment for having beautiful American-born, Romanian babies, who by the age of two would already speak three languages and play the violin.

Lizette had a Svengali-like effect on Marni, manipulating her every move, inextricably linked to her unstable psyche. Marni's sole professional desire was to have her opinions, thoughts, Post-it notes, and e-mails recognized and worthy of corporate advancement. Marni longed for the day to have the fear power that Lizette possessed.

Lizette had an uncomfortable way about her at work and at home. She was one of those types of people you never quite felt comfortable around, even in a casual setting. She was off-putting in unnatural, often egotistical ways, and used this approach in everything she did. It wasn't clear if this illness was self-induced or medically treatable, but she would claim ad nauseam that she had been stricken since her Catholic school days with a bloodcurdling, ghastly condition known as *misophonia*, defined as a hatred of sound, a condition characterized by a diminished ability to tolerate certain noises, including everyday sounds such as talking, chewing, or yawning. Mealtime was absolute torture. Any foreign chomp or slurp triggered outrage, sending her into an instantaneous blood-boiling rage, yet the sound of her own chewing was like a choir of angels on Christmas Eve.

Screwzette was drunk with power, always on someone else's tab. As the firm's puppet master, she had an overwhelming control over the other members of the hatchery. Her tentacles reached up the ladder to the firm's three founding partners: Kline, Allen, and Robbins.

Partners were neither willfully nor readily available to employees, well-meaning or not. Lizette constantly operated from behind the curtain, in Wizard of Oz mode, taking clandestine meetings with clients, always moving or adverting from one media crisis to another behind forty-five-degree blinds, usually for the firm's biggest retainers—like Client #9, Grangeway Trucking, and Client #2, Meyers & Tucker.

Lizette and Marni had a twisted little sidecar named Sasha Ruberg, a Five Towns, Long Island, Goth queen who seemed to have a penchant for anything drab or off-drab. Sasha was from a well-to-do, manufacturing family that came to this country from Eastern Europe and quickly rose to the top of the fashion game.

Her grandfather Saul brought the business from the Lower East Side to the Garment District in 1927 to build his cut-and-sew empire. Sasha didn't need to work. Rather, she threw herself into the hatchery to avoid employment at one of her family's factories.

Sharing an office with Lulu, Sasha would stare at her like she was the last piece of kosher chicken in Manhattan come Friday at 4:30 p.m. Sasha's favorite pastime, when she wasn't toiling over some pathetic task from her enslaver Sergeant Screwzette, was to comb through the eateries of West Chelsea, dining at places like Tenth Avenue Cookshop and Bottino.

The hatchery was run from the forty-seventh floor of 1211 Avenue of the Americas. Sergeant Screwzette and her disciples held dominion over 90 percent of the forty-seventh and forty-sixth floors, and in their minds, each floor of every media outlet from Times Square to Tokyo.

KAR PR played expense account host to the hatchery and their more-than-demanding seventy-plus-hour workweek. The firm's clients consisted of high-visibility Fortune 50 companies and their cadre of needy executives who on many occasions had the maturity level of girl scouts.

In order to subsidize the lavish expense accounts, dinners, parties, and bonuses for the firm, the assorted, unsavory, not-to-be-mentioned-around-boardroom type clients that honestly funded most of the legitimate activities of the firm, cloaking the extravagant expenditures.

The girls of the hatchery and their well-meaning interns were relegated with the task to bury the black ops paperwork for clients like #9, #26 and #13 1/2—so in the end, their clients would garner billions in stock options and golden parachutes, more concerned with the buzz on the *Daily Beast* than shareholder profits.

Infighting inside the hatchery was more common than the incessant coffee breaks by the Keurig. They would go at it, usually led by Screwzette, clawing at each other and themselves. These PR menaces would fight in a way that would make a hormonally imbalanced cage fighter blush like a giddy schoolgirl. In fact, any well-meaning man, woman, child, or Shih Tzu that got in their way was doomed to an irreversible, polarized PR ride from hell. No one was safe from these bitches. I mean no one: not a policeman, fireman, politician, schoolteacher, airline attendant, or prostitute was safe from the wrath inflicted. Should any service person trickle a bit of red wine on Lizette's favorite ivory Italian silk blouse, purposely or not, she would work successfully and in mysterious ways to get that attendant deported. She would uproot hard-working well-meaners just looking to provide for their families, throw them into a van, and fly them back to whatever hell-basket (according to Hansen) they migrated from. She was fiercer than a tyrannosaurus rex on Eighth Avenue and could shop faster than Ganesha, the elephant god with a dozen arms.

One altercation that sticks out smartly on the top of the heap is Jet Black and Blue flight 1052, illustrating the audacity of her piranha-like ferocity and the extent to which she chauffeured people to their wits' end. This incident garnered significant media attention upon landing, due to the crack efforts of Screwzette and her minions. Wikipedia refers to the incident as:

> Date: August 9, 2010
> Type: Flight attendant altercation
> Survivors: 104 (all)
>
> A flight attendant announced over the plane's public address system that he had been called an obscenity by a passenger, quit his job, deployed the evacuation slide at the terminal gate, and slid down. He later claimed to have been injured by a passenger when he instructed her to sit down. His account of the event was not corroborated by others.

One passenger recollects that the flight attendant went on the plane's public address system screaming profanities and concluded, "I've been in this business twenty years. And that's it, I'm done."

As the scheduled flight arrived at JFK from Pittsburgh, the flight attendant told the passengers to "go fuck themselves," grabbed two Blue Moon beers, deployed the escape chute, slid down, and then drove home in his car that was parked at the airport. Later that night he was arrested and taken into custody.

What the media failed to report was the cause and the real details surrounding the altercation. It was Screwzette who demanded a glass of wine from the flight attendant.

"Ma'am, I am going to have to remind you that you are seated in an emergency row," the attendant said calmly.

"Yes, I am aware of that. I paid extra for these seats," responded Screwzette.

"S-s-o you will understand that I cannot serve you three glasses of wine while sitting in the emergency row, e-e-specially before noon, ma'am," stuttered the Midwestern attendant in his folksy drawl.

"Listen, you little QUILTBAG, I've been drinking wine, not vodka. And for your information, missy, I am on doctor's orders for the antioxidants, because you have no resveratrol here!" screamed Screwzette.

"Missy! Resveratrol?" Naturally, the attendant began flogging Screwzette repeatedly on the right side of her face with an in-flight pillow that he grabbed from the overhead compartment.

It was at that moment he took hold of the microphone and blurted out over the PA system a pithy "Go fuck yourselves," pulled the emergency chute, jumped out, and took off in his baby blue VW Beetle.

Another member of the hatchery was Alice, an aspiring starlet from a Texan trailer park in the sky, a bottle-blonde pixie doll, who was a cross between Twiggy and an annoying Kmart cashier. Alice Pullman started with the firm as a summer intern, but after a few sordid evenings with Lizette's only son, Phil, she was soon hired full-time.

Playing hot potato with the pixie weeks later, Phil handed her back to Lizette, trading up for a British tart named Bobby. Lizette was bewildered how bombshell Alice could have swayed her football star son so easily. Her incessant Blanche DuBois histrionics sent Phil into wild fits of narcissism. Thus, he fell in love with anyone who vaguely resembled himself, which soon came in the form of a young Knightsbridge menswear model named Bobby.

Shortly after the breakup, Lizette learned Alice's grandmother was the first woman in the CIA. Lizette immediately felt threatened, which was very uncommon for her, but she had a respect for duplicity, and so she felt compelled to hire the wannabe starlet full-time, knowing full well she would last only until her next big audition at the Hawaiian Tropic Zone.

Lulu, a cross between Audrey Hepburn and Mary Anne from Gilligan's Island, was always the first one in the office and the last one to leave—she was the one that kept the KAR PR behemoth running.

For the first year of her career at KAR PR, Lulu was zookeeper for Sergeant Screwzette and technical officer for her Power Rangers floor model plastic punching bag, which she brazenly worked over from the forty-seventh floor on a semi-hourly basis.

She would slug at the Toys 'R' Us door prize mumbling under her breath names of clients, such as Client #9 and #27. The fighting one afternoon got so fierce that the bag smacked her back in the face when she took a call from her cell phone.

Lulu, an only child for seven years of her life, grew up outside of Orlando, Florida, and was forever altered by the arrival of her younger brother, Kip, which shifted attention off of her and her Malibu Barbie to Huggies and Hot Wheels. Living within earshot of the Magic Kingdom brought childhood responsibilities that her cousins who lived in Connecticut couldn't understand. Young Lulu was expected to be like Cinderella and Mary Poppins, practically perfect in every way, and it was tough for chubby Lulu to live up to her hometown competition. She was even pitted against Snow White and the seven dwarfs in a junior varsity soccer game her sophomore year of high school, and came up with an embarrassing loss in the face of her parents and her "you're not the boss of me" younger brother. This loss left her socially immobile for several months, and it wasn't until she knocked Snow White out for homecoming queen later that year that she felt comfortable again.

Lulu attended the University of Miami and rushed Alpha Chi Omega, which paid off in spades socially, until Hell Night broke loose. Her hair and thirteen other pledges' scalps were infused with a mellifluous, gooey garlic paste that seemed to follow her through her summer internship, where she got her first taste of truth bending and propaganda. The art of public relations seemed to come naturally for Lulu, for it reminded her of how she would bend the truth as a child to throw her younger sibling into an extended time out.

Since her days of Malibu Barbie and *Muppets Take Manhattan*, Lulu always dreamed of moving to the Big Apple in search of her Kermit to kiss into a prince. And she knew she needed PR to get there. PR equaled social events, and social events equaled opportunities to meet and greet more Kermits. At the age of twenty-three, Lulu traded the Magic Kingdom for Murray Hill, a place where many twenty-somethings begin their Manhattan existence. The freak, fraternity populace that sloshed through Third Avenue in the East Thirties quickly played on Lulu's nerves, forcing her to the tranquility of the Upper East Side, to a semi-affordable apartment in a tenement building. Her brother Kip reminded her all along the way that she was "Moving on up!" just like George Jefferson.

Within just a few days of moving to the Big Apple, Lulu landed an entry-level position at KAR PR, where she would be introduced to the puppet master herself, the lizard queen, Sergeant Lizette "Screwzette" Hansen.

And just like that, after a few short months in the hatchery, Lizette felt a level of confidence in Lulu's ability to put out fires and make things happen. She often used her willfully as a pawn in her Christmas list of dastardly deeds that broke, bent, and ruptured the firm's code of ethics, inter—and intrastate laws, and even a few international laws.

Dilettante Interrupted

"One drop or two?" Sasha sheepishly asked as she turned toward Lulu.

Sasha always looked for a second opinion before she performed the high-wire act better known in the henhouse as the Bombay Talkie, sharply squeezing droplets of Visine into an enemy's unsuspecting beverage. For Sasha, one drop meant her mark would graciously endure thirty minutes of mind-altering agony. Two or more drops translated into an afternoon ravaging the body and soul, feeling like a cross between *Cape Fear* and *Saw III* for her victims, atop a cold porcelain throne. Lulu, who never wanted to be part of the indigestible and undetectable crime, always cleverly deflected Sasha's question toward someone else in the group, like Marni. But then Marni would always manage to up the ante. "Make it three!"

"Is a trifecta really necessary?" blurted Lulu, always trying to be the voice of reason.

The victim that blistery summer afternoon was a marshmallow-headed business prick named Billy and his Where's Waldo trader buddies, busily accosting a group of Swedish models. They were at the bar of Pastis, a chic brasserie in the Meatpacking District on the corner of Little West Twelfth Street, a trendy neighborhood made up mostly of boutiques, bars, and bistros that lined the quaint cobblestone streets and turned deadly at 4:00 a.m. Those walking in heels have a very different experience than the ballet-flat-wearing women who gracefully glide across the street, clueless to the living hell that women endure as they hobble over the uneven obstacle course in search of their knight in shining armor, which comes in the form of an available taxi, to give them a ride home or to someone else's.

In recent years, the streets and shops of the Meatpacking District have been completely romanticized by a string of HBO hits; however historically the district has had quite a checkered past. In the early seventies, the area was a seedy zone for pimps and outlaw bikers. To some extent this legacy still remains. And before that, in the early 1900s, slaughterhouses and packing plants filled the district. By the 1930s those houses produced the nation's third-largest volume of dressed meats. Few meatpacking companies operate in the district today. Boutiques and bars have replaced the endless slabs of dry aged beef.

Toasting Irish Car Bombs to their success in shorting the market that afternoon, Boxcar Billy made his way over to Lizette Hansen and company after being shot down by the Wilhelmina girls. Billy was attracted either by Lulu's adorable green eyes beneath her black-framed Gucci glasses, or most likely by the large, steaming basket of steak frites that were placed in front of the unglimmer twins like a trough. Let's face it, Billy was a drunk bastard, and everyone knows a drunk bastard can never ever pass up greasy French fries in front of a woman that he has no interest in, so he could act like a scarfing piglet—which he did, and unwittingly sat down beside the Satan of Sixth Avenue, clearly to his own intestinal undoing.

"Beautiful, mind if I have most of these?" Billy said, grabbing for the basket of fries with the smugness of a corrupt politician and the hands of a steel crane, looking directly into Screwzette's dripping makeup with his bloodshot eyes. "You're cute for a panther."

"And you're an asshole," Sasha interrupted as her forefinger twitched, feeling the sensation coming on for a Bombay.

"Can you give us a break?" Marni said as she watched Sasha nonchalantly reach into her watermelon-colored LeSportsac, pulling out a tiny bottle of Visine, cuffing it in her suit sleeve like a Vegas card shark.

"We would rather have the pigeons eat these than you!" Lulu chimed in as she moved the basket of fried potatoes away from Billy's claws, complete with his Dalton pinky ring.

"Hey, take it easy, Thelma," Billy cried as he peered past Lulu's dark frames.

"You need to leave! Now!" Marni demanded, throwing in a bit of her tough girl, Romanian accent, as to scare Boxcar Billy on the next train out of there.

"Do you know what I did today, Thelma? I just made two and a half million dollars in one hour," he said, slurring his words.

"Ohhh, you're so handsome, I figured you can make that in fifteen minutes sucking dick in the West Village," declared Sasha.

"We must be in the wrong business, ladies!" blurted Lizette as she downed another Ketel One martini while motioning for the waiter to bring her yet another. "Do go on."

"Do go on," were the watchwords. Those three, simple words signaled the chaos to commence in any one of the little dastardly deeds—it was always the "do go on"—those were the words that would ensnare for their victims their well-deserved desserts.

Two bottles of chardonnay, twelve Ketel One martinis, and several shots of Frangelico later, the hatchery listened attentively as Boxcar Billy continued to brag about shorting the market, and how this son of a bitch that worked for some jagoff brokerage firm told him that the whole downgrade of the US credit rating could really shake up his earning potential. Shamefully repugnant, he bet against the country and won big.

The hatchery sat back, and for one hour twenty-two minutes and thirty-six seconds give or take, let Boxcar Billy devour all the papas fritas, and a few shots of Frangelico, all the while making googly eyes at him, pretending to hang on his every word. And it was at this precise moment that he and his baboon buddies in Brooks Brothers suits turned a whiter shade of pale: 3:02:36 p.m.

Sasha was just going to serve up the sons of bitches a Bombay Talkie and call it a afternoon, but when Billy started with the anti-Semitic remarks, she was morally commanded to up the ante, proffering up a rip-roaring, gastro-ride of an evening for the four men.

Four drops was the well-deserved order and honestly a first for the girls—for only those who try to bring down the country's credit rating and manufacture misfortune have karma for some real red-eye ass kicking. This was just the hatchery's own little way of settling the score: a bit of corporate decorum in step with the sludge before them.

Screwzette had long graduated from Bombays, yet on occasion was tickled when it was property executed by her team. She had more of a penchant for a broader swath of terror.

* * *

The firm's most sought after client, Grangeway Trucking, was in town for a media luncheon that the hatchery spent the last two months planning. The cold snap in the October air was a foreboding sign that the luncheon would turn repugnant in one of the most insidious instances of egregious corporate misconduct at the behest of Executive Vice President Lizette Hansen, ten years with the firm.

One of the last beacons of the blue-blood era, the 21 Club stood proudly in the middle of the block on Fifty-Second Street between Fifth and Madison Avenues. Once a glamorous speakeasy, today the four-story townhouse is one of the more celebrated restaurants in New York City. Considered one of the most decadent dining rooms in Manhattan, the hatchery decided they needed to hold the luncheon in the legendary Prohibition-era wine cellar. All the luminaries from the top news outlets, including CNBC, CNN, Bloomberg TV, FOX Business, FOX News, the *Wall Street Journal*, *Financial Times*, the *New York Times*, *Huffington Post*, and the *Daily Beast* were in attendance.

It wasn't long after the executive team at Grangeway Trucking began to arrive that Lizette knew she would have to come face-to-face with Amy Wallingford. If Lizette hated anyone, it was Amy Wallingford, a mother of two young boys that lived in St. Louis. Born and raised in Iowa, Amy was in her early forties, married, and looked like a cross between Blondie and Garfield on a good day.

White Collar Slavery

The reason Lizette hated Amy so much was because she felt threatened, not by her brain, but by her internal role at Grangeway Trucking. Amy was poached from T-Mobile by Grangeway to lead their in-house communications team. But there was one *big* problem—Amy knew *zero* about PR, and each call between Lizette and Amy felt like PR 101, which Lizette had *zero* tolerance for.

Amy arrived in the coveted wine cellar. She quickly took the bait as planned in the form of a colossal country club shrimp cocktail. Lizette and the others couldn't hold in their laughter, as Amy looked more like an overgrown otter with a flipper full of the catch o'the day than a corporate executive.

The girls nicknamed her Famy, which stood for *fat* plus *Amy*. And she was a great candidate for the girls' faux reality show, *Less is More*, a cross between *The Biggest Loser* and *Saw IV*. Making it past midseason was dicey, unless you got rid of the baggage by way of Black and Decker. *Ouch!*

Reporters kept filing in one after another like a Chinese New Year's parade, with the perfect diversion set. The dilettantes interrupted their feeding frenzy of Caesar salad and steak fries with shaved truffles and went to work. They set a plan in motion signaled by Screwzette and hatched by Marni. Alice served as the pick, with Sasha and Lulu as unwitting scouts, simply told to fill in empty seats at the press conference and alert the hatchery if Famy was to head to the coat check, knowing that in a conference such as this, the coat check is rarely monitored. Marni, with her innocent doe eyes, looked around and began walking backwards into the coatroom. Alice later recounted the act to Sasha and Lulu. The conference droned on with the executive team of Grangeway Trucking answering a barrage of questions regarding the future of the company to projections for the upcoming fiscal period.

A cherub-faced reporter from CNBC who bore a close resemblance to Chris Matthews shot out a question based on uncorroborated facts concerning Grangeway filing for Chapter 11. It was like a can of corporate whoop ass opened up on the historic wine cellar, and a media circus ensued with Bloomberg, CNN, CNBC, and several print reporters choking on their petite filet.

Marni, wearing her trademark Isotoner gloves, filched Famy's Missouri state driver's license and nonchalantly moonwalked away from the scene of the crime. By the time the luncheon was over, Bloomberg and the Associated Press already had wire stories quoting Roger Sloane and his remarks.

"Ladies, I wish I had more time so that we could grab a drink to celebrate another successful luncheon, but I have a flight to catch," said Famy as she entered the elevator, clueless to the hellacious next few hours she would undoubtedly endure at JFK when she realized that her driver's license was missing. It was just a few months ago, when in Pittsburgh, that her passport went missing, and she was still in the throes of replacing it for the third time.

"Oh, not a problem at all, we will definitely have to catch up next time," Lizette replied with the stare of a Nile crocodile, clad in boardroom black Donna Karan.

"So where are we dumping this pig?" Marni asked. "Shhh!" whispered Alice.

"Look, I'll tell you when to be paranoid," said Lulu.

"Yeah, like when we are getting checked into Rikers," said Lizette.

"No one has any idea what we are talking about," Marni chimed in.

"It just sounds like we're dumping off some bad barbeque, not committing a crime," said Sasha.

"Shhh. we *cannot* get in trouble here," whispered Alice.

"Marni has this under control," Lulu maintained, lowering the register in her voice ever so slightly. After learning what had occurred at the 21 Club, Sasha and Lulu had little freedom. They were cleverly duped into the Amy Wallingford affair and like so many other dastardly deeds, had no choice but to play along with Screwzette at the helm.

"Let's split this rig," Lulu joked.

"Lars has really got you brainwashed," said Sasha as she turned to Lulu.

"I can't believe you're letting him go on Kathy Winger's stupid fucking dating show," Lizette said as she grabbed Lulu's arm. "Have you lost your fucking mind?"

"He's just doing it to get some airtime for his own reality show," Lulu defended.

"Yeah, what? *To Catch a Predator—Dateline?*" mused Alice. "Uh—last time I checked, you're the one dating a married man with two children," cracked Lulu, giving her the evil eye.

"You know, that reminds me, Lulu, I had this dream the other night that you went to go work for Lars, helping him with his fashion line," Lizette interjected.

"A dream? More like a nightmare," replied Lulu, yet secretly she wanted that more than anything. She wanted to leave these petty bitches in the worst way, but wouldn't let on.

As the super-posse entered Barnes & Noble in Union Square, they made a beeline over to the literature section. Walking past the wall-to-ceiling columns on the ground floor, the group headed to the escalator up to the second floor and straight over to Joseph Conrad's famed book *Heart of Darkness*, the mother of all modern war novels, and slipped the license of Famy's better years into page twenty-two of the book, for a vain game of "hide-and-go-fuck-yourself." Famy Wallingford would clearly have her own little Vietnam when going through security at JFK, for she would surely have an apocalyptic moment at the Jet Blue counter.

This bit of emotional terrorism doled out by Sergeant Screwzette and the hatchery would foil Famy's weekend plans with her husband, whom Lizette also detested. It wasn't until that incident with Client #9 that the firm really began to unravel from inside the hatchery outward.

As a bit of courtesy, the girls scrawled on a yellow Post-it note, each taking turns with different letters. The note read:

Check page 22, Heart of Darkness—Ladies of the Hatchery

They slipped the note into a random page of Joseph Heller's novel *Catch 22* as if by some perverse wicked twist of *Twilight Zone* fate, they would offer Famy a fighting chance at making her tenth anniversary dinner with her husband in St. Louis.

Ding, ding, ding went the trolley, and Famy wasn't going to be on it. There would be no meet-me-in-St. Louis, but there would be tears and a heart of darkness for whoever stole her license and ruined her anniversary dinner.

Feeling guilty beyond words, Lulu thought this stunt had gone a bit too far, ruining that poor woman's anniversary. But what could she do? She was a soldier in Screwzette's foot army. She made her way to meet Lars at one of their favorite neighborhood haunts, the Half King, a West Chelsea gastropub known for the galleristas, artists, and other literary types that frequented it. The pub, erected from the royalties from Sebastian Junger's *The Perfect Storm*, had become as popular as his book and the movie it inspired. Walking west on Twenty-Third Street, Lulu fumbled through her oversized navy-colored Michael Kors satchel in search of her Blackberry Bold that was chiming in.

"Hi, Mom," Lulu said as she answered her cell phone. "Lulu darling, we need to talk."

"I'm on my way to meet Lars for dinner. Can I call you back when I get home?" Lulu questioned.

"I don't think this can wait. Your father and I were at Publix, picking up an Entenmann's coffee cake for the morning, some Sanka, and my prescriptions; so I'm putting my items on the counter, and I look to my left to grab one of those separators because these freakin' hippies were encroaching on your dad's Kashi Go Lean, and picked up a copy of the *National Enquirer*," she said with her Westport, Connecticut, by way of Orlando retirement accent.

"What? Why? Since when do you read that rag?" Lulu asked.

"I don't, but maybe you should, dear. Your father picked up several copies—Oh my God! He's more than disturbed."

"Wait. Why?"

"Ask Lars. Gotta go," she sang, quickly getting off the phone.

Just then, as if his ears were buzzing in a kismet cradle of cadence, Lulu clicked over to answer Lars calling in on the other line.

"Hi, I'm walking Kingsley now, so I may be a couple minutes late," said Lars frantically as he tried to keep up with Lulu's café au lait–colored Havanese pup, scurrying down the street.

"Okay, will see you soon. I need you to stop by London Terrace News and pick up a copy of the *National Enquirer* on your way to Half King," Lulu requested.

"Why?"

"I don't know, my mom wouldn't get into it, just grab as many copies as you can—she said my dad was mortified."

"What? I'm getting another call. It's Gwen. Will meet you at the restaurant," Lars said.

Lulu never considered herself to be the jealous type. Her relationship with Lars was completely secure. And in fact, she could never be jealous of Gwen, because Gwen was code for Dick. Dick would call

Lars incessantly, sometimes thirty times a day, and Lars didn't want thirty missed calls from some Dick popping up on his iPhone. Dick was Lars' executive producer buddy, who came out of his retirement to land Lars a development deal for his reality TV project about the art world.

"Hey, babe, have you seen the *Enquirer*?" questioned Dick.

"I just heard that from Lulu's mother. What in the fuck is going on?" Lars angrily asked.

"Kid, all I'm going to tell you is this is outta control. This could cause some confusion with the networks."

"Huh?" Lars began mumbling unintelligible grunts as Lulu's pup, Kingsley started to squat. Lars went into his manic-panic, Jerry Lewis-Dr. Jekyll jerky mode that typically started with a few grunts, followed by several sighs, building into a full-blown, as Lulu dubbed it, kvetch-a-thon, which occurred within seconds, usually when Lars was overwhelmed by menial tasks, caught off-guard, or in a spat with Lulu.

"Ek oh, poop, Dick, hold on, shit, ek, ah, good boy, shit, ah, Kingsley," Lars, realizing he didn't have a poop bag, began panicking.

"You're on the front page of the *National Enquirer*," said Dick. "What?" said Lars.

"There is a picture of you on the cover," said Dick.

"Of me?" Lars interrupted. "How in the fuck is that possible?" He pulled out a crumpled Shake Shack napkin spotted with strawberry stains from his painted jeans pocket to pick up Kingsley's mess.

"Yea, clearly," Lars responded to the tourists. He now noticed Kingsley's white fluffy tail under his hind legs, which meant big trouble. Lars' eyes widened as he realized Kingsley had a huge poop ball matted on his poor little hiney, and this meant a ghastly bath for the both of them. He quickly picked up his pooch and shot into the phone, "I gotta call you back, I got a situation here."

"The *Enquirer*?" Lars mumbled under his breath, rushing back to his apartment.

As Lulu crossed Seventh Avenue, making her way past the Chelsea Hotel, she spotted an oddly familiar figure: a man wearing a gray suit and skinny black tie. He was lighting up a cigarette under the awning of the infamous hotel, known primarily for its history of notable residents. The twelve-story red brick building has been the home of many great writers, musicians, artists, and actors, including Bob Dylan, Janis Joplin, Jack Kerouac, Thomas Wolfe, Edie Sedgwick, Jimi Hendrix, and was the Bohemian playground for Sex Pistols' Sid and girlfriend Nancy. Lulu couldn't quite place her pinky finger on where she had seen him before, but she was having a déjà vu experience all over again. Lulu was big on déjà vu. In fact she was big on anything related to the occult, ghost stories, or the proverbial X-Files. She believed that there were some strings in the universe that were yoga-bent on tugging at one another, turning this into kinetic, free-flowing, holistic energy, like an acupuncture needle piercing the tender sinews of fate, like transcendental tectonic plates shifting into a vacuum of a love-filled but stern universe, where fate doesn't always end up in a pretty little bow like a Hollywood film. No, rather it tugs at the consciousness of those who have the power to see through the darkness, sensing untoward thoughts; disingenuous by their inception. And to recognize this was a true gift. Cynicism plays no part in absolute discovery, for people and things make themselves evident through clear, definable actions of themselves and their close counterparts, leading Lulu back to her senses. And every fiber of her being alerted her when something felt strongly familiar.

Did she recognize the man with the cigarette from Barnes & Noble? Or was he one of the reporters who attended the Grangeway luncheon? Or maybe it was in line at Starbucks? As she continued walking west on Twenty-Third Street, the warm sun dropped behind Chelsea Piers. Lulu fixated her now weary eyes on the window and followed the man's reflection, feigning interest in the fabled *Rocky Horror Picture*

Show and other offbeat art films that are regularly featured on the placards, windows, and walls of the neighborhood theatre.

Speed-dialing Lars, in a calm, collected, clear tone, she whispered, "Lars, can you hear me?"

"Yes." Lars was hovered over the counter, devouring a bag of Famous Amos chocolate chip cookies, staring catatonically at the *Enquirer's* front page.

"I think I'm being followed; what do I do?"

"Eh, huh? What? Huh?" he continued to grunt, not believing what he was seeing on the page before him. His face turned from a whiter shade of pale to a ghastly green in a matter of a page turn, when he noticed page nineteen.

"Hello. Lars, are you there? Are you even listening to me? What do I do? Can you meet me at Lucky Burger?"

"No, I got a serious situation here. I can't. Just meet me at Half King."

"What? I may not make it. He could kill me. I don't know who this guy is."

"Talk to him."

"What? Fuck you," Lulu said, slightly raising her voice.

Seated at the wooden bar made from a two-hundred-year-old Pennsylvanian barn, Lars pounded his second Guinness in a matter of seconds. He sat stewing over the scandal he was now embroiled while Stevie Wonder's "Superstition" blared over the pub's PA system.

"Hey, thanks a lot," Lulu sarcastically shouted, as she threw her bag on the bar and hopped into a hand-hewn backless barstool beside Lars.

"Will you fucking look at this? I am on the front page of this fucking rag, right above Whitney's 911 call," cried Lars as he slid a copy of the magazine in front of Lulu. "Oh, sorry, I forgot to order your drink."

"And I need one! I could have gotten killed out there!" Lulu screamed. "I'll have a dirty martini," Lulu ordered as she turned toward the bartender, whom Lars had dubbed the "Hai Karate Kid," a slender, blond Asian twenty-something who regularly sported a goofy Flock-of-Seagulls eighties hair-do and made a mean martini. A platinum Ralph Macchio sans the karate but with plenty of cologne.

"What? My career is toast; would you look at this?" Lars gasped.

As Lulu examined the cover, the headline read, "Streisand Turns Her Back on Gay Son—Why Barbra's Sick of Him." And there smack dab beside it was a porthole photo of Lars.

"Ohmigod! That's insane. That's you . . . How did they get that?" Lulu, still in shock, continued, "Ohmigod, I have to call my mom right now."

Lars sighed, "Keep reading."

Lulu rifled through the rag and stopped dead on page nineteen, mortified to find a full frontal shot of Lars, with the pull quote stretched across his chest that read, "She wants him to fall in love with a nice boy and settle down."

"What the fuck?" Lulu blurted out. "It says you're Streisand's Casanova, party-boy son. How can these people get away with this? This is crazy! Well, one thing is for sure, if you are her son, we're getting a bigger apartment."

"I'll drink to that," Lars mused.

Just then, the Hai Karate Kid interrupted to take the couple's order. "What can I get you two breeders for dinner?"

"I'll take the fish and chips," Lars sheepishly requested.

"No. No. He'll have an open-faced turkey burger, a side salad, no fries," interrupted Lulu. "And I'll do the Caesar salad with chicken."

"What? Just let me die quickly with this canola oil coronary," Lars implored. "I'll have the fish and chips."

"Well, make it two," Lulu demanded. "I'm the one being followed."

* * *

A close confidante and special friend to Davis Kline, Client #27's daughter was to be married in a June wedding.

The bride's parents, Michael and Cheryl Withers, hosted the June wedding at the Metropolitan Club. Withers, the son of a Connecticut congressman, now chairman of Withers & Walker, a Wall Street hedge fund with roots in Greenwich, CT epitomized the one percent of the one-percenters. This affair was sure to be a who's who of the Hamptons and Martha's Vineyard crowd.

The warm rays bathed the club's tony courtyard, casting soft crimson shadows from the Corinthian columned gates that proudly addressed Sixtieth Street on the northeast corner of Fifth Avenue. In response to the rejection of his friend by other exclusive private men's clubs, J. P. Morgan erected the Metropolitan Club in 1891. The Vanderbilts and the Roosevelts were among the founding members along with Morgan.

The newlyweds, Lauren Withers-Mason and Philip Reed Mason had quite a crowd assembled for their grand reception, as an endless black sea of limos and town cars besieged the members only club.

The room was full of conservative custom suits and other bloated marshmallow-heads with names like Langford, Nash, and Keating, and their wives, girlfriends, and dysfunctional family members.

It is some odd bit of justice that the progeny of extremely wealthy men end up living under such an enormous shadow, which more often than not drives them to a life of drinking, drugs, gambling, and prostitution, usually all before noon. It's not the son of the great man, nor the son of the son of the great man, but typically some fifth generation trustafarian misanthrope, expelled from junior college by way of prep school, that trades on the family name ad nauseam, to the chagrin of their immediate family. They'll manage to get themselves into more trouble and infamous headlines than the great-great-great-grandfather, running full circle, and often managing to squander their family's fortune by their mid-thirties.

All the top brass from KAR PR were in attendance sans one Lizette Hansen, and the fact that she was literally uninvited to the event of the summer season at none other than the Metropolitan Club, after working tirelessly for Michael Withers and his crusty firm going on seven years now, sent her into sub orbit. This dilettante was going to interrupt the blissful union in the worst way.

Like a holy sixth grade science experiment, she would create a volcano and let the lava burn up the love. The lava came in the form of Holly Michelle, the craziest girl with two first names on three legs. Holly, born Henry, received a call Thursday morning from Sasha.

Holly grabbed the cell phone that was sitting on top of the latest copy of *Out Magazine* on her bedside table. "Better make it good," she said, sounding hungover from a wild night at the Eagle Bar.

"I have a really big favor to ask of you," said Sasha.

"You always do. Well, if you want me to sew my dick back on—forget it, I'm going back to bed. I lost out on Davio last night. The wheel was against me."

"Look, I have $1,000 with your name on it!" exclaimed Sasha.

"It would take a lot more than that to sew it back on, honey," Holly declared, desperately wanting to go back to bed.

"Stop playing around. I need you to pose as a photographer for this crazy punk rock wedding this afternoon," Sasha anxiously explained.

"Uh . . . I don't own a camera, and the only picture I've ever taken in my life is when they cut off my cock."

"What? You were awake?" questioned Sasha, momentarily confused.

"Hell yeah, girlfriend, want to see it?" Holly proudly responded.

"Uh, no thank you. Anyways, I'll be by in a couple of hours with a rented Hasselblad. This client is insisting on using old-school film," said Sasha, quickly hanging up the phone before Holly could say no, and before she could get sidetracked from the assignment at hand.

Sasha was tasked with literally pulling Holly Michelle's name out of a hat the previous night at the Asia de Cuba bar in the Morgans Hotel. Celebrating a small victory, with a piece in the *Wall Street Journal* for Client #9, Screwzette, after a few caipirinhas, hatched a wicked plan to take revenge on the Withers wedding. They would feel the wrath of what it meant not to invite Lizette Hansen to the wedding of the season. Dubbed "Operation Wanderlust," the plan broke down in the following manner:

9:00 a.m. EDT—Sasha and Marni met at the Starbucks on West Fourth Street to concoct a fresh batch of the Bombay Twister, a bottle of Visine with a shot of stool softener: a silver bullet for the Withers wedding photographer.

9:30 a.m. EDT—The hatchery had been tracking Chuck Mondo, wedding photographer to the stars, for the past three weeks and followed him on his routine Saturday morning visits to the Doma coffee shop, a trendy West Village writers' nook on Perry Street, where he worked exclusively on his novel, amidst other young writers of screenplays, novels, and self-help books, making him feel connected with the New York literary community. And the ladies of the hatchery were going to connect him in a whole new way. He'd soon feel like a hallowed American writer atop an American Standard.

"Excuse me, aren't you Charles Mondo?" questioned Marni in her best shy-girl tone, eyeing up her prey and his chai tea.

Chuck smiled surreptitiously and nodded.

Marni blurted out, even before she realized she was still wearing her wedding band and four-carat diamond ring, "I'm getting married in five months, and my photographer canceled on me. Are you—I mean, you wouldn't know your schedule—that's silly. On second thought, do you have a card?"

Looking down at her princess diamond, he shot back in his smug, jaw-clinched Connecticut accent, "It appears that you are already married."

"Oh, d-did I say me?" stuttered Marni. "I meant my sister," she added, motioning to Sasha, who was seated at the adjacent table. "She's a lesbian."

Sasha, hearing all of this, smiled wryly, raising her eyebrow. A nervous wave ran over Marni's body. She saw herself being fired over and over again by Lizette in a taxicab ride home. They had to dose him and quick; they were running out of time.

Chuck, just wanting to get rid of these two, reached beneath the table and rifled through his black leather Tumi attaché. In that split second, in a lightning cobra move, Marni revealed the Visine bottle concealed in the sleeve of her well-worn Yale sweatshirt, and quickly trickled four full drops of the Bombay Twist into Chuck's chai tea. The calculated fourth drop would ensure that the water closet at the Doma would be his residence for the next seven hours straight, completely knocking him out of contention for the Withers wedding.

10:00 a.m. EDT—Marni went to Think Pink Nails on Seventh Avenue South for a manicure and pedicure. Sasha arrived at Holly's apartment on Jane Street where she practiced her lounge act. Sasha handed off the rented Hasselblad with five rolls of semi-exposed film, shot at Black Abyss, a camp for sexual proclivity and those who deviate from there. The camp was a three-day trek into the superego of the sexual experience, where a seven-hundred-person gang bang wouldn't raise an eyebrow. In the brochure, when they say abyss, they mean it. Set in the outskirts of the nation's capital, the playground attracts fetish heads of all types and interconnects them in a tantric web of exploration, specializing in BDSM, bondage, discipline, sadism, and masochism. Not to be confused with DBMS, database management system. The Withers wedding would get some saucy superimposed bride and groom photos with a gang-bang in the background, courtesy of Lizette "Screwzette" Hansen.

Holly (Hank) Michelle arrived through valet in a black-and-white—checkered Karmann Ghia, circa 1972. Exiting the car, she was wearing a multicolored eighties frock with a pink boa, looking like a cross between Cyndi Lauper and Mario Cantone. With a spiky fire engine red wig surrounding her face, her hard, androgynous features broke through her edgy punk rock makeup. It was the perfect fit for the most conservative wedding of the season.

June wedding at the Metropolitan club	$1 million
Tiffany wedding bands	$5,000
Wedding invitations	$12,000
Oscar de la Renta wedding dress	$23,000
Honeymoon in the South of France	$30,000

The look on Michael Withers face when he saw his only daughter's wedding photos—a snapshot of the groom feeding his daughter wedding cake, with an orgy of seven-hundred naked bodies ghosting behind them:

Priceless!

Millionaire Matchup

"I just don't understand why you would have to go to Barbados this weekend. It's my cousin's wedding," Lulu shouted into the phone receiver.

"I'm just letting you know that I may have to go if I get picked for the next round. It's not real. It's a reality show. It's all bullshit. I am not going to like the girl and she is definitely not going to like me," admitted Lars.

"That I believe!" Lulu screamed into the phone. Slamming down the phone receiver, she blankly stared at her computer screen.

"What's the matter, Lulu?" Marni asked, clearly eavesdropping on Lulu's conversation. That was Marni's MO, she was covert, which came in handy, working for Lizette.

"Nothing," replied Lulu, trying to determine if she was more peeved at Lars or Marni.

"It didn't sound like nothing. You sounded upset," said Marni. "Well, it was nothing," Lulu remarked, as she tried to focus and get back to her work. She tried not to think about the fact that Lars might be going to Barbados this weekend with some reality show slut, for his little fifteen minutes of fame.

A few moments later Marni, Lulu, and Lizette rushed out of the office. As usual they were running late for a client meeting. Lucky for them the client was nearby on Fifty-First Street and Madison Avenue, a ten-minute walk from their office in Rockefeller Center.

Wasting no time, Marni blurted, "Lars is going to Barbados this weekend on *Millionaire Matchup*, and Lulu is pissed, but she's acting like she's okay with it," like a rapid-fire machine gun on crystal meth.

"What? Is that true?" questioned Screwzette.

"No. W-e-e-l-l-l. Not really," Lulu hesitated, growing more and more irritated by the ambush.

"I thought everything was okay between you and Lars?" Screwzette pressed on. "What makes you think it isn't?" Lulu questioned.

"Well, if it was, then he wouldn't be going on that fucking TV show! Hello?" Marni egged on.

"Lulu, what's really going on here?" Screwzette demanded.

"It's nothing! He may or may not go to Barbados. He made it to the next round filming *Millionaire Matchup*. And only *if* he makes it to the final round, *only* then would he be going to Barbados. So really, you see, it is nothing!" Lulu declared, irritated now more than ever.

"Well, if my boyfriend ever pulled a stunt like that, you know where you would find his things," Marni cleverly chimed in.

"Boyfriend? Don't you mean husband? Last time I checked, you were fucking married!" Lulu shot back.

"Yes, I have to agree with Marni on this one. This is absurd. Now, he has brainwashed you to think this is okay. Lulu, it is not okay. Have you lost your fucking mind?" asked Screwzette as she checked her CrackBerry.

The word *brainwashed* rang in Lulu's ears as she climbed the steps to her fourth floor walk-up apartment on east Sixty-Third Street, right next door to Bawarchi Indian, one of the reasons why Lulu and her roommates took the apartment. One taste of their tikka masala sent the girls straight to their Bikram yoga class on east Sixty-Fifth Street.

"What do you think?" Lulu asked as she turned to her roommate Sabina.

"Well, I'm with you. Maybe your relationship isn't where you think it is," Sabina replied.

Sabina had wiry long, blonde hair and blue eyes. She stood five foot ten, a hundred and seventeen pounds. She was originally from Armenia, before Sabina's mother had moved her and her three sisters from Yerevan to Los Angeles at the age of five, where she lived most of her life—that is, until she moved to New York for college. After graduating from Touro College, Sabina had a fluctuating linty list of odd jobs from dog walker to dominatrix—her most challenging transition yet. Lars' friends aptly gave her the moniker the Armenian Delight. Sabina's favorite pastime was to chase metrosexual men, and when they ultimately rejected her, she turned to foraging the city's eateries with her roommates.

Lulu met Sabina one night a few years back, outside the trendy Soho House in the Meatpacking District.

"Oh, honey, I am going to have to go. This is my very best friend from high school, and I just ran into her. She's leaving, and I'm going to go with her," Sabina said as she turned to her date that night.

"What?" replied her overeager suitor.

"Well, thanks for a lovely evening, gotta go," Sabina sang as she jumped into a cab with Lulu.

Lulu can still hear the poor guy pleading from the street, "But you don't know her. I just heard you . . . You just met!"

Sabina and Lulu laugh about that night often. They were instant friends.

"We'll be here analyzing this all night. And the game is about to start, so I'll give you my two cents and that is it. He wants to do the show to help his career. Nothing—absolutely nothing to read into. He's doing this purely in hopes that it will help him get his own show," said Kayla, Lulu's rational roommate.

"A show about what? About how to be a dickhead boyfriend?" Sabina playfully questioned. "He's typecast!"

Kayla was a petite, Southern Californian suburban surfer girl who moved to Manhattan to pursue her dream of eating her way through the better Korean delis of the naked city, which was a love the girls all shared, one macaroni and cheese, chicken wings, and Ben & Jerry's Schweddy Balls ice cream at a time.

As Monday night football blasted from the flatscreen TV in the living room, Sabina and Lulu camped out in their tiny kitchen, hovering over the counter, enjoying a heavenly plate of Brie, Manchego, and Gruyère from Murray's in the West Village and a bottle of chardonnay that Sabina sent back from her recent trip to Napa Valley. When looking for apartments, the girls were so laser focused on how to divide an apartment by three, that the kitchen somehow was grossly overlooked—so much so that when the girls arrived on move-in day, movers in tow, they thought they had the keys to the wrong apartment. It wasn't ion Lulu called the leasing office to learn that it was not a joke and that they were, in fact, home sweet home.

Lulu and Sabina vowed to make the most of it. They both lived by the same mantra: "Sure it's cramped. But this is New York. What isn't cramped?" And just like that, they turned their wine and cheese parties into a weekly ritual—a ritual that included only the two of them, mostly because that's all that could fit, and even that was pushing it.

Lulu could always count on Sabina to analyze any problem with her. Even though Sabina loved to watch football, she loved drama even more, and lucky for Lulu, the San Diego Chargers weren't playing that night. After an hour of analyzing the Lars scenario, Lulu's cell phone rang with the ringtone, "Have Love Will Travel" by the Black Keys. Lars jokingly programmed the ringtone into Lulu's phone several months back, and it was quickly becoming the bane of her existence.

"What is your problem?" Lars asked.

"What are you talking about?" questioned Lulu.

"Screwzette called, harassing me! I don't need this! I have enough stress in my life!" Lars screamed.

"What?" asked Lulu.

"I just got off the phone with her. This bitch had the nerve to call me up on the phone while I was in a meeting with the executives from Saks to tell me that I had to pull out of the show and basically kept threatening me, repeating that I would be on a real PR ride. Lulu, what are you telling this woman? You need to make it stop!"

Oddly enough, Lulu was not mad at Lars; she was furious with Screwzette. She had gone too far.

"I said it was nothing. Marni was eavesdropping on our conversation, and told her everything. I didn't say a word to Screwzette," Lulu convinced Lars.

The next week was a living hell for Lulu. The hatchery was rocked by the text war between Lars and Lizette. A thousand irate text messages and seven days later, Lulu was summoned to Del Frisco's. On the ground floor of the McGraw-Hill building, the restaurant was located only a few blocks away from their office. Since Bobby Van's was their regular watering hole, Lulu had an odd feeling that something was amiss.

Typically, the steakhouse was reserved for the most important client lunches or business deals. Lizette had an odd sense of humor and sensibility. It was dirty and raunchy like an English comedian; her jokes were always tied to some scathing, literal, underground meaning, and this thought played on her as she entered the building of higher learning. Lulu knew there was a psych lesson coming, but wasn't sure whether it was in the form of a Rorschach test or Screwzette ready to tear her to shreds.

"Soooooo, Lulu. What happened? Did he make it to the final round or what?" Marni asked inquisitively.

"No," said Lulu.

"Yeah, figures," said Marni.

"What are you trying to say?" Lulu asked.

"Lars had no right to text me. That was way out of line," interrupted Screwzette turning toward Lulu.

"Out of line? You're out of line," Lulu fired back, secretly proud she was finally able to quote one of her favorite movies. Well, almost—if you changed line to order, but she didn't care; she was defending her loving boyfriend Lars. "He's trying to get his own reality show, not a date," Lulu continued, trying to think of what else Al Pacino's character in *And Justice for All* would say. She could feel her blood start to boil and her cheeks felt flush. It was then that Screwzette's CrackBerry chimed in with another text. Picking up her phone, Lizette removed her glasses from her hair and slid her arm like a trombone until she could focus on the message. It was yet another toxic text from Lars, which read:

"Why don't you go back to what makes you drink every night? You can't control me like your little minions."

Lulu could see the steam coming out of Screwzette's freshly coiffed Frédéric Fekkai blow out, crumbling like a demolished building right before Lulu's very eyes. Her blow out, feathered Farrah Fawcett curls imploded and looked more like a matted Chihuahua than a wannabe Charlie's Angel. Lars text incensed Screwzette into a frenzy as her voice deepened, "He's f-i-i-i-n-i-s-h-e-d."

Her "cankles" gave way as she buckled into the nearest seat at the bar, just swearing minutes earlier that the last thing she wanted was a seat before dinner. Lulu had never seen Lizette this enraged. This was one for the books. Her warm, powdered cheeks went sallow within seconds of reading Lars' dig. The Withers wedding non-invite paled in comparison. Lulu immediately feared for her life. She suddenly had a vision of being on the Serengeti, charged by a wild rhinoceros with only a Starbucks latte to arm herself. She stood no chance against the snarling beast in the red Pucci dress. She could see herself skewered like fresh meat on a shish kebab; her career was clearly char-grilled.

Lars was a champion at getting people to go off the deep end. Getting under their skin was his specialty. He was actually better at this than Marni was at concealing her fat ass. He had a sideshow talent for pissing people off and was often invited to parties to get back at an ex-boss or ex-lover. He had a real gift. People would often come to him by word of mouth and seek his advice at how to get someone to snap. It wasn't just one type of person. He would advise on how to piss off anyone, from a congressman to a car attendant. He would find their weakness and pick at it oh so slowly, like a withered scab. He also had great charm, but that was not what moved Lars. It was his caustic side that gave him the most satisfaction; for he could move mountains with it, and Screwzette was his latest experiment of something he dubbed "emotional terrorism." He considered it a type of verbal waterboarding.

Screwzette awarded Lulu an earful and her walking papers. Lulu left the steakhouse, her eyes welling up with tears as she walked west down Forty-Ninth Street. Walking past the bright lights that made up Times Square, Lulu played back the events in her mind, trying to think if there was something she could have done differently. She was coming up empty. She needed Lars now more than ever, so she headed to his Chelsea loft.

Purple Raincoat and a Pink Thong

Working for high profile clients was demanding. Working for Client #9 was more like trying to power New York City on Christmas Eve with a broken-down BIC lighter as your only source of fuel. So was the upwardly mobile well-meaner trying to placate the demands of his enslaver like a mighty salmon swimming upstream only to be ensnared in the gripping claws and jaws of a burly brown bear, in this case, Client #9—as Lulu's misfortune would have it, was also sleeping with Lizette "Screwzette" Hansen.

Lulu landed grizzly Client #9, a cushy reoccurring gig on one of New York's leading business television networks. So, the bear and the lion, Mark DeLyon, leading anchor for *Bloomberg*, traded juicy business barbs and lunch notes before the closing bell.

The group moved over to Nello's for a post-production meeting, arguing the finer points of an '86 bottle of Beaujolais. Nello's was the upper crust of the Upper East Side. Dining next to royalty and A-listers wasn't atypical for a Tuesday night. Impossible for them to resist the hints of gardenia mixed with the fresh basil wafting from the main dining room, the hatchery nestled into a banquette in the corner of the restaurant, led by Nello himself.

"Thanks again, we always receive great feedback from our viewers about your advice," said Mr. DeLyon.

"I always love doing the show. In fact, I received a call this afternoon as soon as the show was over. And we have a potential new investor wanting to come on board," said #9.

"That's great news! I'm so glad that we were able to finally get together tonight. So, tell me more about your family," said Mr. DeLyon.

"Well, I have four beautiful girls," said #9. "They keep me pretty busy. The oldest is twenty-five and the youngest is four months."

White Collar Slavery

Lizette heard through the grapevine that Client #9 had had another baby, but the details were never confirmed until tonight. Lulu strategically sat closest to both the bear and the lion; she knew she had to proffer up a very clever diversion or risk being devoured like fresh meat.

"Four months. Congratulations. I have two children myself. They are eight and twelve, so I know you're not getting much sleep," continued Mr. DeLyon.

"Yes, between the NoDoz and the Pampers at 3:00 a.m., my nerves are shot, but my overseas trading has gotten better," laughed Client #9. "So Marni, how old is your little one now?"

"Ian will turn one next month," Marni proudly proclaimed. "Then what are you still doing here?" joked Mr. DeLyon.

Mr. DeLyon was unaware of the amount of control Lizette had on both Marni and Lulu. Lizette had a maniacal, social-stabbing grip on their psyches. Like Piggy in *Lord of the Flies*, holding the conch, Screwzette held the coveted Lana Marks aqua-blue sports bag and reminded Marni and Lulu every morning they were too poor to afford one of their own. She treated herself to the bag, or so she maintained, but the girls of the hatchery knew that it was a gift from Client #9, who beneath the sheets, Lizette had affectionately dubbed "St. Stephen," and whom Marni and Lulu nicknamed Raincoat, for the Burberry trench coat that Lizette always kept on the back of her office door, in case a quick visit was in order.

Lizette influenced the girls' decisions so strongly that neither one of them ever questioned a task for fear that their job would be in jeopardy, which was made pretty clear very early on. If one of the girls ever questioned her, she was treated like one of the subjects that betrayed the queen in *Alice in Wonderland*.

Marni nervously chuckled as Lulu looked at Lizette out of the corner of her eye, gauging her reaction to the obviously normal question Mr. DeLyon posed to Marni. Feeding into the pressure, Lizette turned to

Marni and sympathetically asked, "Why don't you have the car drop you off, and we'll stay a little bit longer and have dessert?"

This was the type of mind-control chicanery that Lizettte always pulled; making it appear as if Marni was there on her own free will as if it was her choice to stay out so late with a young baby at home. Marni thought for a moment and then quickly excused herself from the table and left.

With Al at the wheel, trusty car #48 waited in a long line of black town cars and sedans that were perfectly parked on Madison Avenue in front of Nello's. Al was the only person on earth allowed to drive Screwzette anywhere. He received this plucky job because he was the last man standing at Big Apple Limousine. Literally, he was the only person that Screwzette hadn't had deported. After a series of seedy drivers and experiences, Screwzette grew to trust Al for all of her "dirty deeds done dirt cheap." She had Al on speed dial. And for Al, that was a very dangerous thing. Even on his days off he was still implored to pick her up. Lucky for Al, the trips with Screwzette and her hatchery never lacked a dull moment.

Al's first stop was a luxury high-rise building in Battery Park City. As he pulled up to the circular drive, Lulu glanced over at Screwzette, feigning as if she had been seeing St. Stephen's building for the first time. As Client #9 exited the car, Screwzette turned toward Lulu and said, "Did you like how I didn't even acknowledge the fact that he had a baby?" Screwzette always needed reassurance.

"Yes, that was played off perfectly," Lulu's usual response to Screwzette, trying to make her feel better. "And the fact that neither Marni nor I even reacted to him when he said it, you could tell that really got him mad."

Screwzette still never fully admitted to Lulu that she had had an ongoing affair with Raincoat, but Lulu knew.

The purpose of the next morning was to relive every moment of the dinner the previous night. Marni usually brought breakfast that consisted of coffee and three egg white turkey bacon English muffins.

This type of reenactment happened quite often, as the hatchery needed to exhaust all conversations word by word, vivisecting the meaning of everything. Two hours later, Screwzette exclaimed, "We need to get him back! And it needs to be good!"

It was a bone-chilling November morning when the air was so ice cold that it froze your batteries the second you stepped outside. It was the kind of day the girls had been waiting for—they were revenge ready. Plotting and exploiting was what Screwzette and Marni lived for. It was what they knew best. They had been stewing over the news of Raincoat's baby for months and their perfect plan was born that winter day.

This revenge came in the form of a fluorescent-colored think-pink thong. Screwzette had come up with the award-winning plan, upping previous amorous exploits by the hatchery.

Marni and Screwzette whirled out of the office, on their way to Bloomingdale's, like two Tasmanian devils in a glazed doughnut factory fighting over the last Boston crème éclair. They clearly couldn't orchestrate any field operations without a full and proper burial of several frozen hot chocolates from Serendipity, a bacon burger and steak fries, wading in a cheesy goulash of heart-stopping cholesterol. Screwzette alternated sloppy bites of her bacon cheeseburger with sips of her frozen hot chocolate. However, Lulu was unable to stomach yet another one of their flash-mob feedings, so she opted out for reconnaissance to find the perfect "think-pink" thong for Raincoat.

As Lulu rounded the corner into the lingerie department on the fourth floor, she spotted a pink berry-colored lace thong that would be the perfect pairing for the personalized Hallmark "I love you" card with the quaint, faint recording of "I think I'm freakin' pregnant with your baby."

According to Sergeant Screwzette, the plan was for the dirty bomb to be delivered at precisely 10:35 EST the next morning at Raincoat's penthouse and for the bomb to detonate shortly after, in the arms of his Brazilian baby mama. Screwzette knew full well that Stephen "Raincoat" Walker would not be home. He was out of town dancing around another M&A deal. Ah yes, the perfect accompaniment. Suddenly a text from Screwzette popped up on Lulu's CrackBerry.

Get here now with today's WSJ. We are at Dylan's Candy Bar.

Lulu found the dessert divas nestled up to the Cotton Candy Bar like two cartoon pigs waiting for mother's milk. Fortunately for Screwzette, she had her Tuesday beauty pack in tow, made up of a travel-sized container of Bac-O Bits, a broken down bottle of Bobbi Brown bronzer, a hijacked Nabisco snack, a copy of the latest *Barron's*, and her autographed copy of *Revenge for Dummies*, which she usually kept hidden at the bottom of her aqua-blue bag. She would reveal the weapons in her arsenal as needed. Today it was the Bac-O Bits. And as Screwzette sprinkled a few on her pink cotton candy, she relished in the thought that they had found the perfect lace thong. Writing the copy for the card was not as easy as it sounded—it called for their best thinking. Out of her Tuesday beauty bag, she pulled out a pair of disposable latex gloves that she passed to Lulu and insisted that she put them on as she started to pen the note. Screwzette methodically planned every last detail; even up to the timing of the pregnancy to be sure the faux baby was conceived on Raincoat's last business trip to France. The think-pink thong supported breast cancer research, so somehow Screwzette justified to the hatchery that all of this was done in the name of charity. After all, the thong was purchased using the firm's credit card. A clever hour later, Marni assembled the package, also donning a pair of latex gloves, and gave it to Lulu to mail, but not before she sprayed Lulu's perfume on the sealed envelope.

Lars gave Lulu a bottle of Christian Dior's Addict as a present the month before. Luckily for Screwzette, Lulu was carrying the seventy-five milliliter bottle in her bag, though not so lucky for Lulu, because she resented Screwzette highly for making her use her perfume, thinking that the scent might give it away. Next, Sergeant Screwzette ordered Lulu to go to an obscure, out-of-the-way Fed Ex to be sure there would be no trace. Ninety-Sixth Street and Second Avenue would be the destination drop site. The brisk winter breeze cooperated rather smartly as Lulu slipped on her Isotoner gloves. Everyone in the hatchery had matching monogrammed mauve and black gloves, which were given to them one Christmas by the firm. Making her way to the Upper East Side, Lulu quickened her step, reminding herself that at least this twisted field trip was happening in November and not July, for she certainly would have looked quite foolish wearing fur-lined gloves in the middle of summer. As Lulu snuck into Fed Ex, Stevie Wonder's song, "Signed, Sealed, Delivered I'm Yours" warbled over the speaker system.

Later that night, Lulu awoke in a cold sweat, with visions of the unglimmer twins smirking at her through the shatter-proof glass window of some pathetic visitors' booth at Rikers, like two fat-cat Mafia dons sending a made man up the East River. Lars, being fast asleep, meant he was up all night pushing paint around for his upcoming Condé Nast art and fashion exhibition. She could see he was stressed out by the way he was listlessly laying on the bed like "the other guy" in a bare-knuckle cage match. Through his curly espresso locks, Lulu noticed a new alopecia patch. The new arrival must have cropped up since the weekend, when she lovingly shampooed his entire body as they had steamy sex in the shower. She delicately kissed the quarter-size bald spot, hoping to calm his nerves. Lulu absolutely, wholeheartedly loved Lars.

As she escaped to the gym, she looked back at Lars, her little creative pet; the thought of real trouble danced in her head. She could not shake the Stevie Wonder tune. It kept repeating itself over and over again in her head like a twisted infomercial for "a hard bed and some soft time."

Lulu increased the resistance on the elliptical machine to the death-climb setting, as if to somehow sublimate her Catholic guilt over the dastardly deed of the love letter and think-pink thong. That morning the Asian markets were up and so were two of New York's finest parked in front of their apartment building. Lulu almost spit up her SmartWater as she glanced out the huge bay windows that overlooked Eleventh Avenue to find two NYPD officers entering the building. She felt an Eleventh Avenue freeze-out coming on—they were waiting for her. Her sweat glands broke in a nasty storm, and she could smell her own demise.

Don't or Da Silvano

Screwzette clopped past American Apparel on Sixth Avenue just past Bleecker Street. Admiring her reflection in the orange-tinted store window, she licked the crimson Bobbi Brown lipstick off her front crown, badly worn from too many martinis and cigarettes. She sneered at the colorful T-shirts in the window for the common folk. She was carrying the Lana Marks sports bag, which she could trade for every piece of cotton merchandise in the store and then some. And the power of knowing this made her feel like she was on top of her game, despite still feeling a bit sluggish from a nutty Wednesday morning, where the firm's biggest client, Roger Sloane, CEO of Grangeway Trucking, rang the opening bell at NASDAQ, to only divulge later that the company was "retreating"—filing for bankruptcy. He needed St. Stephen "Raincoat" to restructure the money that was hemorrhaging out of the market on the stock ticker symbol GNWY.

Da Silvano was the premier "seen and be seen" West Village Italian eatery, a mecca for celebrities, paparazzi, and everyone stuck in the middle. The food was outrageously delicious, authentic, and semi-affordable, like every other restaurant in New York, if you work an eighty-plus-hour workweek.

As always, Lulu was early. She waited for Marni and Screwzette to arrive. The debonair Silvano, a white-haired restaurateur with arched eyebrows and a jovial smile, began chatting Lulu up in his thick Italian accent.

"Lulu, my darling, *che cosa hai fatto*? Your dress is *bellisima*. Is it one of Lars'?"

"*Grazie*! Yes, he has a collection in Saks."

"Wonderful news, I will send some of my lady friends over."

"Oh, Silvano," Lulu replied with a wry smile, "and I know you have them."

"Ah yes, but they are just friends. Not to worry, your table will be ready momentarily. Ciao, Lulu."

As Lulu glanced over to a table tucked away in the corner of the restaurant, she found several dark-haired Italian busboys frantically setting the coveted table seven for three. She sent Lizette a text.

They are about to seat me. How close are you?

Just as Silvano was making his way over to Lulu from the kitchen, Screwzette and Marni made their grand entrance. To Lulu, Screwzette looked more like a broad-faced billboard for Diet Coke than a president of KAR PR. She was packed tight in her Pucci dress. Marni, wearing a black empire dress from Pea in the Pod, expertly hid the fact that she had a five-month baby bump. Marni had a rare gift. Like some people who can see the future, some people who can swim the English Channel in their skivvies, and some people who can knit a sweater in twenty minutes while standing on their head, Marni, even prior to her second pregnancy, was able to conceal her cellulite. She was an interstellar champion, one of the best, in Lulu's opinion. Completely true story: Her husband had no idea, even on the night of their nuptials, how truly heavy his bride was. But one wouldn't know simply by looking at her. However, her groom was in for a rude awakening when he lifted up her Vera Wang, only to find his wang went completely the wrong way.

If Marni was a god at concealing her fat ass, Screwzette was the polar opposite. She was the sloppiest, most disheveled corporate dunderhead in all of New York. Somehow, through the grace of a miscalculated corporate merger, she fell into a position of power. She acted as gatekeeper and supreme plunderer, lording over Lulu and the rest of the firms' well-meaners, brainwashing the minds of young men and women, trying to make a difference in the world. Like Lulu in college, they picked up the mantra, "We have to do better than our parents and leave our children with more than just

TV, marijuana, and rock and roll music," the legacy bestowed upon them by the last generation.

These well-meaners work night and day, day and night to have a few good meals, their assembled Ikea furniture, a 401(k), landing eventually with a two-bedroom apartment, two dogs, two kids, and too much to handle. They submerge themselves in their work, willfully committing to a form of "white collar slavery." Working eighty-plus-hour work weeks, they grind away their ambition, charity, and goodwill, all because of some corporate "greedheads," who willfully clog up the wheel of corporate advancement, progression, and betterment of the lives of the employees and the goods, services, or products they create, all for a few more dollars.

These greedheads—both male and female—are created early on, most likely in junior high or high school, when they are excluded from some type of social or sporting activity. They harbor this resentment and carry a sophomoric feeling of alienation throughout their lives, manifesting itself in forms of corporate vasoconstriction, stifling creative thought and advancement by the well-meaners. Unfortunately, they are in positions of power in corporate America, enslaving and breaking the backs of the youngest entry-level millennials all the way up through the baby-boomer executives. It is usually middle management that adopts this attitude rather than the top executives. More often than not, top-level executives are in positions of influence because they know how to treat and respect their employees, peers, and communities. It is something about those stuck in middle management, daily repeating the very same inter-office nightmares and corporate infractions that turn the well-meaners into numb lemmings, ready to toss their morals into the Hudson River in exchange for a good table at Morimoto's.

Lulu stayed the course—always at hand, and the first one to be sucked into a speed texting match of nonsensical insecurities by her enslaver, who only wanted to check her own cell structure every twenty minutes, using Lulu as her shrink, fashion consultant, nutritionist, and fact checker. She vainly used up every ounce of nights, weekends and energy that she could possibly reap out of Lulu's body and soul, only to reward her twenty-four-hour-a-day, seven-day-a-week, three-hundred-sixty-five-day-a-year devotion with a backhanded compliment and a somewhat stylish costume trinket from Henri Bendel's that somehow in Lulu's mind swept all the dirty water under the corporate bridge, where Screwzette's fat ass was permanently docked.

Lulu's seven-day-a-week enslaver trotted into the restaurant wearing a retro, red Pucci dress. Lulu thought to herself, *Why, pray tell, did Lizette think she could wear a bold-printed, geometric Pucci dress, like scores of other well-heeled women who did so unknowingly, all comically sporting the unflattering geometric print, like a superhero underdog of fashion, looking more like a sea of Lego blocks rather than a smart, tony dresser?*

As Screwzette made her way into the restaurant, she passed Jeff Goldblum and an attractive, young woman who looked like a cross between Carla Bruni and Marion Cotillard. Grabbing the attention of Silvano, Goldblum and company were escorted over to Lulu's awaiting table. With a hand on Lulu's shoulder and a nod, she knew her friend had to give up the table to the Fly, or else one might wind up in her bowl of minestrone.

Lulu felt a quick, sudden wave of panic overcome her entire body, a warm, dulling sensation, like being pricked by hundreds of hot acupuncture needles in a litany of hellish painful moments to come. For Lizette considered herself a grand patron, confidant, and personal friend to Silvano and certainly had spent enough of the firm's dollars to be considered a VIP. But in his mind, she was a hellish, evil woman who regularly upset his other customers, often becoming unruly after having a couple sips of Chianti. She was one incident away from being banned from the Zagat-rated Italian bistro.

Silvano grabbed Lulu's panic-stricken, numb shoulder gently, his eyes saying simply, "*Addio*, Lulu; I have to give the table to Mr. Goldblum."

Silvano gaited off to the kitchen to avoid Lizette. Clearly she was a loose cannon at his establishment, who often ran her little corporate junta from table seven, now occupied by Goldblum and his lovely guest. With fire in her eyes, Lizette peered down at her CrackBerry and scrolled through her messages to find Lulu's text stating that they were setting table seven for them.

Often these situations make these greedheads feel that they are corporate rock stars, worthy of attention, adoration, and excess flattery. More often than not, the greedheads create more harm than good by intentionally wreaking havoc on their employees and creating unnecessarily tense situations over the most trivial nonsense unrelated to corporate matters because their self-appointed-rock-star status has not been recognized or catered to.

This behavior stems from a long-rooted, socially learned bad attitude, often resulting from the enslaver being excluded from an event because of their own doing, lack of accomplishment, or skill. How often does a midlevel manager walk with swagger in the halls of a company and then walk like a mouse on the way to the subway? It is only within the corporate walls that they violently beat their chest to show that they are top gorilla. They are their own lawgivers in their own *Planet of the Apes*, where humanity has no place.

When this act of social or corporate exclusion is repeated in their adulthood, it creates a firestorm of discord for the well-meaners, devoted employees, serving willfully as white collar slaves—all for a weekly paycheck and a 401—*"I can't take any money out until I'm nearly brain dead"—(k)*.

Lizette's face flashed from Diet Coke silver to fire engine red, back to silver, back to red again, all while muttering under her breath some ultimate threat. She motioned for Marni and Lulu to hastily evacuate the pasta stand.

"Wait 'til my friends at FOX hear about this. You'll be on some big PR ride!" Screwzette screamed, and just like that, she stormed out with Marni and Lulu, who seemed to say "sorry" to Silvano with her lovely, endearing, green eyes. The next stop was Bar Pitti, an Italian restaurant just twenty feet north of Da Silvano. The two eateries, Da Silvano versus Bar Pitti, like the Vesuvius feud, had all the classic elements: deception, greed, and penne alla vodka.

Making their way past the sea of paparazzi peppered along the sidewalk and the Bar Pitti habitués dining al fresco in the crisp, cool November air, the ladies ducked into a tinted Lincoln Town Car. Because of the bistro feud, it was a clear taboo, verboten to exit one eatery and enter the other. So Screwzette ordered car #48 to spin around the block and let them out in front of Bar Pitti. As they rounded Bleecker Street, something told Lulu to crane her neck to the left. In what seemed like a whisper of a moment, out of the corner of her eye, she caught a glimpse of the *Matrix* man, her stalker with the gray suit and skinny black tie. Her heart swan dived into her stomach, as she had the sinking suspicion that they were all dead wrong on this one. She was being followed. This was one feeling that she would like to have ignored.

Lulu's thoughts began racing. *Why in the fuck was this marshmallow man after her? Was this related to Zirko? Or was she completely and utterly out of her mind?* Perhaps she was having a Lars moment, a fit of unbridled enthusiasm.

The ladies discreetly made their way inside Bar Pitti, past the Chianti-enhanced volumes of the loyal patrons. They were seated at a fairly decent table. Both Lulu and Lizette could tell this by the amount of big money seated around them. The hierarchy of seating in Manhattan was simple. If you were a celebrity, as in Hollywood, you ruled the lines and the kitchen. And from there it was the regular VIPs, then everyone else lumped together, including the blue bloods that once ran this tiny island with a faux iron fist until the late seventies, when they fell asleep at the wheel. If you were not part of the mobocracy, those were the tough breaks in the naked city. If you were a regular customer or a big money spender and liked by the restaurant staff, you might get seated nestled between two power lesbian tables, and that was only if you tipped well the last time, putting you on the short list.

To the left of the hatchery was a table of two power lesbian fashionistas who appeared to be gossiping about the most decadent wedding ever conceived in the tri-state area.

"I think this is going to be the wedding of the season!" exclaimed a woman, who looked like a cross between Johnny Cash and Donna Karan.

"Personally, I think Manhattan Mini Storage had it right when they said 'if you don't like gay marriage, don't get gay married,'" said an androgynous-looking woman with short blonde hair, wearing a thick ivory and black voodoo warrior necklace that screamed "I am primal woman—hear me roar."

"I thought they were having the ceremony in West Hampton?" asked Donna Cash.

"No, they wanted to be in the city, near the cause and effect," replied the warrior princess, as she brought a glass of red wine to her metallic-shaded lips.

"Better shopping than the beach," replied Donna Cash.

"Barneys!" sang the two women in unison, clinking their glasses together.

Screwzette, with a maniacal grin, pretended to listen to Lulu wax on about turning thirty and her mysterious *Matrix* man as she eavesdropped on the table nearby. With pinpoint precision, she calculated the value of the women's outfits in her head like a freak show human abacus, all while shoveling down a plate of pappardelle and a few glasses of chardonnay.

Step right up, folks. See the human jealously machine as she adds up your net worth right before your bloodshot eyes.

Warrior Princess:

Prada black lambskin runway pencil skirt, circa 2012	$3,200
Jimmy Choo yellow patent leather pumps, circa 2011	$1,900
Spanx black silk pantyhose, circa 2012	$65
Céline black leather tote, circa 2012	$4,500

Burberry ivory silk blouse, circa 2011	$2,295
Beatnik voodoo necklace from Brooklyn Flea, circa 1912	$12
Giorgio Armani Eyes to Kill For eye shadow	$32
Sephora air brush machine bronzer	$350
Chanel hot pink lipstick	$35
Mani-pedi: nail color Guchi, Muchi, Puchi by Essie	$95
Chanel black clutch circa 2009	$4,700
Frédéric Fekkai blow out and fresh tint	$325

Give or take international exchange rates and salons, the warrior weighed in at $15,877, well beneath the threshold that Lizette Hansen had set for "queen bitch" status in the room with her Lana Marks aqua-blue sports bag coming in at $100,000; and that was not even considering her Cartier tank, Pucci dress, and her cache of accessories stashed away in her day pack.

Next, she went after Donna Cash, with her laser price checker that would make any department store floor manager proud.

Donna Cash:

Hugo Boss embossed goatskin battle jacket, circa 2011	$3,200
Checkered vintage Buffalo Exchange jersey, circa 1978	$40
Prada dark denim Jeans, circa 2011	$1,200
Stella McCartney leather bag, circa 2009	$2,200
Smashbox eyeliner, shadow, and lips	$110
Tiffany two-carat diamond studs	$2,900
Hugo Boss suede black boots, circa 2011	$3,100
Bedhead faux hawk from Astor Place, circa 1982	$350

The total for Donna Cash was $12,900—still coming in well under the ceiling set by Lizette. So Lizette turned her attention, considering that her assessment of their wardrobe basically was up-to-date, and she felt that perhaps she could learn a thing or two. What she needed was a wardrobe redux and remix.

Lizette had the memory of an elephant, remembering the celebrity stylist who ruthlessly makes over your closet, purging all off-trend items and updating your closet with the latest must-haves for the season, then creating your own chic personal lookbook to share with your most intimate friends.

"Lulu, what was that thing you read me the other day? I need the number of the Chic or Eek lady now," demanded Lizette.

"Oh, I love that woman, she's ruthless when it comes to a closet!" Marni chimed in.

"I didn't ask if you liked her. I need her number. Now!" Screwzette demanded. "Getting it, one second," Lulu replied.

"Now, you get that little blogging bitch Debbie Brillstein from Brooklyn on the phone and have another glass of pinot grigio, or you're fired!"

"I think you're absolutely crazy! If you think for one second that you don't need any anesthesia, you are going to change your mind," Lizette said and Lulu agreed. "You can't exactly find a midwife on Craigslist."

Marni replied, "Alan's boss's mother is a midwife so that's the option we're looking at."

"I don't understand. Doesn't your primary care doctor have any recommendations?" questioned Lizette.

"And you're gonna trust your baby to your boss's mother? Alan's late to work every day," mused Lulu with a wry smile.

"I'm sorry," interrupted Donna Cash in a sheepish tone, even for her faux biker look, "I couldn't help but overhear," as she turned toward Lizette, who after a few plates of pasta started to morph into true Octomom proportions. "I heard you were considering natural childbirth."

"You go girl! At your age!" chimed in the Warrior Princess, sounding more like Wendy Williams than Helen Reddy.

After hearing this comment, Lulu could have sworn that against the warm, bathed light inside Bar Pitti, Lizette's highlights flashed an emergency warning flare. As she choked, her penne shot out of her mouth like a torpedo coming from the *USS Virginia*. Lulu took great pleasure that Screwzette finally would get a much-deserved comeuppance. As a daily dirt disher, she rarely received her just desserts.

What would come out of Lizette's lips next would scare even the most seasoned LA gang leader. "Listen, you silly bitch, go back to drinking your appletinis, you dumb fucks! Esther over here is the one that is pregnant!"

Lizette used the taboo word on these two like she had been working on an oil rig since the age of two. The next ten minutes would turn into a firefight on par with anything on the eleven o'clock news: a grotesque mixture of loose body parts, whirling around in an odd concoction of olive oil, marinara sauce, spit, Grey Goose vodka, and yellow Jimmy Choo's. It was just then that two stocky Latino men burst through the double swinging doors of the kitchen and dove towards Lizette like two linebackers on Super Bowl Sunday. Lulu, in lightning speed texted Sasha, who was back at the hatchery, to have car #48 ready to pick them up for their great escape.

On the car ride home, Lizette was so far down Marni and Lulu's throats, one would think she was filling their cavities, drilling into them, leaving poor pregnant Marni pissing in her penny loafers, sobbing in waves of uncontrollable tears. For Screwzette, her troops did not sling enough flaming arrows in retaliation. Their plunderer had been plundered herself.

"How dare those fucking bitches tell me I'm fucking pregnant? I don't look fucking pregnant. Marni, do I look fucking pregnant to you?"

Screwzette's eyes scornfully seemed to say, "If you weren't such an international champion at camouflaging your cellulite, those dumb bitches would have easily known you were the baby mama!"

"Stephen says I look like Sophia Loren. Fuck those severe bitches in their metallic lipstick!" Screwzette continued screaming at the top of her lungs.

Actually, to Lulu, Screwzette's highlight flashing, children's Benadryl and chardonnay chugging Hansen looked less like Sophia Loren and more like Alf.

Occupy "Maul" Street

For both conservatives and liberals, Occupy Wall Street set a precedent, knotting diverse ideologies together in an unruly bow tie. This movement reared its Medusa-like head, stemming from New York's Wall Street and spread to Atlanta, Dallas, Oakland and other major cities. Under the smoggy Californian sky, yogis replaced socialist insurrection, mirroring the sixties flower power movement of "peace, prosperity, and pot." In some cities it morphed into a sinister scene, like the vicious riots that broke out in Oakland, California. What started out as a multi-headed, leaderless outcry, bought and paid for by both the left and the right, morphed from an innocent Paddy Chayefsky "I am mad as hell and I am not going to take it anymore" demonstration over ATM fees into an odd rally for fringe politics and socialism, undermining the American dream.

These protestors, feeling stymied by capitalism, desperate for economic change, huddled together, the working poor versus the impoverished with plenty of tear gas to go around.

What do you have to lose when you've already lost your mind? read one sign held up by a young teacher for the FOX News camera, which Lulu photographed with her CrackBerry. Another read: *Let Them Eat Cake.* A beleaguered young woman, wearing a tattered suit, cradling a baby in her left arm, held up a sign that read: *White Collar Slavery.* The sign said what her maudlin face couldn't. To Lulu, this woman appeared to be the poster child, the corporate face of the overworked and underprivileged. Her matted hair and dirty nails signaled to all that she had been one of the diehards living in the makeshift village with her iPad as a security blanket, Gerber baby food, and a Coleman tent and heater.

In the crisp, frigid air, Lulu felt a new dampness as the temperature began to drop. A radio blared that an unseasonable storm was barreling across the Midwest and promised to blanket the Northeast. With tears in her eyes, Lulu turned away from the woman and child, and looked toward the construction of the Freedom Tower standing defiantly in the proud skyline of lower Manhattan, trying to determine what had become of her generation. Society was ripping apart everywhere in the world. Lulu wondered what was to blame for the unrest. *Was the world just molting into a new form of inhumanity? Intolerant of despotism and diversity? Yet on the flip side, society as a whole had never been so informed and alive.*

As a light dust of snow fell over the financial district, Lulu felt like she had to do her part to even the score. She would have to take matters into her own hands and be the clear voice for the voiceless; a rock in a sea of turtles; a beacon of hope in despair. As Lulu hopped on the subway, she headed uptown to Lars' apartment. She began to reflect on her own life and her own enslavement. Those three words were forever Etch A Sketched in her brain, she could not shake the image of that woman's sign: *White Collar Slavery.*

A wave of panic rocked her body as a homeless man in a full-length fur coat, reeking of raw fish and Jameson, entered her subway car with an empty Starbucks cup in hand, begging beside her as he sang the familiar Rod Stewart song, "If you want my body and you think I'm sexy, come on sugar let me know." Exposing his hairy, nylon-clad right leg, he continued his act for the next four stops, collecting a total of what appeared to be four crumpled dollar bills. Lulu had seen enough for one day. As the Union Square stop approached, she quickly exited the subway car. Coincidentally, so did Rod Stewart. As the snowstorm began to roll into the city, Lulu could see rather large flakes falling onto the turning auburn leaves.

The vendors at the farmers' market began packing up their green-and-white-checkered canopied tables and the unsold, still colorful bounty of produce from the neighboring farms. Majestic brown and yellow tones of picture-perfect eggplant, acorn, and butternut squash proudly displayed alongside award-winning state-grown Granny Smiths that lined the northwest corner of the square, a brilliant example of New York City in agricultural synchronicity—all under the approving, watchful eye of the Empire State.

Knowing Lars was at home, Lulu let herself into his apartment. "That's it! I'm quitting!" Lulu screamed.

White Collar Slavery

"Whoa! Whoa! Whoa! What happened now?" questioned Lars.

For as long as Lars had known Lulu, she had been threatening to quit. Usually an expensive dinner or an afternoon of shopping sucked Lulu back into the hatchery.

"I know. I know. I sound like a broken record. But *this* is *it*!" Lulu said, standing over the kitchen counter and flailing her arms as she began to describe that poor woman with her child.

"I wanted to see what all the fuss was about, so I went down to Zuccotti Park," Lulu began.

"What? Are you crazy?" Lars interrupted.

"It was completely insane! There were mobs of people and tents everywhere," Lulu continued. "They had their own library with people checking out books. And there was food. Gourmet food everywhere! Then there was this cute girl standing with her daughter who couldn't have been more than two years old, and she was holding this sign: *White Collar Slavery*. I can't get them out of my head! You spend your whole life slaving; working like a mule, only to find out your child's health care has been cut off! This is it!"

Lars interrupted Lulu, trying to calm her down, "Why don't you just sit down? Let me make you some tea."

"There isn't even a comfortable place to sit here!" From floor to ceiling, Lars' apartment was covered with his expressionistic paintings. The furniture, made of molded plastic, was so uncomfortable that it was like sitting on a hellish beveled milk crate. Lars thought that since it was a Frank Gehry design, it must be hip. And the fact that it was beyond uncomfortable was the ultimate example of houseguest prohibitive.

"This is *so* uncomfortable," Lulu cried as she slid off the gray tugboat-shaped couch. "I just want a comfortable sofa! I don't want to be miserable anymore! I was looking at this woman in

Zuccotti Park, and it wasn't until I began talking to her—Melinda Mendelssohn—that I realized—basically, she could be me!"

"Honey, it's not you," Lars lovingly interrupted.

"She started her career as an accountant for Meyers & Tucker. She worked her way up the corporate ladder, played by all their corporate rules and political bullshit," Lulu explained, as she excitedly brushed back her long, wavy locks with her right hand.

Lulu continued ranting. "She put in no less than seventy-hour work weeks for ten years, expecting for the last three years of her career that she would make partner, but her firm would push her out for a first-year associate, always passing her over for partner. The economy was tanking. The firm was being audited themselves. The list goes on. And the first-year associate rose through the ranks in two short years and made partner."

"Now honey, where exactly are you going with this?"

"Remember when we were doing the crisis work for that division of Meyers & Tucker, when they were going through their reorganization? She was one of the casualties. I didn't start it, but I certainty lit a match to the village—covering up all the stories about the people that were out of work. I feel terrible about the whole thing."

"I told you—you're working for the Satan of Sixth Avenue. Are you really surprised? That kind of thing happens all the time. You aren't the only one in that position."

"I know. I know. But it really hit home, and it just makes me sick. This sinister corporate cycle had to end. A single mother lost her nanny because the benefits wouldn't pay, her condo went into foreclosure, and she basically could not afford child care, so it was either stay at work and put all the money into day care or take care of her newborn. All along she played by the corporate rules, and where did that leave her?"

"Broke and on the streets, evidently!" blurted Lars. "You gotta relax! I mean, we . . . you are going to settle the score here; I'm just not sure how. I don't want them firing you," he said as he pulled Lulu near and kissed her on the cheek.

"Well, Lizette is pulling me off Meyers & Tucker and Grangeway." Lulu, getting more indignant by the second, pulled away from Lars and started to pace around the high-ceilinged loft, glowing with a radiant shade of iridescent turquoise from Lars' body of blue paintings.

She stormed into the bathroom and started forcefully brushing her long, auburn hair. "You know, I'm going to get that bitch for tormenting me and making me do all that bullshit."

"She's a fucking criminal, and if you're not careful, she'll turn you into one. She stole that client's license and goes through other clients' purses."

"They're fucking *clients*! And now she's forcing me to do another bullshit caper and fuck with Raincoat's baby mama again in another horrific display of vanity," Lulu continued as she moved from the bathroom to the bedroom, where she laid down on his fluffy white duvet, leaning up against the back of the iron bed post.

Lars moved to her and began rubbing her feet with a soothing touch.

"I feel so bad for Melinda and her baby," Lulu said. "Too many people are falling through the cracks."

"That's exactly why you should to be the voice," Lars said supportively. "Maybe you should write a book!"

"Well—I would be motivated to finish it. A hardbound best seller shoved right up her fat ass," Lulu continued.

"Damn, baby, you're breathing fire. You're so cute. Stay there," Lars pulled himself to Lulu and began stroking her ruddy, flushed cheeks. After a few moments of tenderness, Lulu finally felt calm and began to ponder, in Lars' safe arms, what it must be like to lose everything. She decided that she would not be driven by her contempt for Screwzette, but rather would seek her own salvation in this book. She wondered what all the personal stories were from the other occupiers like Melinda. To Lulu, at first the kids in the park seemed liked disgruntled NYU and Columbia students, smoking pot and getting free food, mixing alongside ex-cons from Rikers Island who were tipped off that Zuccotti Park was the place to be. Then the protesters' feelings morphed into a deeper sense of abject resentment and, in cities like Dallas and Oakland, turned downright scary. The movement was less like Strawberry Fields and more like Kent State. Why would they brave a storm in Zoo-cotti Park just to prove a point that they can organize, but to what advancement? Or is it just that people by their nature are attracted to chaos?

Americans had it quite good. Sized up against most places on the globe, America was and would always be a land rife with possibilities and hope. Yet whenever the country seemed close to real social breakthroughs, a never-ending set of disenfranchised killers, mired in forms of war against democracy, stepped up and sullied the water for the rest of the citizens on real issues, always diverting attention from the key issues with violence. What would break the cycle?

Melinda Mendelssohn would become Lulu's new symbol for the modern woman. Her face, strong, a determined mother who, facing an economic dust bowl, would come out on the other side, baby in hand, a changed woman for having a Kafkaesque struggle with herself and her community. She would be the inspiration for Lulu's book, *White Collar Slavery*.

Lulu wondered where Melinda and her beautiful daughter were at that very moment. She saw visions of the infant huddled around a gas heater, awakened repeatedly by the sounds of beating drums, drunks, and unruly tourists. The storm promised to bring deadly ice and snow that night. Poor Melinda. Lulu had to do something. She opened one eye slowly, looked up at Lars, kissed him, and as their eyes met, they both bound out of bed. Lulu realized she had to go see Melinda immediately so they could plot the course for a better life for she and her daughter and the millions of well-meaners stuck in an unflinching and unrewarding work cycle. Lulu grabbed her coat and scarf and one for Lars, as they scurried out the door.

The brisk midnight temperature was dropping fast as Lars looked north toward the glass-encased mega structure of the Jacob Javits Center on Eleventh Avenue, in search of a yellow cab through the ice-covered streets.

Velveteen Meltdown

If Lulu continued with her tell-all, a swell of criminal injustice would ensue. This she was certain of, for the stories in the right hands would expose Screwzette's lust for corporate malfeasance and illogical fear tactics, which completely and witlessly dominated her would-be professional life. Lulu could hardly contain her excitement, bristling over the satisfaction of penning what she hoped to be her crowning achievement. Night after night, with Lars by her side, she relived and captured the horrors of what it was like to work for a closet monster that operated in such illegal, lewd, and lascivious ways. In a way, it was more despicable than working for Satan, because the Devil's blood dries clear. When you deal with the Devil, you know what you're up against. But having to aid a psychological piranha; masquerade as a corporate partner; sublimate one's own real personality; and carry out Lizette's malicious machinations was, to Lulu, unadulterated torture. This guilt, coupled with her Catholic conscience, kept Lulu quiet—resolute but full of remorse—every two weeks when her direct deposit hit her account. A prisoner of Sixth Avenue from the forty-seventh floor, Lulu felt like her job was always in jeopardy. Her stomach was always stricken with the queasy feeling that she could end up just like Melinda Mendelssohn, jobless and homeless.

Living in New York City was, is, and will always be a daily Darwinian psychological struggle to stay one step ahead of the condo fees, rent hikes, taxi surcharges, delivery fees, taxes, subway increases, toll hikes, bridge closings, and its brightest plan yet: the yoga tax. Naturally, this urban petri dish draws in the best and the brightest, thriving in neighborhoods from Hell's Kitchen to Nolita. In fact, the old Catskills saying "It's a dog eat dog world" rings true no place more than on these mean streets. Martin Scorsese summed it up in *Taxi Driver*: "You talkin' to me?" It's the quintessential mantra for Manhattanites who make it out the door each morning and into the debilitating daily grind that is New York City and its boroughs of Brooklyn, Queens, Staten Island, and the Bronx.

White Collar Slavery

Lulu had had enough of Screwzette's spinning lies, causing cries, and seeing those fat Michelin thighs parade in the most ghastly way every day for as long as she could remember. She had the seven-year itch to get far, far away from that bitch, and this was her chance. Her subconscious will to settle the score was powerless against any fleeting notions of self-preservation. After all, she was complicit in these corporate wrongdoings, and there was little she could do to mitigate that fact. She was a solider committing acts outside the parameters of psychological warfare.

Her worst fears might be realized with this insidious Zirko affair. It was clear to Lulu that she could very well go down in flames, like Snoopy's Red Baron, fighting in the dangerous Manhattan skies. Plus, she had only peanuts to defend herself legally. Lars, her cute and cuddly Charlie Brown blockhead artist boyfriend, was a powerhouse of misguided creativity and affection, but didn't have enough Warren Buffetts in his painted pockets to protect her from any criminal charges that might develop if these stories were published.

Yes, she would be the sacrifice. Lulu would be the martyr to challenge, the dilettante dragon in a death battle on Sixth Avenue. She hoped that in the last few remaining days, while plotting her escape and inevitable revenge, she would not cause any red flags to be raised or have to bite her tongue to avoid any Freudian slips that might dribble out during the calm before the storm.

Lulu sat in her office making press calls and doing whatever might take her attention away from seeing that marshmallow-headed *Matrix* man pirouetting in and out of her consciousness, with that unmistakable furry, coffee-stained, caterpillar birthmark that covered his left jaw. Her neurosis, learned from Lars, made her wonder: if they ever got into a tussle and she had to use her trusty Swarovski crystal-covered pepper spray on him, would the toxins dissolve his furry, freakish birthmark, like turpentine on oil paint? Or would it come alive and eat his face? Or worse, hers? Or morph into a federal agent? Clearly, she had seen too many episodes of *The Twilight Zone, The X-Files* and *Ghost Hunters*.

She sat uncomfortably, working on a Grangeway press release, while considering who to enlist to track her tracker. Lars was too sloppy for this kind of work. He was endearing, irascible, incorrigible, and great in bed but a bit too scattered for investigative work, although she would never let on that she thought this way. Over the years, Lars deluded himself into thinking he was some outlaw Lee Marvin type, with his rock 'n' roll band and ridiculous mod, mustard-colored Vespa. He looked more like a dark-haired Napoleon Dynamite than a Hell's Angel. Although always good natured and there for her emotionally, this was not quite his bag. He was better at playing the rogue scholar. He had many skills, more than the average bear, but a detective was not one of them. Sure, he could conjure up the dead with his annoying behavior, incessant nonsensical antics, and impersonations of obscure television and film personalities, and yes, he was a divining rod for freaks and weirdos—one trait they adoringly shared. But no, for this, Jose from Big Apple Limo would suffice. As Lulu gazed around her beige-colored office, where she had given her heart and soul for so many years, she thought of all the time spent with the hatchery shopping, dining, and vacationing, and wondered if she would miss any of the extravagant expense accounts, decadent dinners, long lunches, and expensive slush gifts. No, she could do without them. She would rather ditch the whole sordid matter than dine in the lion's den another day.

With her renewed sense of vigor, she would expose more than just the tawdry and pathetic dealings of one New Jersey flack and her flock at the firm. Lulu decided that if her book were to have real literary meaning, measured against modern novels, the story would have to somehow calibrate or have a profound impact on the tilted system. It would have to shed light on the corruption and the lewd, immoral, and unchaste corporate activities that precipitated and served as the catalyst for the Occupy Wall Street movement. She would have to incorporate a few of the themes from some of her literary heroes such as Upton Sinclair, whose book *The Jungle* exposed the poor health conditions of immigrant workers in the meatpacking industry in the early part of the twentieth century. Sinclair's observations of the state of turn-of-the-twentieth-century labor were placed front and center for the American public to see, suggesting that something needed to change to put an end to American wage slavery.

Lulu's all-time favorite literary opus was *Atlas Shrugged*, Ayn Rand's most extensive statement of objectivism, a philosophy created by Rand based on the premise that the proper moral purpose of one's life is the pursuit of one's own happiness or rational self-interest. Rand believed that the only social system consistent with this morality is full of respect for individual rights embodied in laissez-faire capitalism, and that the role of art in human life is to transform humans' metaphysical ideas by selective reproduction of reality into a physical form—a work of art—that one can comprehend and to which one can respond emotionally.

Rand's essential philosophy is based on the concept of man as a heroic being, with his own happiness as the moral purpose of his life.

Atlas Shrugged explores a dystopian United States, where many of society's most productive citizens refuse to be exploited by increasing taxation and government regulations and disappear. John Galt, a character in the novel describes the strike as "stopping the motor of the world" by withdrawing the minds that drive society's growth and productivity, leads them. In their efforts, these people "of the mind" hope to demonstrate that a world in which the individual is not free to create is doomed, that civilization cannot exist where every person is a slave to society and government, and that the destruction of the profit motive leads to the collapse of society. The protagonist, Dagny Taggart, sees society collapse around her as the government increasingly asserts control over all industries.

In Lulu's mind, this egalitarian view of a fair and just system should have been at the root of the Occupy Wall Street movement. But the nature of the sinister undercurrent and hidden agendas was unknown to many of the college students and well-meaning workers, who saw the movement as their "tune in and drop out" Timothy Leary moment, an opportunity to wage the war against the machine. The whole movement led to a media meltdown that, in Lulu's mind, drove it straight into the Zoo-cotti zone.

As Lulu tidied up her desk, she e-mailed a draft of the Grangeway bankruptcy release, hoping it was her last e-mail for the company. But as with all other things, Lulu took pride in her deliverables. As far as KAR went and Lulu was concerned, she was the deus ex machina, a god from the machine. She kept the firm's top-shelf clients plumped up with Restylane injections, filling in the fissures of tarnished corporate images with the proper mix of talking points, crisis management strategies, and dinner etiquette. Without her, her clients would be crippled. Lulu managed a labyrinth too complex for an intern or a newbie to tackle; no matter how adept they might see themselves fit for this kind of corporate chicanery. The brainwashing went on—saying white was gray and gray was white, allowing television producers, newspaper journalists, and bloggers to wakeboard through the waves of press releases, bringing them close into confidence—until the sheer, unabashed, corporate waterboarding began. The modus operandi of KAR's tilted system was to turn employees into listless, flatlined, body-bagged business heads.

No episode demonstrates the situation better than that of the recent story in the news of the employee who donated her kidney to her boss, who was in desperate need of a transplant. She had been rehired by the firm with the hidden caveat that she was expected to make good on an offer to donate one of her kidneys to her then boss. A short time after the operation, she was pushed out of her position because of her ailment and was consequently fired.

This audacious, cutthroat cannibalism pained Lulu's heartstrings because she had given her own head, heart, and stomach to the corporate cause—abetting the loathsome, deceptive, maniacal deeds of the dilettante dragon. She regularly had cold-sweat nightmares, and they were about to end. She had to keep it together a bit longer and not get her ire up, blowing her cool like the Jet Blue pilot in the news. Captain Clayton Osbon allegedly had a complete and utter meltdown while piloting a commercial plane full of 131 passengers—men, women, children, and six crewmembers who had to restrain him. Seemingly, this was a result of being overworked by the system. Twenty-plus years of back-to-backs, one-ways and deadheading, turned him into an emotional terrorist, and an episode of yelling jumbled comments about Jesus, 9/11, Iraq, Iran, and terrorists to passengers. He was found not guilty by reason of insanity.

Lulu would work clandestinely on a healthy new goal that she hoped would keep her from divulging her take-no-prisoners plan: sending seventy-five copies of her published book to the firm's partners, clients, associates, journalists, and persons who had been wrongfully harmed by the firm.

She envisioned each recipient in turn picking up the phone and calling Lizette to encounter a bit of hell on earth in a Dante-esque domino effect. This would keep Lulu quiet during those moments when her absolute mistrust and disdain for her dizzyingly evil mentor might break the levy of her nerves and create a watershed that might jeopardize her scheduled escape from Sergeant Screwzette's multiplex prison camp.

She imagined Screwzette's bloodshot eyes welling up with tears, but not because she was struck by the ignominious scorn that would surely be bestowed upon her by everyone she ever happened to rub her chubby little elbows up against, and even some she didn't. What would get her would be the accurate depictions of her grotesque physical shortcomings, descriptions of her pathetic hygiene and illegal and disturbing habits. Her behavior left her alone, bitter, and spiteful, void of real, honest emotion. Screwzette's estranged husband, family, friends, and colleagues would cripple her and put her on a one-way ride to social alienation. *Sweet revenge,* Lulu thought.

Reading an autographed, first-edition hardbound copy, which Lulu planned to shove straight down Screwzette and Marni's throats, respectively, would be just the revenge the psychiatrist ordered. And knowing this was what allowed Lulu to stealthily continue to smile under the oppressive regime. She would hold out like an assassin until her target was in her scope site and fully tranquilized for the kill.

Before Lulu shut down her PC, she made damn sure to check her *Freaky Friday* to-do list and marked off one final item: an appointment for Lizette with the dental diva, Katrinka Tzeka, who happened to be in New York on sabbatical from Albania's capital city of Tirana. The impossible-to-get appointment, because of the heavy word of mouth, was traded for a favor. Lulu promised her one of Lars' oil paintings in exchange for the crazy bit of oral kindness. For anyone unfamiliar with the internet sensation Tzeka, she was the infamous dentist for graciously giving her ex-lover a full frontal toothectomy, stripping every bit of enamel out of his double-talking mouth during a post breakup appointment.

Although less caustic than her earlier predecessor Lorena Bobbitt, infamous for cutting off her cheating husband's pecker with a carving knife, Tzeka's method certainly gives her jilted heart a run for the money. As they say about hand grenades, a close second is usually enough.

As Lulu checked the appointment off her to-do list, she gathered her things and bolted out of the office, hoping to get home before Lars. She wanted to surprise him with his favorite dinner, spicy chicken curry. They were celebrating that Lars found a lawyer that would take his case against the *Enquirer*. Exiting 1211 Sixth Avenue through the cold, crisp, mid-January frost, she noticed a yellow taxicab parked neatly in front, an odd sight, especially at 6:00 p.m. on a Friday night. Without hesitation, she hopped in, looking around as if she had just won the Mega Millions lottery.

Lulu frantically dialed her CrackBerry to call Lars. "I just saw the *Matrix* man again. He's in front of me. I have to follow him."

"Who?" Lars questioned.

"I was stopped at a light and I saw that guy again," Lulu rambled on frantically. "He got into a cab on the corner of Forty-Seventh and Seventh. I swear he saw me. He looked right at me!"

"That's because you're so pretty. You need to calm down," Lars tried to say in his most soothing, calming voice.

"I may be a little late; I have to follow him," Lulu said.

"No, this is ridiculous; just come home. I'm on the other line with the lawyer, I gotta go."

"I can't. I have to follow him." "You need help," Lars pleaded.

"Ohmigod, now he's following me. He just stopped and picked up someone on the corner of Thirty-Seventh Street."

"Take a picture with your phone."

"Ohmigod, I'm being followed," Lulu blurted, now noticing the Asian cab driver, sizing her up in his oversized rearview mirror, squinting, as if he had seen her on a wanted poster. The driver started honking a staccato call in Morse code that made Lulu vainly suspect for a moment that perhaps he was in on it, since there were no cars in front of him to honk at.

"Why can't you let this go? You are so fucking fixated on this guy. Let it go already."

"Lars, I gotta go. I think the driver is in on it too," Lulu whispered as she ended the call.

Lulu couldn't waste any more time. She sent her friend Chloe a text that needed an immediate response. This was urgent. She felt violated. She couldn't turn around, and kept looking into the reflection in the Plexiglas divider, then to the rear view mirror, and back again. She felt like a prisoner. She felt trapped. As the cab driver pulled up to Lars' apartment building, she wanted to wait for the cab to pass, but as she turned around, no one was there. *Did she imagine the whole thing? What just happened? Was Lars right? Was she losing her mind?*

"I guess you don't believe me?" screamed Lulu as she flung open the front door to the loft. Their puppy, Kingsley, ran to the door to greet her. In silhouette, Lars was in front of a large canvas in the far corner of the room, painting with deliberate, broad, strokes.

"Well? To be honest, does it really matter if I believe you or not?"

asked Lars in a rational tone.

"Of course it matters."

"Look—do I think that you were in a cab and that there was another cab behind you? Sure, there are over thirteen thousand cabs in the city. That's possible."

"Well, if you don't believe me about this, then what? This is absolute bullshit."

"Well, you know what's next if you don't stop this: Bellevue," Lars said jokingly.

"Fuck you. I know what I saw." "Okay. Okay. Relax. I believe you."

"No. You. Don't. You're just trying to appease me."

"Even if you saw that guy again, it doesn't mean he's following you. Did you get a photo? Like I said?"

"No! It all happened too quickly." "It always does."

"Ugh! Listen, we're done talking about it," Lulu said, going into her own kvetch-a-thon.

"Wait, where are you going?"

"I have to reevaluate everything," Lulu said, maniacally slamming the door to the bedroom, causing Kingsley to whimper.

"Baby, you're crazy! I just can't believe you're causing an argument over this," Lars yelled through the door as he continued to paint. "C'mon, now you're making the baby upset."

"I can't believe you don't believe me. I'm going to bed."

Lars made his way into the bedroom after a few moments, realizing Lulu might be truly upset. "Baby, I'm sorry, I don't want to argue. I love you. If you think you saw him, you saw him."

"I know what I saw," Lulu shot back.

"My God, you sound like the *Ghost Whisperer*: 'I know what I saw last summer,'" Lars said, mimicking Lulu.

"Ugh! Why do you have to turn everything into a joke?" "I can't help it. It's what I do."

Lars had a professional laundry list of excuses, and like a magician, he would pull them out of his hat as needed. To hear Lars utter any one of them would usually send Lulu into a focused rage. "I can't help it," was a close cousin to some of his other pathetic arsenal of excuses, like:

"I didn't know . . ."

"I don't feel good . . . I'm tired . . . I'm sick . . ." "I got confused . . ."

"I'm doing the best I can . . ."

"Listen, I'm sorry. I love you," Lars lovingly maintained.

"I love you too," Lulu replied.

"You know, I was thinking, baby," Lars said as he crawled beside Lulu and Kingsley on the white dreamy duvet and spooned her, "maybe I could go with you to yoga class tomorrow, and then we can take the baby to the park. Would you like that?" He kissed her tenderly on her lower lip.

Since forever Lulu had wanted Lars to join her at Yoga Nation, but never pressed him because the fear that he would fart in a room full of her friends and fellow yogaphiles in fixed firm pose was too much for her stomach to take.

"Mmmm. That would be so nice, baby," Lulu said, secretly hoping he would change his mind come morning.

Yoga Nation, a second-floor Bikram Yoga studio on Ninetieth Street, neatly overlooked Madison Square Park. A cliquey group of yoga heads and their instructors ran the premier three-thousand-square-foot haven. Lulu, when she was able and not wasting her time on some ridiculous weekend task in the form of an errand, press release, Benadryl buy, breaking Henri Bendel return policies or texting battle, tried to catch as many classes as she could. The classes were mostly full of weekend warriors trying their hand at the hothouse of torture. But occasionally she ran into someone who had more to say than, "I'm knee-deep in Neptune," or "My chakras are on injured reserve," or "Pluto is eclipsing my Aries," and other completely kooky types that Lulu found formidably annoying.

Lulu often subscribed to the old adage from the movie *Barfly*: "It's not that I don't like people; I just don't like when they're around."

Living in New York City is a blisteringly jaded experience no matter what socioeconomic path one is on. Manhattan is a tiny island, twenty-two total square miles, made up of staggeringly competitive beehives of drones fulfilling the financial means to keep the city moving. It's akin to the ant farm, inhabited by tiny creatures toiling for the greater good. Carrying weight a thousand times their body mass to their cubicles, relaying a sense of learned cynicism that adversely affects their every waking moment, as long as they live in the naked city. The iconic cry of "Hey, are you lookin' at me?" is on the tip of every New Yorker's tongue. It would have been, because there are pirates at every port, looking to sell you a lot more than the Brooklyn Bridge.

With Lulu by his side, Lars smiled sheepishly as he looked around the crowded room. Every inch was lined with a mosaic of multicolored mats occupied by perspiring, stinking torsos twisting back and forth in an orderly, dizzyingly, hypnotic ballet of sweaty, juxtaposed bodies. Only the music wasn't Tchaikovsky, but a cacophony of cries for dear life in the Bikram house of love.

Wearing a frumpy pair of faded Fila sweatpants, circa 1986, and his infamous "I want to live forever; so far so good" T-shirt, Lars clutched Lulu's hand in holy fear that he could quite possibly pass out before the class even began. The humid, 105-degree, high-ceilinged studio adorned with hazy, trippy, tranquil paintings of the Taj Mahal covering the ceiling and walls made Lars' stomach do backflips as he fleetingly tried to hold down his lunch. Hot moisture from the room usually created listless bodies by the end of the session.

For those unfamiliar with Bikram yoga: it's not for the faint of heart. It's a back-bending, mind-mending, holistic hell-ride with the best intentions, worst pain, and most intense heat that your muscles have ever perspired over. It usually keeps most of the newbies in the corner eating naan bread for their holy lives. No wussies need apply; Bikram is for the experienced yoga head from start to finish.

Lulu worried that her afternoon might turn into an abject tearjerker because Lars, in some perverse sense of pleasure, against her mighty will, wolfed down a double Shake Shack burger, mac and cheese, and a large chocolate malt.

"Listen, if you embarrass me, I'll never be allowed back," Lulu whispered harshly, turning toward Lars, sprawled out on his yoga mat stretching. "I'm warning you."

"Jesus, you sound like my mother," Lars shot back.

"This is my favorite place. I mean it," Lulu sternly maintained.

"I'm the one that got you the membership for your birthday; I know how much you like it," Lars knowingly answered. "It's so fucking hot in here; this is beyond hell. I'm having my own little Vietnam over here."

"Yeah, well, just keep your voice down," Lulu sternly whispered. "I knew this wasn't a good idea."

"Ha! You're not the only one," Lars said, his face suddenly clinched as if he were about to let one go.

"If you do, that's it. Just leave the room." "Now you sound like a substitute teacher."

"Well, you are acting like a child. Can you shut up?"

"It's possible but not probable," Lars mumbled sarcastically.

Aditi Patel, the most-sought after yoga instructor in the city, was a strikingly attractive, slender drink of water, who looked as if she were straight out of Bollywood central casting. Her calm, resolute, British accent made her a favorite among celebrities, granola types, tourists, students, moms, and businessmen, and especially to Lulu, who adored pushing herself to the limit to work off the weekly hostilities of the hatchery. Plus the celebrity gaze was fun. From as far away as Miami to Montauk, serious yogaphiles of all shapes and sizes flocked to Patel's class, which was purportedly booked through the next decade.

In her soothing tone, Patel began the class with a couple of warm-up moves, as a few last-minute stragglers and the silver-screen legend Susan Sarandon snuck in through the side door, fighting to find a spot on the crowded floor.

"Don't look now, but Susan Sarandon just walked in," Lars whispered quietly to Lulu, motioning silly eyes toward the side door to an attractive, red-haired woman in her fifties who nonchalantly placed her mat quietly on the last bit of hardwood in the far back corner of the room.

"Shut up. Just stretch. Stop annoying me." Lars was forever playing the faux-celebrity body-double game, and she was forever taking the star struck bait, hook, line, and sinker.

Not a day went by, walking Kingsley in West Chelsea, or really anywhere in Manhattan, when Lars wouldn't try to pump Lulu's heart rate up with a "Hey, don't look now, but there's so-and-so the actor" routine. The rotating list included the likes of Robert De Niro, Philip Seymour Hoffman, Matthew Modine, Sarah Jessica Parker, and more. Occasionally, he would even try to tease her with movie stars who weren't even alive anymore like Dennis Hopper and Esther Williams. "Don't look now, Lulu, but Esther Williams passed us on the water taxi," or "Dennis Hopper just pulled up to Haru on his Harley." Or names that he overheard Lulu mention from the gossip columns, like Nicki Minaj or Lady Gaga. Those were the ones that were the real gems that always made her do a double take.

No, this morning Lulu would enjoy her time to relax in Bikram meditational bliss, to get a respite from her pinged nerves, and to realign her chakras, even if for just a few peaceful moments. Lars' stupid shtick would have to be tuned out. Forever finding star doppelgängers among the crowded streets, restaurants, and bars of New York was a regular part of Lars' inane comedy act, which when they first started dating seemed cute, but now was just overly tedious and wildly obnoxious to her.

"She looks pretty good for a Saturday morning," Lars said.

"Just be thankful that my brain thinks faster than my arms, because you could be in a lot of trouble. Shut up," Lulu said in a breathy tone, going into her half-moon pose. Her long, slender arms curved above her head, and her torso moved to form a perfect forty-five-degree angle.

"This time, I'm really fucking serious; it's her," Lars said, going into his best cobra pose, which resembled a broken-down beach lounger at a yard sale.

"I don't want to hear it. Pay attention to the instructor," Lulu said, motioning her head toward the teacher.

"But that's really her. It's so fucking hot. I'm dying over here," Lars said.

"Good, just do it quietly."

"Okay, everyone, let's change it up just a bit. All together we're going to go into our camel pose—ustrasana. It's quite blistering in here, so better take it nice and easy," Patel said.

"Did she just say camel toe?" Lars joked.

"You're disgusting," Lulu scoffed as she stretched her head far back. With her eyes closed, she imagined what it would be like to be on some romantic pilgrimage. She imagined herself being hoisted atop an elephant's back in the broad Mumbai sun. She saw the god Ganesha with a thousand arms of shopping might, and wondered what treasures she and Lars would uncover in the flea markets of New Delhi.

She saw herself watching Lars floating with Kingsley on his back in a tranquil, brick red river, filled with old women, children, and monkeys wearing fezzes on their heads bathing, and the image of Kingsley wearing a pith helmet playing polo atop a wild boar. These images ran across her darkened inner eyelids in her deep meditative state. As Kingsley smacked the polo mallet into Lars' shrunken head, the sound awoke Lulu from her daydream. When she opened her left eye, still in pose, she looked behind her. She was dumbfounded to find her *Matrix* man with the coffee-stained furry birthmark two mats behind, smiling straight at her, with a Cheshire cat grin.

"Achoo!" Lulu sneezed.

"Gesundheit," the whole class chanted in unison.

Jerking her head back from the violent sneeze, she caught a glimpse of Susan Sarandon and began a machine-gun succession of muffled sneezes.

Whenever Lulu would get overanxious, since the age of six, when she won her first spelling bee and nervously sneezed all over the Farmington Elementary faculty, she would break out into a sneeze-a-thon when startled.

This rattled Lars so severely, vainly straining in the heat to keep his cheeks silent, that he had little choice but to let the mac and cheese go, and was damn lucky that his cheese was drowned out by her sneeze.

Lulu was torn between interrupting dear Aditi's class, clearly verboten, which would send her permanently packing, banning her for life, or worse, embarrassing herself in front of Sarandon. Or should she wait until after class to confront her would-be killer? Would he be gone by then? Would he kill both of them, or would he go after the entire class?

She thought maybe it would be better to stay in a classroom full of people, because Lars was no Bruce Lee. She really couldn't see him helping too much past the idle threats of "My karate is not so good," and "Take Sarandon, not us." These thoughts flooded through her mind as she panicked, stricken with the thought she and Lars could lose their lives. Her stomach pretzeled up and she quickly contemplated what to do.

Softly speaking into Lars' ear, Lulu ordered him to crawl over and politely ask the *Matrix* man his business. "Go over there and tell him to meet us outside."

Lars, now profusely perspiring from every pore of his body, questioned, "Who?"

"Ugh! The *Matrix* man—he's here," Lulu said.

"Oy vey. Perfect. This nonsense is finally going to end," Lars says. "He's two mats back to my left," Lulu said.

Lars looked to his right and Lulu anxiously whispered, "Your other left."

Lars flustered easily and broke out into a cold sweat, thinking for a fleeting moment that perhaps Lulu was right and there was something to all of this. The coincidence was too uncanny. *Who was this creepy guy? And why was he in class?* He started to feel guilty for dismissing Lulu's claims. A clammy feeling overcame Lars as he started to size up this freak that was wistfully staring at his girlfriend. He had been in a few tough spots before with his band, and after a few moments decided that this marshmallow-headed man didn't pose that much of a threat.

Crawling over to his mat, Lars on all fours, like a rabid dog, whispered in his best Christopher Walken accent, which sounded more like Richard Nixon, "Hey, pal. Gosh. What are you doing here? Huh guy? 'Cause me and my boys are going to rough you up. Don't say a word, huh guy?"

Before Lars could finish his nervous impersonation, the marshmallow-headed man interrupted, "Why don't we take this outside?"

Leaving their mats, the two scurried out of the room into the narrow hallway. They were practically on top of one another.

"Hi, it's a pleasure. I'm Skip Anderson, from the American Academy of Dramatic Arts, and we've been following Lulu's every move."

"Of course you have," Lars said cutting him off. "What gives you the right to follow someone around like a private investigator?"

"She applied for a scholarship. Hello. We are the Academy of Dramatic Arts, so we have to be super-thorough for our aspiring candidates," he explained, flashing his "Bring it on" spirit fingers, looking less like her marauder *Matrix* man killer, and more like an out-of-work choreographer.

"Ohmigod," Lars shot back, letting out a guttural laugh.

Lulu, overhearing the exchange, exhaled a grand sigh of relief, closed her eyes again, and imagined herself the star of a Bollywood blockbuster.

Paranormal Paranoia

To the quick, Lars, with his patented and completely overeager, "I told you so," gloating smile, wistfully went for the last of the couple's arctic char tartare. They were dining at a romantic table tucked away in the corner of the Red Cat, an invitingly eclectic eatery that caters to West Chelsea's well-heeled art crowd, nestled amidst the galleries. The dining room simmers with a funky aesthetic of hanging Moroccan lanterns and barn wood siding that panel the long, narrow walls. It was a *New York Times* review that turned Lars onto the tavern, upon the recommendation through an uptown art dealer and long-time friend that consigned Lars' ceramic and bronze sculptures regularly to Bonhams & Butterfields Auction House. The couple always had a "purr-fect" meal there, reserved for special occasions. And finding out that good ole Skip was hardly a threat to their tartare definitely counted.

"Clearly you're gonna shelf all of this spook stuff now, aren't you?

'Cause I really can't handle any more," Lars pleaded with Lulu.

"Well, how do you explain the police car parked on the bridge in front of the apartment building this morning?" Lulu questioned.

"Look, let's just sublimate all this energy here. No more maudlin looks," Lars waxed on, using his five-dollar vocabulary. "And let's look on the bright side. You got accepted to one of the best acting schools in the world. Kirk Douglas, Grace Kelly, and Robert Redford went to school there, for Christ's sake."

"I know. I know, you worked for Redford in Georgetown on *Quiz Show*, fifteen years ago," Lulu remarked. "After you worked on *Pelican Brief* with Denzel Washington."

Since his days studying film at American University, Lars always found work as a crewmember on feature films, music videos, documentaries, and very rarely these days in between art sales would take on such work. However, his buddy Bobby Broadwater worked as a coordinating producer on *Millionaire Matchup*. He introduced Lars to a production company that hired him for Barbra Streisand's *One Night Only* performance at the Village Vanguard. Lars had a grueling two-day shoot. In the rain, he was tasked with bringing the A-listers, including Nicole Kidman, Bill and Hilary Clinton, Barry Diller, and James Brolin into the intimate West Village jazz club, where Streisand would perform inches away.

The paparazzi on assignment managed to snap a photo of Lars, and since he was directly in the mix of things and looked strikingly similar to a young Elliot Gould, that he must have been Streisand and Gould's son. As legend goes, Lars maintained that some odd years ago, Elliot Gould himself approached him at JFK and started talking to him like he had known him his whole life. And shortly after, he met Oliver Stone at the Nash Hotel in South Beach, who asked him if he was Elliot Gould's son. Lars had one of those comfortable, familiar faces with soft puppy-dog eyes and is constantly being recognized and stopped on the streets, mistaken for somebody else.

Mostly, it started with "Hey, didn't I see you in that movie?" meaning a character actor that you couldn't quite place—much to the consternation of Lulu, who grew tired of these street antics.

"Grace Kelly went to the academy, so you'd almost be one degree of separation from Hitchcock. So let's be happy for what we have," said Lars.

"I do love *Rear Window*," Lulu shot back.

"Because you're a paranoid freak and like to people-watch too much," Lars retorted.

Rear Window was one of the couple's favorite films. Combined, they must have seen the classic, starring Jimmy Stewart and Grace Kelly, over twenty-five times and could easily recite every line. It played perfectly into their people-watching proposition, which plagued the afternoons they spent in the park, Chelsea Piers, or perusing uptown. Lars was an Olympic champion at it, a professional. In Lulu's opinion, he was as good as they come. He could size people up, not in a sordid, gold-digging way like Screwzette, but in a more comprehensive, uncanny, comedic kick-in-the-ass way that was always spot-on. It was a rare gift. Ironically, he couldn't make much money off of it to support his art lifestyle unless, of course, he became a TSA profiler at La Guardia. From a hundred meters away, Lars could tell where people were from, why they were there, who they were with, and what they did for a living, and sometimes even what they were saying to one another, mouthing their words, like a *Mystery Science Theater* routine, mad-libbing funny moments. It was a completely innocent, low-cost, quirky, quasi hobby; recalling and regurgitating funny lines was something they both fondly shared.

"I'm paranoid; so what?" Lulu continued.

"Don't you think that's putting it rather mildly? You thought the show of force yesterday was for you," Lars joked. A post-9/11 counter-terrorist measure for the streets of New York consisted of a daily convoy of cops spreading assurance to the 8.2 million city residents through a parade of force. Dozens of cop cars linked in a long protective procession combing through the streets, warning would-be terrorists to take their crime elsewhere.

"Well, they were following me for a few blocks, weren't they?" Lulu questioned.

"You were on a one way street," said Lars. "When does this end? You have to give this a rest, honey."

"Okay, so I'm not being followed by that guy," Lulu said.

"Right, tonight we are celebrating the fact that no one is following you, and I have the biggest lawyer in Hollywood taking my case," Lars said, referring to his case against the *National Enquirer*.

For the past few weeks, Lars had been in several awkward and embarrassing situations due to the *Enquirer* mix-up. Besides Lulu's mother and his own family, it didn't play so well in Palm Beach with his mother's octogenarian jet setters, who went big on this bit of gossip. Lars even had a couple of events in Palm Beach and New York canceled. And perhaps most horrifying of all, he ended up on BoyCulture.com, which was great fodder for his band mates.

Lars hired Stuart "Lenny" Fine, one of Hollywood's most powerful attorneys, representing Hollywood's elite writers, directors, producers, and actors, and had been named one of the top five A-List entertainment lawyers. Fine was beguiled by Lars' cold call, and after hearing the sordid story, believed it was an important case and decided to take it on. Lenny became a lawyer to help people and realized an artist in New York City needed all help he could get.

"Let's toast to a beautiful night, our health, and Lenny Fine," Lars said, raising his pint of Brooklyn Lager.

"I love you and appreciate that you're always there for me," Lulu lovingly said as she adoringly gazed into Lars' big brown eyes, raising her glass of Grenache. "But you have no idea what it's like working for that monster. She makes Meryl Streep in *The Devil Wears Prada* look like a shoe salesman at Daffy's."

Waiting for their main course of salmon and short ribs, nibbling on some sourdough dipped in olive oil, the couple peered around the room. Lars motioned to an adjacent table of three, an elderly couple and their flamboyant male friend, clutching gallery catalogues, waiting for their appetizers to arrive.

Lars turned on his shtick. "Get a load of Myra and Murray over here and their designer pal Paco. Murray's an accountant who has given up golf and is looking to fill their house in the Hamptons with the worst bullshit art their money can buy in Chelsea. And Paco knows exactly how to spend it."

"Ugh, I can just see the art now," Lulu agreed with Lars.

"Paco wants them to buy a pink chair turned upside down with a box of Brillo pads glued to the left leg for eighty thousand dollars," Lars continued.

"But Murray had his eye on a foreboding steel cube covered in faux snakeskin for the foyer," Lulu quickly chimed in.

It infuriated Lars and his group of art buddies to no end, how ultra-insular the galleries in Chelsea were. And how unwilling they were to take chances on anything new, or for that matter, on anything decent. When Lars moved to New York from Philadelphia nearly ten years ago, he called a major Manhattan gallery and told them about his work, to which they replied, "We don't accept living artists; call us back when you're dead," and graciously hung up the phone. The New York art scene was just that tough. To break a new act, you either had to be famous or dead.

So Lars decided on a different tack and created an art group whose mission was to promote new ways of expressionism in a group setting. And they were making waves, exhibiting their work all over Manhattan.

Due to Lulu's close ties at the NASDAQ, she managed to have Lars and his art group preside over the closing bell a few summers back.

It's tough to be a working artist living in New York, or anywhere for that matter. Since the beginning of time, the system has been designed merely to enslave the artist to the church or state, like a feudal sharecropper, toiling over the canvas, for patrons and critics yearning to see suffering and signs of insanity in their creations. Yes, art is one of the few professions whose devotees applaud and relish the creators' deaths, exponentially raising the value of their pieces of suffering.

Francis Bacon's "Three Studies of Lucian Freud," recently sold at auction for $142 million, the most expensive artwork ever sold at an auction. This triptych was a big shot in the arm for the art market. And oddly enough, the sale gave contemporary artists hope that there is life after Picasso, who reigns as the quintessential maestro of modern art. If a picture paints a thousand words, and all the world is a stage, then it is the artist, not the actor that needs better lighting. More often than not, the artist sits at the bottom of the economic food chain, embodying the term *starving artist* for many, for most of their career. Lars was constantly pointing out that Van Gogh, the godfather of modern art, sold only a few paintings in his lifetime, and now in the twenty-first century is regarded as one of the greatest artists of all time. All of this kept guys like Lars dreaming and working into the wee hours of the night, so that if they were lucky, someone may look at their work hundreds of years later and see their abject suffering.

Tying into themes of objectivism, creators should refuse to allow their inventions, art, business leadership, scientific research, or new ideas to be taken from them by the government or by the rest of the world. According to Lulu's theory of creative relativity, if they did, that would fix the system.

"You see that guy over there at the table near the end of the bar?" Lars asked.

"Uh huh," Lulu admitted.

"The guy with the Aviators on his head, talking to the girl," Lars continued.

"Yeah, talking to the girl with the Katy Perry do, that are now looking this way," Lulu added.

"Yeah, probably looking for their appetizers," Lars unabashedly maintained. "Detective Mark Watson. Now, that guy looks like a federal agent. Straight out of CSI."

"You think? He looks more like an architect to me," Lulu said.

"Yeah, but he's not after you," said Lars. "He's after Katy Perry. Looks like they're on their third date."

"It could be a cover," Lulu retorted.

"If that guy is after you, I'm Andy Warhol," Lars lovingly joked.

A tall, slender, dark-haired waiter resembling Adrien Brody interrupted with dessert menus.

"I'll do the strawberry rhubarb crumble. With one fork. Thank you," demanded Lars.

"You're so rude," Lulu said.

"We were gonna share. I was gonna feed you," Lars shot back, caught and cornered.

"They don't know that," Lulu said. "You're such a freak. Since when do you like strawberries? I wanted to buy them the other day and you said no."

"They reeked of E. coli," Lars joked.

"Yeah, but it was three baskets for like four dollars; I've never seen them that cheap," Lulu said.

Lulu loved a bargain. She would swim with sharks to save seventy dollars on a Tory Burch bag or climb Mount Fuji for a "free gift with purchase." It wasn't that she was cheap. She just detested wasting money. It was tough living in Manhattan. Lulu considered herself a modern spendthrift, among other things. And the thing that irked her most was paying full price for anything—period! She was always on the lookout for any semi-available swag from the agency—theater, movie tickets, restaurant, or sporting event passes.

Sharing the same theories on artistic fairness, Lulu and Lars believed entertainment in NYC should be more like a fine-dining experience: if you don't like your meal or have a bad dish, because the acting or writing sucks shit, then you should be given a new dish or simply not pay. The couple had walked out on countless shows over their seven-year courtship and developed this creative economic theory based on a whole lot of bad plays and movies.

In the brisk January air, the couple headed east on Twenty-Third Street past London Terrace, the prewar apartment building that occupied the entire block. London Terrace was a luxury apartment complex built in 1928. When Lars first moved to New York he rented a tiny studio apartment, cramming all of his artwork inside the closet-sized pad. The apartment was so small he had to leave the apartment to change his mind.

London Terrace was the dream of real estate mogul Henry Mandel, a flashy real estate developer. In the late twenties, he acquired the land on which to build the largest apartment building New York and the world had ever seen. In financial ruin, during the Great Depression, Mandel leapt from atop his dream building, plummeting to his death. This was the selling point for Lars. For if the creator believed in his work that much, he felt he owed it to Mandel to reside there.

"I saw Annie Leibovitz a couple days ago. She must still live in the building," Lars said.

"Speaking of photographs, I meant to show you this at dinner," Lulu said as she handed Lars her smartphone with a photo of one of her estranged high school friends, wearing a wedding dress and heavy eye makeup. "Look, Ellen is getting married next month."

"Oh, here we go, I'm in trouble now," Lars interrupted. "Your friend looks like Linda Blair!" Lars winced as he grabbed Lulu's phone from her hand and stared at the photo. "Her freakin' head looks like it's gonna spin around."

"Ugh! Well, at least she's getting married," Lulu sighed. "And having an exorcism at the same time," Lars joked.

The couple pined to see Woody Allen's *Midnight in Paris*. Woody, Scorsese, Coppola, and Eastwood were about the only filmmakers Lars and Lulu were willing to shell out their hard-earned cash for. The film promised to be a poignant and romantic romp through the streets of Paris.

With an oversized tub of popcorn in hand, extra large Dr. Pepper, Milk Duds, and Twizzlers that Lulu smuggled in from Duane Reade on the cheap, they began the grueling process of agreeing on two seats together. Lars longed to be in an aisle seat, close to the back of the theater, but not too close to be interrupted by jag offs like himself that incessantly need to run out for more soda, candy, or bathroom breaks. Lulu preferred to be in the centermost seat of the theater. She felt that this location maximized the surround sound. With such specific seating needs, the two rarely agreed on a seat. It usually ended with some sort of bribe in the form of a foot massage to settle the seating skirmish.

Juggling his bounty of snacks, like a drunken pirate, Lars caved to Lulu's seating demands, as they scooted their way across a string of crowded seats to the middle center of the theater.

"Uh—do you think we missed anything?" Lars whispered to Lulu.

"Uh—the previews are still playing. Doubt it," Lulu said, motioning her hand toward the screen.

"Just want to make sure we didn't miss anything," Lars whispered to Lulu. "*Rolling Stone* said it's the Woodman's best movie since *Manhattan*."

"What are you talking about? I showed you that article. I just hate it when you do this," Lulu said.

"All right, settle down," Lars mused. "I forgot; I've had a lot on my mind with the lawsuit and all."

"Shhh! It's starting," Lulu said as they settled into their seats. The signature black-and-white credits began to roll on the huge screen.

"Do you plan on talking through the whole movie?" Lulu questioned, shifting her body weight, turning around to give a group of Columbia kids wearing school pride the evil eye.

"They're probably doing their dissertation on Woody Allen as a case study in Freudian filmmaking," Lars joked. "Give 'em a break."

"Ugh! I can hear them now: 'He hasn't made a sophisticated comedy since *Hannah and Her Sisters*,'" Lulu whispered, quietly mocking the college students that were seated two rows back.

Lars, turning around to size up the ruckus, nearly choked on his Twizzlers to see the couple from the Red Cat behind the group of Columbia kids, near the aisle.

"We have a definite type of situation here," Lars said. "Shhh. I want to watch this," Lulu said.

"So do I, but I don't think we are going to," Lars said, trembling and finally believing Lulu for the first time. Maybe those feelings of hers, though misguided, had some merit after all. Or was he just getting sucked up into her paranormal paranoia? The coincidence was too uncanny. Lars was a bit erratic, but when he needed to, he could focus precisely like an intense shot of cortisone. And he felt that the couple from the Red Cat spelled trouble. Or was it maybe they were just having dinner and a movie?

"If you say one more word, I'm never going to the movies with you again, ever," Lulu quietly promised.

"Uh—but the couple from . . ." Lars, visibly shaken, whispered as the film began.

"Not another word, or that's it," threatened Lulu, interrupting Lars. Lars' heart sank as he slumped into the high-backed, cushioned seat.

Was he just buying into all this spook shit that plagued Lulu's nerves of late or was his baby Lulu really in some sort of trouble that she was trying to explain and he just wouldn't listen? A wave of remorse was followed by a sudden jolt of fear that his beloved might be in real jeopardy. Lars was confused about what to do. Knowing Lulu, if he tried to warn her, she would just continue to shut him down. So he quickly downed the rest of his Dr. Pepper and shot off to the men's room to get a better look at the suspicious-looking couple.

From what Lars could tell from watching movies, this stocky fellow had all the right makings of a federal agent—the Aviator sunglasses, golf pro preppy concealing an ex-military look. He couldn't make out his shoes, usually the dead giveaway. Jackbooted thugs always wear shinny black shoes with brand new laces—or so he had read. He would make a pass by him and his date to see what he could learn, pretending to need a refill on his soda.

As he passed the couple up the aisle on the way to the exit, he caught a glimpse of a shiny metallic object peeking out beneath the man's navy blue suit jacket. Was it a gun? A cell phone? Could it be some sort of cigarette case? Maybe it was an iPhone case? It was too dark in the theatre to tell. Lars, panicking, circled immediately back to his seat and painstakingly scrawled out a note on the inside of his empty Milk Duds box, using the sticky chocolate from his index finger, "They have a gum!" He meant to write *gun,* but was so nervous that he messed up the "n" and made an "m" by mistake.

He passed the note to Lulu, who glanced at it, immediately tossed it down onto the theater floor, and irately mouthed, "I don't want any gum. Shut up."

As an excuse to turn back around to the would-be agents, Lars cracked his neck. His eyes practically popped out of his head, and he was mystified to find two empty seats with the couple nowhere in sight. Lars tightly clutched Lulu's left hand, kissing her gently on the cheek.

* * *

Slapping shut the white paneled blinds, Lulu frantically peered out of the floor-to-ceiling windows of Lars' loft spotting a Grangeway truck parked ominously on the Hudson Yards Bridge directly facing the apartment on Tenth Avenue. Holding Kingsley in her arms, she began pacing back and forth in the living room. The north-facing windows, once a selling point, provided just the right amount of light, but not today. Yes, today the light revealed too much.

"I can't believe you would just sit there and not tell me," Lulu said. "I tried to. You just ignored me," Lars pleaded.

"They have a gum? Of all the crazy things. You are really something, you know that?" Lulu said, catatonically bouncing Kingsley up and down in her arms.

"Keep your voice down," Lulu whispered.

"I said I wasn't sure if it was a gun," Lars maintained.

"What was it then, huh? A WMD? Of course it was a fucking gun!"

"What did you want me to do?" Lars questioned. "Fend them off with my freakin' pack of Twizzlers?"

"You really should have told me," Lulu said. "Uh—I did!" exclaimed Lars.

"Why would you do that? Why did you let me sit there the entire time? Why didn't you say anything?"

"I tried to tell you, but you said you would never go to the movies with me again, and that's my favorite thing to do. I love going to the movies with you," Lars lovingly maintained.

"Ohmigod!"

"I dunno, it could have been nothing, like Skip Anderson from the Academy," Lars admitted reassuringly.

Looking out the window again, Lulu muttered with eyes aglow, "I'm going to walk Kingsley. Text me if the Grangeway truck moves. I mean even an inch."

"Oh boy! What do you think? There are people in the back of the truck with listening devices trained on you? I think you're taking this to the extreme."

"Well, as a matter of fact, I do. So just tell me if it leaves, okay?" Lulu maintained.

"You've lost it. I'm calling Dewey; we need some sound advice," Lars said.

Dewey Arnold Yates was the couple's conspiracy theorist from Southampton that Lars knew from his days in DC. For some time, Lars had helped Dewey with his spirits project, an "extraterrestrial ale" that Yates purported was made from UK barley fields and touched by the aliens' crop circle formations. This barley was used to create the ale dubbed "Cloud 51 Ale: The truth is in here."

Yates was a fanatic on fringe matters and an aficionado for anything related to aliens and the occult. He carried with him more conspiracy theories than anyone cared to remember. So when the couple had an emergency and needed a double dose of crazy, they called in the captain of conspiracy theories—Dewey A. Yates.

Lars was forever astounded by Yates's latest discoveries. Yates, a child of privilege, grew up on Manhattan's Upper East Side and spent summers on Dune Road in Southampton. Dewey's mother, Carol, bore a striking resemblance in her day to the lighter side of Linda Evans. She adored her international jet-set lifestyle and all that Manhattan had to offer in the 1970s. When Dewey's father passed away in the early eighties, his maniacal Uncle Jimmy took over the family reins, forcing young Dewey into indentured servitude to his lobbyist lifestyle, demanding that he leave New York and move to Chevy Chase, Maryland, enslaving him as ball massager to his two bull mastiffs, Tucker and Tyson.

Carol, seduced by the single, socialite lifestyle, like many of her girlfriends began accompanying handsome, successful, gay men out on the town to the opera, ballet, theater, cheeky affairs, and chummy restaurants. Men that posed zero threat to her *Town & Country* sexuality—just her wardrobe. And they loved doing all the things her deceased husband had little time for when they were married.

This went on for years. Her life was hijacked by her Madison Avenue boyfriends like Bobby Finch and Jeffrey "Jet Set" Oaks, that admittedly spun Carol out of control for so many years attending one fabulous party after another that she had a snowball's chance in hell in ever meeting any eligible man to remarry, thus getting off of Dewey's back.

Uncle Jimmy's financial iron fist hold on Dewey's trust fund forced him to abandon his beer-making dreams and pushed him into a life of semisolid squalor, living in a small shack outside the tracks of Southampton. He resided there with his plethora of passionate manifestos on many subjects, including but not limited to: reptiles living among us; society is *Soylent Green*; and aliens run WalMart. He has operated in a least favored nation status with his mother and friends since she pulled out of the beer business, refusing to back him any longer due to his wild, out-of-the-box political views. She was concerned that if her son had his way, guys like Art Bell, George Lucas, and William Shatner would run the world, waiting for the aliens to attack.

So naturally, when Lulu was cursed with some criminal chicanery, the couple called the Consigliore of Craziness. And as luck would have it, the Dewster was in town at his mother's Upper East Side townhouse, which undoubtedly meant she was on an extended holiday to some stinking fabulous destination or another—probably Sri Lanka or Kuala Lumpur with the likes of Jerald or the group's newest flavor of the month, Marty Trudelo. Like so many times before, Dew snuck into his mother's townhouse, with his spare key and was holed up drinking his alien brew, smoking pot, and eating well from her oddly stocked fridge.

Lars found the Dewman like a twisted Wonka in a land not of chocolate, but of conspiracy. Lars and Lulu hopped a cab uptown and knocked on the door to Carol Yates's townhouse. Visibly shaken, they heard a faint, choking, "Come in!" And went inside to find Dewey on the balcony smoking a joint, halfway hacking up a lung, his tall figure silhouetted by the bright lights of the clear East Side night. Carol's townhouse was a fine assemblage of antique objects, art, and furniture that epitomized an upper-crust lifestyle that Dew spurned for so many years. But now in his mid-forties, he was missing the comforts that come with clean clothes and edible food. Lars liked going there because Carol, a friend of Lars' mother from Palm Beach, had a few of his early figurative works and proudly hung the oil paintings in her living room.

Dewey, a lanky guy with grayed-out temples, wearing a shabby Brooks Brothers charcoal sweater and an old pair of faded Lee jeans, drew open the sliding glass door. Inviting Lars and Lulu to join him on the balcony, Dewey offered Lars a hit of his roach, and his customary survivalist theories of relativity on current matters of the state. He would address his friends, or anyone he met for that matter, as though they were in a holy closed-door White House briefing on psycho-germ black ops warfare, and they were damn lucky to be privy to his secrets, theories, and beer.

Yates embodied an overly casual, prep school beach bum look that mostly left one questioning whether he was an eccentric millionaire or a well-spoken homeless fellow. By design, this allowed him to operate a stealth wardrobe, and saved him lots of cash on trendy clothing. It wouldn't be out of the ordinary to see him wearing flip-flops in February. That was all part of his folksy charm.

After hearing him speak for just a few moments, people could quickly wrap their head around the fact that he wouldn't be fit to babysit. Not that he was unfit to be around children, or a creepy guy, or a marauder of some type, but he expounded on principles that would make even an AM talk radio show host blush. In twenty minutes he could take a two-year-old and turn him into a conspiracy theorist, the toddler crying out that Fisher Price is an alien takeover plot. Once, pulling his young nephew's broken See 'n Say from under his bed, slow-motioning the altered grunts of the pig, the horse, and the cow, he equivocally admitted that one could quite distinctly hear the ragged toy whisper, "Paul is dead." The explanation as to why the talking toy alluded to the Beatles' *White Album* was a discussion for another time.

"It's G13 mixed with Girl Scout cookies. It's kinda creeperish, so be careful, like a Kush," Dewey said hacking up what now sounded like his second lung. As Dewey continued to describe the high, he handed the fat, dirty, resonated roach to Lars as Lulu intercepted it, sucking down the smoke as if she were a member of the Rolling Stones. She hated marijuana, the smell of it, all of the accouterments, the mess, and most of all the stupid names associated with it: Mary Jane, grass, cheeba, nugs, chronic, kind buds, giggle bush . . . the list went on. It just wasn't her thing. She tried it several times in college, and the only thing that it ever made her feel was paranoid—acute, mind-altering transcendental bouts of Chicken Little theorist paranoia, like seeing ninjas falling from the sky, ready to raid her mind. Admittedly, she was not a weed enthusiast, but thought that the smoke might offer her a fresh perspective—fighting paranoia with paranoia—a negative ion charged with another negative ion might produce positive results, and she figured when in Rome, do as Dewey did.

"In the next couple of weeks, by the middle of April, it will have happened. It could be tomorrow. It could be February 20. That's a good day. Or it could be April 16. But sometime between now and April 16, I would say. It will be televised. They will arrest basically like a good percentage of the top bankers and politicians and other important people—celebrities, actors, anyone that they have got the goods on."

Lulu and Lars stared at Dewey with disapproving eyes, scared that he just may well have slipped past earthly bonds into the hereafter. Lars, shivering in the cold with his hands in the pockets of his Banana Republic twill parka, noticed Dewey wearing flip-flops in the frigid temperature, and motioned to Lulu to look down as the Dewman continued with his diatribe.

"It runs in the thousands most likely. They will be hauled off to jail. It will be a mass arrest and will be referred to as 'The Happening.'" Dewey's eyes began to glaze over in a catatonic state.

"There is a guy named Drake. It's actually corroborated by many different sources, but a guy named Drake. He's a Korean vet. He's in touch with the top people. It will be local law enforcement backed up by the federal marshals and the military, but really it's the military. It's the top personnel at the Pentagon that have decided to go ahead and do this. They're tired of fighting wars for profit on behalf of the modern lizards. They are going to reestablish civilian control over the military, not shady corporations, and basically they are weeding out the criminal element that has thoroughly infiltrated Washington, DC, and pretty much the state as well."

With the dispassionate monotone quality in Dewey's voice and preacher-like posture to his psychobabble sermons, you weren't sure whether to Baker Act him or embrace his holy words as gospel.

He was a convincing chap when you were smoking his weed, but outside of that he was just plain scary. For those unfamiliar with the Baker Act, it's a loose standard of sanity that allows two family members, friends, or even acquaintances to call into question a third party's sanity like a mental power of attorney, giving the rights to other individuals to question their mental health. Needless to say, Dewey was on the couple's short list. When he wasn't on a quasi tirade spouting off about his Uncle Jimmy or his mother, he was pushing the social envelope with his theories on the future of our fragile society.

Dewey continued, ever more convincing to Lars and Lulu, that he was a candidate for this year's freshman class at Bellevue.

"Drake is going to be on the radio tonight. He lives in West Virginia, and he has been authorized by the Pentagon to talk about this and prepare people for it, so they don't panic afraid that the criminal element might escape jail time and create some type of chaos in the country, whether it's a race riot, taking out infrastructure, or like whipping up religious static or communist infiltration. It's reestablishing the world law in the United States. Just Google *Drake* and *world happening radio*," droned Yates, bringing a droll, emergency-broadcasting tone to his alarmist rhetoric. "He has Elvis singing *Dixie*, and eventually . . ."

"Dixie?" interrupted Lars, who now had heard about enough, but couldn't really escape this onslaught.

Lulu mused, "Now Elvis is taking over the government?" Lars began whistling the tune to *Dixie Land*.

"No, you'll hear Elvis," Dewey continued.

"Dew, this is all very interesting," interrupted Lars, "but we don't have a lot of time here. What do you think Lulu should do about her boss and this Zirko guy?" he said as if he might actually have some paranoid insight. "Did you listen to my message? She believes she may have passed some insider information that may have crashed the market. And she thinks that these people are chasing her. And if there is anyone that knows about paranoia, it's you."

"Is this going on in the book or in real life?" Dewey questioned. "Both," Lars and Lulu said in unison.

"I need you to do some investigatory work with me this week," Lars continued. "We are going to follow this guy down to Wall Street."

"Let me think about it, I don't know if I can do it this week," Dewey replied.

"What's up with your boy Pearlmutter? When was the last time you talked to him?" Lars questioned.

As Dewey waxed on about his prep school pal, Remi Maurice "Pinhead" Pearlmutter, the group moved inside and sat down on Carol's French antique sofa and cordovan leather hassock.

"Haven't seen him in a few months," Dew said finally. "Maybe we need him on this?" questioned Lars.

Remi "Pinhead" Pearlmutter began innocently as Yates's gifted second-year roommate at Choate. But by the end of his junior year, he must have eaten one too many magic mushrooms, because he had a complete meltdown one night. He literally tuned in and dropped out. He self-administered tiny silver acupuncture needles to his eyelids, ears, and cheeks and strolled around the campus library like Pinhead from *Hellraiser*, as if it were nothing.

Pearlmutter unabashedly admitted that he was able to catch radio frequencies by calibrating the needles to his tuning fork, which he found in his sixth-grade cello case. This was a compelling sight to see. He would customarily tune his face while watching reruns of *The Big Bang Theory*, simultaneously snorting rails of Ritalin or anything else he could get his hands on. Bath salts and Sudafed were also ways for him to understand more, or so he ghoulishly believed. He maintained he could decipher the high-pitched sounds into some sort of Morse code, and believed the CIA was behind these intermittent, interplanetary decoded transmissions. He was quite a mess even by Dewey's standards.

"Someone from the CIA was attacking Pearlmutter with radio waves, making him sick, protesting his treatment in their hands. That was the story, I don't really know. Maybe he was just trying to fuck with me, I don't know," Dewey continued.

Lars noticed one of Dewey's irises go chameleon-eyed crazy, rotating a weird 180 degrees. Overhearing a faint knock on a distant neighbor's doorway, he went on, "Pearlmutter would eat only at Chinese buffets, because he thought the CIA was poisoning his food."

Lulu, sick to her stomach and not able to keep a lid on her laughter any longer, nudged Lars' corduroy chinos like she wanted to head straight to one of her favorite places in her old neighborhood, to have a glass of wine with Lars and make love. She was feeling high from the joint, not paranoid.

It was a high she had never experienced before. This was undoubtedly the first time in her entire life that she was able to think three steps ahead and see clearly past facial expressions and into someone's psyche and superego. Lulu lovingly looked at Lars' six o'clock scruff, defiant chin, and hard-working hands, and realized why she put up with all of his crazy friends, because she could see clearly now, as she always knew, that Lars was a terrific and lovely soul. And he put up with her assembly line of anxieties on a daily basis that even her own family had trouble dealing with, aside from holidays and her birthday. She had heard enough and was tired of Dewey's schoolboy tall tales of medicated twits.

Feigning interest into Yates's crock of certifiable crap, because through the haze there was always some shrapnel of inner truth, Lars said, "Maybe we need to reach out to Pearlmutter and get these acupuncture needles for Lulu to keep these people away from her."

"Yes, that's a thought," uttered Yates quietly.

"The reptiles have been in charge of the world for a long time," Dewey continued rambling. "They basically have been knocked off their perch. But, all this is going to be common knowledge within . . . I would say three to four months. There is a schedule."

Lars always joked that with Dewey there was always a schedule for a train that never seemed to arrive at the station. He had a rye field full of reasons why none of this insurrection and social chaos of doomsday scenarios ever played out for the populace. It remained—and thankfully so—in the bowels of his twisted mind, which constantly stretched out the timeline—his "schedule"—into an infinite thimble of excuses. But Yates was not alone. Many others shared this sentiment of a dawning of a new social paradigm. They would welcome this new order to be as accessible as the Internet.

"It all really starts out with the mass arrest. There are going to be revaluations. I could tell you. If you buy some dinar you can make yourself rich."

"Actually, we already ate," Lars mused.

"Buy some Iraqi dinar. Buy it online and they send it to you," Dewey explained.

"Dinar? C'mon, Dew," Lulu replied.

"It's their money. It's like the dollar. It's Iraqi dinar." "Uh huh," Lulu said.

"You can buy it for twelve hundred dollars, they send it Fed Ex," Dewey continued. "They are saying it's going to come out in double digits. That means over a million dollars."

"Uh huh. Dinar." Lulu sarcastically shot back. "Yup," Dewey said.

"Hmmm."

"The dong is another one that is supposed to go wildly. It's supposed to appreciate through the roof," Dewey says.

"So, back to the lizards, what were you saying about them?" Lulu questioned.

"Well, a lot of the newscasters are lizards," Dewey continued in a calm and resolute tone about such revealing subjects and had a clear, almost inside knowledge of fringe matters that usually led the average Joe to believe that he was some sort of ex-paramilitary. His vast knowledge made him an authority. An authority on *what* was at question, other than he might deserve a long, white, linen dinner jacket that just so happened to tie his hands, in a straight-talking tuxedo-like way.

"A hologram starts to break down, and they actually start to appear as lizards," Dewey explained. "Their face gets spotted and all sorts of crazy shit. You can watch it on YouTube all day; it's pretty crazy. You need to look at the underground base in New Mexico. There was a shootout between the lizards and some of the troops down in the subterranean level. A soldier actually shot and killed two of these things with his government-issued semiautomatic. Then they fired back with some sort of heat gun and basically melted off two of the soldier's fingers."

Dewey now formed a decapitated peace sign, raising it up high in the air, as if there were a huge sea of people around him. Craning his neck back, he stared off into the sky, as if he were transfixed on a passing starship.

"They killed them many years ago when they knew what was going on with the reptiles. What they were saying in a radio interview is that they are going to be on the loose. So if you see one, get out of its way. They are much stronger and faster than we are. We don't have a prayer against them unless we are armed."

"Actually, I'm going to hold off," Lulu said as she waved her hands up toward Dew and his joint.

"Yeah, I'm good too," Lars said.

"Well, I will tell you that after the mass arrest starts, we are going back to common law. And common law says that if there is no victim, there is no crime."

Assorted Nuts

While Lulu planned her departure from the firm, she enlisted Lars, the Dewman, and a guitar player from Lars' band, D-Key to help her ready. Recently separated, D-Key moved to New York six months ago to live out his lifelong dream of becoming a rock 'n' roll star, but instead wound up selling Life Alerts on Canal Street. His career was flailing, and he couldn't get up, so Lars employed him with odd jobs, whether it was stretching canvases, buying paint supplies, or the latest task at hand—trailing Theo Zirko, to find out exactly what kind of trouble Lulu was mixed up with.

D-Key worked stealthily and his rates were modest. An eighth of weed, two signature sandwiches at Katz's, and two hundred bucks usually was the barter. Lulu and D-Key normally went on brisket benders and had pastrami parties at Katz's when the band would go late night and needed a quick cholesterol fix. But lately, D-Key was holed up in Connecticut with a flax-seeded, mousey-blonde yogini named Belinda, where he would expound on their new organic kombucha swill lifestyle. They would carry around their elixirs in tiny concentric mason jars in their backpacks, and make love on yoga mats while drinking them. Together they made Lars and Lulu sick to their stomachs, forever and constantly bending and contorting into folds of off-putting behavior that was stomach churning and outrageously inappropriate.

Dewey drove a secondhand red Cutlass station wagon, complete with creepy wooden side paneling that somehow suggested that sketchy things had once taken place in there. His mother Carol, who kept it in a friend's garage for many years and after a few gin and tonics, forgot it ever existed, passed it down to him. Dewey took it out one Sunday afternoon in a desperate attempt to cart around his collectibles to a flea market in Hampton Bays and has been driving the jalopy ever since, dubbing it "the Carol Burnett."

Lars in the backseat had a makeshift office with his iPad and pocket printer. D-Key in the front seat had Lars' HD camera cradled in the nook of his elbow and had it trained on the revolving doors of 101 Water Street. With Dewey at the helm of the Carol Burnett, made famous by an entry in the *New York Post*'s "News of the Weird" column:

"A man in New York has been charged with leaving his Cutlass wagon illegally parked—for three hundred years. The man learned of the accusation when he got a $20,500 bill. The city was billing him for unpaid tickets going back to 1999, but a clerk typed the year 1699 into the computer."

"You still paying this off, pal?" Lars joked, referring to the red steel ride that reminded him too much of Stephen King's *Christine*.

"Yeah, I'll be paying these parking tickets off until the rapture," Dewey replied.

"I don't understand. Why don't you just get rid of this thing?" Lars asked as he lit up a bored-out green apple packed with G13, took a hit, and then passed it to D-Key.

Parallel parked a hundred meters away from the target, the car quickly clouded up in the frigid air with bilious smoke that wafted past a throng of suits in long coats penguin-ing past the group on their morning commute.

"These are all future customers for my device," D-Key pointed out as he blew smoke toward them.

"For your anal probes or something else, dickbag?" shot Lars.

"Life Alert, oh bilious one!" chimed in D-Key, not wanting to overplay his hand and jeopardize his next hit.

Dewey, responding late to Lars' dig about ditching the Carol B., tousled his hair in the rear view mirror a bit too long. "Are you kidding me? This baby?" he said, letting out a snide chuckle. "This baby is a real eighties delight."

"And it makes you look like the preppy killer," Lars admitted, actually frightened by the red steel monster. And he hated riding in it, especially around Southampton to places like Shelter Island. Not because it wasn't fancy enough, he didn't care about that. What he hated was to break down, and the Carol B. had a rather spotty record, at least when he was in it.

"Fuck you," Dew replied. "I don't give a shit about what you think. I don't need a fancy car to get chicks to go out with me."

"You don't?" D-Key chimed in, taking a supersonic toke off of the Granny Smith.

"I'm going to Funkin' Gonuts for us and to make a call. You two private dickbags stake out the target," Lars said as he held up his iPad, showing a photo from Theo Zirko's LinkedIn profile and then quickly closing it and peering around as if they were the ones being followed. By whom or what he wasn't sure, but he wasn't going to take any chances when it came to his baby Lulu.

Dewey handed over a short, detailed list of breakfast demands on a Post-it note: doughnut options, coffee, creamer, sugar combinations, the numerical possibilities scrawled out like Nash in *A Beautiful Mind*. Not having his specific breakfast needs that morning might set Yates off and thwart the mission. He pulled the breakdown from the torn pocket of his pinstriped oxford polo tucked beneath his plaid Axe man Cometh Paul Bunyan parka and handed the note to Lars through the side triangle window. He was unable to open his window since the Carol B. hit a twenty-point buck a few summers back.

Yes, the Dewman's sense of entitlement was staggering, strong-arming his friends weekly, and using guilt tactics to get them to shell out real cash for tune-ups or bodywork or gas cards. By the end of an innocent five-minute trip to the fish market or the beer store, if you weren't careful, you might be anteing up seven hundred bucks or more just to turn off his faucet of contempt.

At dinner, Dewey was a true sight to behold, ordering like he had just been freed from prison, requesting freaky à la Carte items with wild abandon. He and D-Key were international jivers when it came to money. They both subscribed to this "celebrities never pay" philosophy and applied it to everything they did. And they did it with such unabashed fervor that it was truly unsettling to witness if you were meeting them for the first time. But soon you got over it . . . or not.

Lars turned down Pearl Street and headed toward the familiar brown-and-orange sign at the end of the block to grab a Box O' Joe and some munchkins for the fools aboard the Carol B. Lars picked up a call from Lulu. He expected her to be hyperventilating with her typical Monday morning mantra of "I have had enough," but instead, she was as collected and clear as a copy written sound bite: pithy, emotionless, and calm, but carrying a fiery undertone. Lars hardly recognized her voice, expecting it to be full of high anxiety.

"I have decided: this is it. I've downloaded all my contacts. I'll be taking a long lunch to decide about acting school, and when I get back, I'll be meeting with Kline to give him my two weeks. I'll see you later for dinner. I love you," Lulu said calmly, in a robotic *Manchurian Candidate* tone and ended the call, cracking a wry smile.

The weed the night before opened up a Tiffany box full of prismatic thinking for Lulu. The floodgates of enlightenment had been opened. She finally was able to see her caustic situation with Screwzette in the clearest of lights. She had been prepping her departure since forever, but actually doing it was exhilarating.

Truthfully, she now understood why pot was illegal. It made you feel like you should take a stand against injustice, like in the sixties, and now with the Wall Street protests, however misguided. Today would be the day that she would settle the score. She would take a long lunch with scary old Skip from the Academy and decide if she would really enroll next semester, come back to see Kline, and give her two weeks notice, which would almost certainly amount to a work-from-home situation. High-power firms prefer not to have employees stew around at the office after quitting or being fired for fear of what might go bad or end up missing. Instead, they box up your things like a corpse and escort you out on a walk of shame or glory, depending on how you left the war.

Now completely frozen, Lars approached the Carol B. with an armful of rations, feeling pretty good that Lulu was finally quitting the firm. Lars grabbed the jimmy-rigged handle on the left-side rear passenger door, yanking it as if he were pulling a fat old man from a fiery barn. He practically ripped his arm off. Yates forgot to tell him that it had recently been welded shut due to some structural damage suffered in a snowstorm by Dew's neighbor's plow. He swung his arm around in sheer agony as he fell back, slipping on a patch of ice.

D-Key swung open his door and jumped out. "Say, Cap'n Dickbag, let me take those sea rations off your hands. What happened?" he asked, bending down to pick up the Box O' Joe and the white Dunkin' Donuts bag from the sidewalk.

"Owww! What the fuck!" cried Lars, holding onto his shoulder for dear life, attempting to get to his feet.

Dewey, rolling down his window, shot back in his slow, droll, I-forgot-to-tell-you voice, "Uh—it's welded shut! My fucking neighbor hit the undercarriage with his shitty snow plow."

"Fuck. Why don't you tell someone?" yelled Lars, shaking his arm out. "Jesus Christ, just don't miss this target going in. Make sure you just keep the camera rolling at all times, dickbag. You can't do this? You're doing this!"

D-Key was always fucking everything up, fucking up gigs, fucking up his marriage, fucking up Lars—anything that he could get his hands on. He was a natural. He was just that kind of friend. You always knew you were in for a ride, financially and emotionally, a trait that he and the Dewman merrily shared. On the schnorrer-meter these two slippery cats gave each other a real run for the money, which was ironic, because neither of them ever doled out a single cent, no matter what the occasion. They were what you call in the business "wholesale jivers." To get D-Key to ante up cash for a bar bill was like asking Gandhi to join the Green Berets; it just wasn't happening. He would make out with an old lady or a doorpost to try to get out of his part of the tab.

A slovenly, hairy-backed jammeister, freaky D-Key's only saving grace was that he could play the six-string guitar and wah-wah like he was the Devil of the D'Addarios. Funk was his backbone. He would beat his feet to the syncopated sounds from his semi-borrowed, quasi-broken Silvertone twenty-five-watt tube amp. He figured it was good enough for Zeppelin.

D-Key had been arrested more times than he cared to remember, and had a petty rap sheet on his driving record that read like a bad filmography: careening around South Florida in a beat-up Ford Focus wagon full of dope smoke with knobby snow tires like he was a tour guide at Lion Country Safari; coming to a complete stop on highways; driving on sidewalks in residential areas; and going the wrong way on a one-way street—that was his specialty. He was a magnet for cops, like he had a GPS up his ass. They would root him out in the strangest places and haul him in, always asking the same question: "Uh—son, when was the last time you were arrested?" as his arms were lowered before he was cuffed and read his Miranda rights.

Most of the time he would escape unscathed 'cause he was just so damn charming, in a loose cannon kind of way that would constantly crack you up, until you were stricken with an overwhelming sense of pity for him and were just damn happy he wasn't married to your daughter or dated anyone you ever knew. Lars had actually seen parents pack up and leave the country with their college daughter following a measly ten-minute coffee date at Starbucks.

Lars met D-Key while playing his guitar in South Beach with Dewey and Lars' art dealer pal, Paolo Fisher. Paolo had a crazy loft by the train tracks in West Palm Beach, a private art gallery where the band did some of their earliest recordings.

During the winter of 2009, for a charity fundraiser at the iconic Breakers in Palm Beach, an oceanfront resort known for its legendary hospitality and magnificent one-of-a-kind Italian Renaissance–inspired design, Lars had managed with Paolo's help to mount a solo exhibition in the Grand Ballroom for the wealthy donors of the Alzheimer's Foundation in town for the season. Lars' parents were to attend, along with some of his most important collectors who lived in season on the island. No more than ten minutes into the cocktail hour, quite inappropriately dressed, wearing a Bob Marley Smoke Me Up T-shirt, black frayed jeans, and a jacket borrowed from the club, D-Key in his infinite wisdom managed to sneak into the gala. He managed to insult the head of the charity, two of their biggest benefactors, and blow three silent auction bids for two of Lars' large, figurative impasto works, while simultaneously damaging a one-of-a-kind, fifty-thousand-dollar vintage screen. All while he was sprawled out behind the antique tapestry like a pregnant walrus, surrounded by a schooner full of seafood hijacked from the raw bar, ring tossing empty shrimp tails into champagne flutes, and splattering cocktail sauce across the screen, like a brutal slaying at Sea World. Lars' mother's face when she got the bill: *priceless*. Chasing D-Key across the eighteenth green with the bill in her hand was an absolute Kodak moment.

Why he couldn't stay at Paolo's gallery as planned, setting up for Lars' *Into Space* exhibition for the following day, was beyond his glib answer of, "Sorry, I forgot; I must have early onset Alzheimer's." His answer horrified the gala chairwomen, Lars and his family, Fisher, and the thousand-dollar-a-plate patrons that came out to support the worthy cause. D-Key, testing a wireless microphone for the horn section of the band, forgot to leave it at Paolo's, or to turn it off for that matter, and when he walked into the ballroom, it cross wired with the charity's loudspeaker as he made the off-color comment.

Paolo Fisher was an odd bird, too. He considered himself to be one of the sexiest vegetarians over fifty on the planet. Paolo and his Russian bride were constantly on a worldwide social media campaign, traveling to uncharted countries year round to pump up his profile, hoping organically to make Fisher a gluten-free celebrity. With his mild mannered, milquetoast looks, vegan complexion, small oval specs, and salt and pepper close-cropped Afro, he looked more like a guy from the Geek Squad than a blisteringly badass Bujinkan.

Paolo was a Shihan ranked instructor, studying exclusively with the eighty-one-year-old grand master in Japan since the early nineties. Fisher possessed the strength of a leopard, and on the morning of Lars' *Into Space* exhibition, he would come face-to-face with an animal out for more blood than a bargain hunter on Black Friday.

Paolo dealt mostly in highly sought after Andy Warhol works and the Baron of Blown Glass, Dale Chihuly. Then he got hip on Lars' paintings and bronze sculptures, focusing on suborbital travel.

On the night following the Alzheimer's gala, Paolo planned quite an affair. He invited all of his A-list collectors and friends to Lars' solo show. He also folded in his birthday bash into what promised to be a wild event, with models dressed in Lars' galactic garb, and Clusterfunk live, laying down tasty, improv grooves and his space-inspired paintings. Fisher officially dubbed it "The First Art Show in Outer Space."

Paolo decided to break away that morning before all the chaos ensued. The plan was to help D-Key pick up a small bit of stage equipment for the band, which was near an animal sanctuary that Paolo regularly supported.

Paolo, a champion for wildlife often donated to many Florida charities dedicated to the preservation and humane treatment of animals.

Wending their way through the big-cat sanctuary, D-Key drove up to the small terra-cotta villa; losing his nerve, he decided to stay in the car while Paolo went inside. In an area immediately adjacent to where the African leopards were kept, sat a holding cage where staff members worked with a recovered leopard. The following was Paolo's account as told to Lars, his parents, Lulu, and the two hundred invited guests as he returned from the Good Samaritan Hospital on the eve of Lars' solo show.

> There was a female leopard, about two hundred and twenty pounds that had been agitated and restless all morning. I was in the caged area adjacent to it. There

was an overhead cage access point where the cats could jump into the big, open area. I was in there when all of a sudden I heard D-Key's voice scream, "I'm going to have a look around. Here if you need to move my car . . ." As he yelled "car," billowing dope smoke escaped from his lips as he hurled the keys through the fence to Fisher just as one of the handlers in the other area with the leopards screamed, "Get out! Get out! Get Out!"

From about twenty yards away, I saw the big cat charging toward me. I took a couple steps forward to where the animal was, and in the time it took me to take three or four steps toward the gate, the leopard crossed the distance, looked right through the fence, crouched to the ground, jumped up in the air, and flew about nine feet. I had just enough time to raise my left hand, putting the palm of my hands on the back of my neck so that my forearms were across the side of my neck and my throat. The cat pounced on me from three quarters on her side. Her bottom two teeth sank into my cheekbone and my temple, and her top right tooth landed to the back of my head as I went crashing into the ground, her tongue wrapping around me like a tube top. Luckily, after thirty years of martial arts training, I knew how to hit the ground just right, so I didn't break anything. I knew that as soon as the cat had me, I had to play dead. I had to relax completely. If I blew an adrenaline rush I would die in seconds; the cat would shake and finish the kill. So I completely relaxed and my heart rate slowed down. I knew that there were people coming to rescue me. Someone was there almost immediately, trying to get the animal's head off of my face. All I could see at this point was the inside of the leopard's mouth.

As I lay there, I felt my skull start to compress, and knew that she was getting ready to bite right through my skull. So I had to reach my hand into the cat's mouth. I stuck the tip of my thumb into a pressure point in the roof of her mouth, and applied pressure to relieve the crushing force on my skull. I knew that if I didn't do it hard enough, my skull would crack and I would die. But if I did it too hard, the animal would bite my thumb off and come right back at my face, and it would be over. I managed to get that point just right. After twenty to twenty-five seconds on the ground, I suddenly felt her come off of my face. I immediately sprang up, rolled forward, and made it to the closed latchkey door.

I didn't feel any emotion at this point. I was soaked in blood but didn't feel any fear, anger, or physical pain. Then I saw D-Key look at me, and he had this cartoon expression of horror on his face. So my first thought was he's kidding around, and that he's making a joke, like "Whoa! That was close!" Then I thought maybe nothing happened, but then I saw my reflection on a glass surface. It looked like I was missing a good portion of my face from my temple to my cheekbone and below. My cheekbone was totally exposed. My next thought was that I had to find this piece of skin and take it to the hospital. Then I realized that it was just lacerated and that all the skin was pushed down to my jaw. So I found a clean paper towel, and put it on my right hand. The wound was on the left side of my head. I took the four fingertips of my left hand and pushed it below my jaw. I pushed into my face and worked all the skin up my face again, until I was able to flap it back into place. I made sure to carefully line up all the edges and apply direct pressure. "Just get me in the car and get me to the hospital," I said. The bleeding stabilized at that point. I lost enough blood that I felt tired and lost color, but I wasn't in danger of bleeding to death; it was only a facial wound, not an arterial wound.

On the way to hospital, D-Key, priding himself on his Rolodex of excuses, came up with the only plausible scenario that wouldn't cause alarm at the hospital. He told them a ferocious dog had attacked Fisher. If they told what really happened, the cat would be put down, the sanctuary would be closed, and it would be all over the Palm Beach papers—and possibly make national headlines.

Later that evening, Fisher arrived at the crowded gallery wearing a pair of Foster Grants that masked the 166-tiny-stitched gash that ran the length of his face. D-Key obnoxiously closed the show, riffing "Cat Scratch Fever" by Ted Nugent, which Lars and Lulu thought was in terrifically poor taste but terribly fitting. Meanwhile, Fisher tried to close a deal on a painting called *Space Port Landing* for thirty thousand dollars.

For Fisher's fiftieth birthday, his wife had a vintage convertible rolled in—ironically, an XJ Jaguar. Fisher, crying and barely able to see his new silver dream machine, admitted to Neke Carson, a longtime friend and fellow martial arts buddy that he knew firsthand, "It's damn better to be riding in a Jaguar than the other way around."

Carson, a karate man and a renowned artist, was famous for painting a series entitled "Rectal Realism" in which he painted a portrait of Andy Warhol with a paintbrush stuck up his ass. It currently hangs in the Andy Warhol Museum along with Polaroids and a movie made by Warhol himself. The *Village Voice* commented, "I don't know whether it's art, but that apple sure can paint."

* * *

Assholes of another kind: the guys in the Carol B. went gonzo on the news about the *National Enquirer* mix-up, razzing Lars, especially about Lars' full body shot. As they were about to break for lunch, Dewey had almost finished with his two-hour mind-bending explanation of why the Carol B. was a testament to his virility. If anyone could get laid in a town like Southampton, where money isn't the only thing, it's everything, with a cursed ride like Carol B.; then he was a deity of sorts. This idea rang true for D-Key, the roguish womanizer, who felt the same way about his Ford Focus.

Dew needed a break, so he stumbled into a Greek diner on Water Street to use the bathroom. As he entered the restaurant, he immediately spotted Zirko at the counter buying a cup of coffee.

Alerting Lars on his cell, they both tracked Zirko from 101 Water Street to a black Lincoln Town Car parallel parked on Pearl Street. The Town Car then pulled around the block to a federal building just a few streets up. Stepping out of the limo was Zirko and another man whom Lars realized after closer inspection was the man with the furry, coffee-stained birthmark, Skip Anderson from Yoga Nation.

It was now clear that he was offering Lulu a part not in a student play but a starring role as a pawn. Lars just about did a Betty Boop in his pants as he watched the two men walk into the building together. Lars shot an SOS call to Lulu who was gathering her things at the office, readying to meet Skip for lunch at the Palm in Battery Park City.

"I am out the door. I'm running late. I didn't change my mind, I'm still leaving," Lulu rambled in a rebuffing tone, somewhat annoyed.

"No. No. I'm with Dewey and the dickbag. I mean okay, you're right." Lars, getting flustered, put his words together frenetically, as he tried to explain spotting Zirko and Skip Anderson together. "Uh—I saw Zirko, and okay, I am absolutely positive it was fucking Skip Anderson, he looked nothing like . . . he's a fucking federal agent, a blue suited G-man."

"So. I guess I'm not getting that scholarship?" Lulu replied. "Lulu, are you listening to me? Did you hear me?" Lars pleaded.

"Yes, I heard you! But you can't be serious!" Lulu screamed.

"I'm telling you, don't meet him for lunch. It's a setup." Focusing in, like he was famous for, Lars shook off the abject stupidity, thought for a moment, and pulled it all together. "Listen, Zirko is either a Fed or working for them, because, good ol' Skip with the spirit fingers ain't no fucking guidance counselor. He's a G-man."

A wave of paranoia toppled Lulu like a tiger net as she frantically decided her next move. As crazy as it sounded, she needed to dig deep into the abyss of conspiracy to fight this insanity. She definitely couldn't go to any conventional authorities like the cops, the ladies in HR, or even a freakin' fortuneteller. As pathetic as it sounded, the only person she could turn to was Lars and his cache of self-medicated merry pranksters. And the thought of that depressed her.

Lulu grabbed her flash drive, a souvenir MLB team jacket promised to Lars, and two Amy Winehouse CDs and bolted down the stairwell to the forty-first floor, hearing her heart Cirque du Soleil as she skipped steps, tripping over her suede Sam Edelmans, tossing on the Yankees team jacket. She knew they wouldn't be looking for her at Robinson, Brill & Marks, or the law firm on the forty-first floor, especially after donning the Yogi Berra number eight jacket. From there she took the service elevator to the street, hopped a cab and headed downtown.

Approaching the Carol B., which was parked on the corner of West Broadway and Canal Street, Lulu could see the Dewman arguing with a tiny Asian meter maid, needling her for the senseless $150 "standing in a no-standing zone" ticket, flapping his arms in the mid-day sun, making gestures like a psychotic pigeon getting ready to have a triple coronary because of the pricey ticket she was issuing.

"This may be a rhetorical fucking question, but are you guys total assholes?" Lulu screamed. "Why would you call attention to yourselves?" she barked as the meter maid handed Dew the ticket and she hopped in the backseat beside Lars.

"Start talking, Nancy Drew, how exactly did you clowns figure this out?" She continued motioning to D-Key. "I want to hear the whole thing."

"Can I interest you in some vintage kombucha?" he offered as he raised a mason jar and graciously brought it toward Lulu, as if he were a sommelier at Le Bernardin.

"Knock it off, will somebody tell me what happened?" Lulu asked, becoming frustrated.

"This is hard for me to admit, but you've been right all along," Lars confessed.

"Always am. Just tell me exactly what happened," Lulu insisted.

"What we have here is a failure to communicate," Dewey chimed in. "We're going to have to take a ride."

"Look, we can't go home. They're going to be looking for you. That bitch is behind this. She's ratting you out!"

"They're probably there right now," Lulu added.

"Let's just start driving. You don't want to get another ticket," Lars urged.

"Well, I'm not paying it," Dewey said as he handed the ticket to Lars in the backseat.

"Hold onto it, they're like savings bonds, the longer you hold onto them, the more they're worth," Lars continued.

"Ohmigod! Just drive!" Lulu yelled. "And start from the beginning." The Carol B. pulled out like a dragster at the Dover Downs, peeling out, riding up on part of the curve, and nearly hitting a hot dog vendor who was pushing his cart across the street. Dew hung a Louie and headed toward Chinatown.

"If you want to talk conspiracies, look at these guys. None of them are American, running the streets of the city," Dewey explained, pointing at the street vendors.

"I ate a dirty bomb from one of them the other day," D-Key joked. "Stay focused!" Lulu screamed.

"What? Don't look at me," Lars replied.

"What in the fuck happened?" Lulu screamed as she slapped Lars in the face.

"Actually guys, can you give us a few minutes? I kinda liked that," Lars joked like he wanted more.

"They're all in on it, I already told you on the phone," Lars maintained.

"I knew it, see," Lulu said.

"Dewman, any ideas?" Lars questioned.

Before Dewey could get a word in edgewise, D-Key interjected, "Turn right here, yeah, two blocks down, right there, uh huh, yeah, right there," as if someone were scratching to find the itch on his hairy back. As Dewey double-parked in front of AcroYoga, they found Belinda waiting outside, shivering in the cold, wearing only a wafer-thin windbreaker and carrying a tattered navy blue North Face backpack.

"What the fuck are we doing here?" Lulu yelled.

"I can't believe what a swinging dickbag you are," Lars said. "What in the fuck are we doing picking up Daisy dickbag? We have the fucking Feds chasing us, and you're picking up granola Jane? I am going to kill you!"

"Oh, yeah," D-Key retorted. "She has these pecan diamonds you have to try."

"Yeah, they're freaky-deaky," Belinda said as she suddenly popped her head into the driver-side window.

"So where's your yoga mat?" Lulu questioned, overly suspicious of anyone now.

Belinda was a slightly cross-eyed, bowlegged, twenty-two-year-old ex–beauty queen from Connecticut who adored single motherhood, yoga, and D-Key. She attended the Culinary Institute of America and graduated as a certified CIA chef.

She met D-Key late one night at a Ziggy Marley concert at the Hammerstein Ballroom, much to the horror of her well-meaning working mother, whom she lived with in Greenwich with her three-year-old son. Belinda fell head over heels for D-Key and had him move in a couple weeks later.

"My yoga mat is in my mind." Belinda's lips curled up in a wacky beak as she spoke.

"Of course it is. Why wouldn't it be?" Lars interrupted.

"I do AcroYoga. It combines acrobatic concepts with yogic consciousness," Belinda continued, her voice sounding as if she were a tour guide on Cloud Nine doing hits of helium while her head and eyes tilted in opposite directions like a Felix the Cat wall clock.

"Let's get the fuck out of here already," Lars said.

Before Lars could say fuck, Belinda belly flopped into the front seat of the Carol B. and straddled D-Key like a carousel horse. As the beat-up Cutlass wagon hiccupped and backfired, it gunned, belching down Canal Street, heading deep into Chinatown.

"I have an idea!" blurted Dewey as if he rarely had any. He turned toward the backseat, now with his crazy chameleon eye doing the dance of the water lilies with Belinda's.

"Watch the car. Shit!" cried Lars as the Carol B. nearly hit a yellow hybrid taxicab swerving to the left, quickly changing lanes.

"Boy, this is some crew; this is how you're protecting me," Lulu said turning toward Lars.

The Dewman, Lulu, and the jivers in the Carol B. wended their way through the narrow streets of Chinatown, stopping in front of an old restaurant supply and noodle factory. Chinese lettering adorned the face of the building. Dewey got out, looked down the block, and shook his head as if he were lost. The sign said "Shanghai Noodle Trade and Restaurant Supply." Belinda and D-Key mauled each other to get their jackets off, and stayed in the front seat as Lulu and Lars jumped out and looked up at the abandoned, dirty, red brick building with its green flickering neon sign.

"Are you kidding me? Tell me he's kidding," cried Lulu looking to Lars.

"Dew, I mean this is too much," Lars confessed as Dewey made his way to the tailgate of the wagon.

"Well, no one would look for me here," Lulu admitted.

"See, see, we're making some progress here," Lars replied, immediately thinking that this might get a lot more ugly.

"As you know, when the going gets tough, the tough guzzle beer," Dewey declared, pulling two four-packs of his alien brew from out of the trunk. And like a homing pigeon, D-Key's schnorrer-meter peg moved; with his tongue still halfway down Belinda's throat, he reached his arm out of the window, like a beer-drinking vine, straight out of *Little Shop of Horrors*, murmuring, "We'll start with two. Feed me!"

"That's mighty swell of you," Dewey retorted, mumbling under his breath. The Dewman liked to keep a close lid on his beer, and it was taboo to grab out of the hands of the brewer. But D-Key, not one for formalities, filched two from Dewey's hands, swallowing the bottles back into the front seat of the scary Carol B.

"Ohmigod," cried Lulu. "I'm definitely going to jail."

"Sweetheart, you're not going to jail," Lars replied. "Don't worry. I'm not going to let that happen. Dewey, are we lost?"

"I think so. Definitely. Let me make a call," replied Dewey.

Lulu and the jivers, with Dewey leading the way like a twisted Tibetan tour guide, trekked up the narrow, dusty, nine flights that reeked of dead rats, urine, and old Chinese take-out to a large door adorned with a slew of signs that were haphazardly taped to the steel door, looking more like a ransom note than a "beware" deterrent.

Stuck smack dab in the middle of the door was a nuclear hazard symbol; to the left of that one read: *Biohazard Medical Waste*; the one below, slightly askew, read: *Smith & Wesson on Premises Beware*. Still another one read: *Dog, Beware of Owner*, and underneath that, one read: *We don't swim in your toilets so don't pee in our pool*. The last sticker struck Lulu as rather odd, because if there was a swimming pool behind that door filled with biohazard medical waste floating in a sea of urine, she realized what the smell was, and thought, maybe with all of her trouble and the bullshit crack team she was with, that she just might rent the Smith & Wesson, swan dive in, and end it all. But thoughts of her pup, Kingsley, and Lars' good intentions made her curious as she looked upon Dewman with her angry eyes, watching him knock on the thick steel door in a succession of raps, signaling some sort of code, waiting for a response.

Dewey turned around to the group. "He wants to know if anyone here is a cop."

"Lars played one on TV once," D-Key joked as they heard the sound of a ferocious bark through the metal door.

Dewey peeled back the flap of the biohazard sign and stepped away, allowing those who dared accompany him to be seen through the large, oval peephole. After a long pause, the crazy metal door slid open with a holy crash, revealing a large, imposing male figure dressed in camouflage pants. He was naked from the waist up, wielding over his big folds of blubber what appeared to be an Uzi machine gun. The light rays from the large room behind the silhouetted man bounced off the silver-tipped acupuncture needles that covered the fat man's eyelids, ears, cheeks, and chin. A look through the open door revealed a madman's lair, a psychotically messy apartment stacked with books, charts, and newspaper clippings pasted to the graffiti-sprayed walls.

Arched in the doorway, a growling German shepherd with fangs bared, foaming rabidly at the mouth, charged at Dewey.

"Plat-plat-plat," went the Uzi, squirting a viscous, lime-colored liquid that struck the shepherd in the face, and silenced the beast's deep bark, stopping the ferocious canine cold. The shepherd sprang off its powerful hind legs and suddenly heeled, inches away from attacking Dewey. Yates felt his heart do a double-gainer into his queasy stomach as he attempted vainly to hold back a truckload of vomit that went spewing all over his new Hilfiger down vest and onto the dirty hardwood floor.

"Holy Jabba the Hutt," D-Key blurted as Belinda let out a gut-curdling scream followed by an even louder one from Lulu. "Ahhhhh!"

"Run, its Hellraiser," Lars cried.

"Pepper spray, and from the second chamber cyanide, so who's fucking next?" uttered Remi Maurice Pearlmutter, raising his arms up in a Rambo pose, holding the Uzi as if he were the holy emperor of all mankind.

"Ugh! Shit! My vest," said Dewey as he stared down on the floor, now watching the dog lap up his vomit.

"That's too much," cried Lulu as she turned away in horror, watching the dog lap up the big chunks of puke. "Just kill me now!"

"Engaging cyanide in 5 . . . 4 . . . 3 . . ." Remi wistfully began counting down.

"Whoa! Whoa! Whoa! She was kidding," Lars jumped in. "It's only an expression."

Remi, now aiming the gun at Dewey, asked in a militant voice, "Just how do I know you are Yates and not some lizard adapting his skin?"

"Uh, well, you roomed with me at Choate, and you used to spank it to Stevie Nicks albums and your Cheryl Tiegs poster when I was in chemistry class."

"Anyone would know that; that was published in my manifesto," fat man Remi replied. "Come in!"

"Dewster, now I know where you get all your shtick from," Lars said as everyone entered Remi's messy loft. "Besides waterboarding, what else goes on here?"

"Don't cha like what I have done with the place?" Remi muttered in a threatening voice, training the gun now on Lars' head with the infrared scope right between his eyes.

In the middle of the room stood a tent made of mosquito netting. Housing a series of old military-issued desks, resting on top of the rusted steel was a hodgepodge of computer screens showing various Google Earth maps of New York, Washington, DC, and Los Angeles. Beside the desks were rows of aquariums radiating a greenish night-vision glow. Inside, swimming around, were Remi's four polygraph piranhas: Ringo, Paul, John, and George, and his octopus Sullivan.

"No. No. As a matter of fact, we were just saying it's stylish but completely accessible—early Rambo meets Jonathan Adler, an absolutely timeless look. Isn't that right honey?" Lulu said, desperately making SOS eyes toward Lars.

"I'm seeing an *Out of Africa* meets Frank Gehry cardboard kind of thing," Lars replied, pointing toward the tent.

Belinda remarked, rocking her eyes looking up toward the ripped tin roof, "I see this big Chihuly glass sculpture coming down in the center."

"Sit down and tell me more," replied Remi, now captivated. He led the group to an off-matching set of ripped cordovan and suede club sofas, a sea of empty Budweiser and Jack Daniels bottles littered the floor. Next to Remi stood a makeshift coffee table made of taped-together FedEx boxes, resting on top were more stacks of magazines and newspapers.

D-Key quickly proffered up the four-pack of Dew's beer to the fat man, displaying it nervously, describing the brew in a game show host voice, as he handed it over to Pinhead, still brandishing the loaded Uzi. "An amber ale with barley harvested from the famed crop circles fields in England. A hearty, extraterrestrial ale . . ."

"Knock it off, Monty Hall, before I blast you into the next Milky Way," Remi said, changing his tone from social to psychotic.

"So, the Dewman tells me you kids are in a little bit of a quagmire," Remi continued, doing his best Colonel Kurtz. "Now, I can help you, but it isn't going to be pretty." His left eye twitched as he uttered the word *pretty*. "Dew says you have some marshmallow-headed Feds after you and you seek answers."

"Can you help us?" questioned Belinda, tilting her head like a curious puppy.

"You mean with your brain transplant? No, I'm afraid you need to go to Mount Sinai. I don't perform those here anymore," mused Remi.

"Have a pecan diamond, they're freaky-deaky," Belinda said, offering them out of her large Ziploc bag.

"Tell Betty off her Crocker over there to get those fucking pecan sandies out of my face. I eat only off of Chinese buffets," said Remi. His face began to swell up with a fiery flushness, exuding trouble as the veins popped and shimmied on his forehead.

"Well, I do love a buffet," D-Key agreed.

"Well, who doesn't," Lars admitted supportively.

"Shut the fuck up," said Lulu, addressing D-Key and Lars, while clinching her teeth.

"They're pecan diamonds and you should really try one. I'm a trained chef from the CIA," Belinda said. "I'll just leave them over here for when you're ready for a taste." She set them down on the ledge of an easel. Resting atop it sat an iconic photograph framed of Richard Milhous Nixon shaking Elvis's hand.

"The CIA? In the cage, now!" he ordered, pointing to the center of the room. "You touch a computer, I cut your fingers off! Dewey, who the fuck is she?" As the German shepherd began barking, he herded D-Key and Belinda, who jumped to their feet and into the netting.

Remi, like he had been suddenly ambushed, pulled from inside his right boot a small pellet gun and hastily unloaded it, riddling the plastic package of sweets into smoking road kill.

"She just jumped into my car, I don't even know her," Dewey confessed.

Cleaning off the hand gun as if he were ready for a real fight, Remi continued, "My polygraph piranhas will fucking tell me if you two are telling the truth. Get your shitty finger in there, before I shoot you both full of fucking holes."

"Wait, what?" cried Lars, as he heard Belinda scream a second time, motioning like she was going to actually listen and stick her finger in the green-glowing deadly tank. But she was stopped by Lulu's retching scream.

"She's harmless. I'll put my finger in there. Use mine. I'm a painter; I don't need it," Lars went on as he stood up.

"He's my boyfriend; he'll give his finger," cried Belinda as she nudged D-Key closer to the tank.

"What? We only met last week!" cried D-Key. "Kidding!"

"Those fish don't stand a chance against him, Remi. Do yourself a favor, use mine!" yelled Lars, trying to think quickly what to do, but not being very successful. Lulu, highly agitated, realized this Remi mess was going south fast.

"Yeah, that's a good idea. You," Remi said, now addressing D-Key. "Get your finger in the green water now, or your girlfriend gets it right in the ass."

"I've been trying to convince her of that since we met," D-Key pleaded. "Any insights, antidotes you could share . . ."

"Shut up! Just put your finger in the fucking tank, jerk-off!" Remi screamed. From the underside of his naked wrist, he barked into a Secret Service type two-way radio and addressed his pet piranhas. "Ringo, Paul, George, John—have at this creep and let me know if these people are all full of shit. 'Cause other than Dewey, and I'm not even sure this is Dewey, this whole thing is starting to stink."

D-Key timidly tested the water with his right-hand pinky finger as the piranhas began circling, eyeing up his digit like a Nathan's all-beef dog. A lightbulb seemingly going off in his head, D-Key switched nonchalantly to his index finger, to which Remi groused, "Hey, pal, by the looking at you with that seventy-two tour Zep T-shirt, your grubby pants, and the guitar pick sticking out of your right pocket, I'd peg you as a wannabe ax man. And we all know, jerk-off, you could still play a bad ass guitar without your index finger, as proven by Jerry Garcia, so put your guitar pickin' finger in there, boy. Now!"

D-Key submersed his arm, thumb first, into the dull, green murky tank. Polygraph Paul danced around the thumb, getting closer and ready to snack on his nail with its razor sharp teeth. Paul's eyes suddenly glazed up as if he had seen a ghost and floated belly up to the top of the tank—extremely dead.

Remi screamed, "Paul is dead! Paul is dead!"

"Holy *White Album*, D-Key, you dickbag. You swinging, fucking dickbag!" Lars screamed. "Let me kill him."

"You're all a bunch of liars. You all will die!" Remi yelled as he spun around a fanny pack from the small of his back, unzipping it to reveal a small, explosive pack with a digital timer, ripping through a five-minute countdown. "You can all die."

The German shepherd barked insanely, like he had discovered a dead body down by the river.

Remi switched gears like a corporate madman trying to placate an important client. "I've never met anyone quite like you. I think you possess a few special powers; I would like you to come work for my operation. I could use—like they say—a dickbag like you."

"I think I have little choice, since I just broke up the Fab Four," D-Key said, putting on an English voice of distinction. "Where did you pick up these Portuguese house pets? Undoubtedly on a trek down the dangerous Amazon, and I don't mean the one that sells the books."

As if by magic, by the word *Amazon*, Paul came back to life, as if he were shocked back by the light of the Grim Reaper, and began fishtailing back to the other Fab Three.

"This guy's good," admitted Remi.

"Does this mean I'm off the hook?" asked D-Key.

"Fuck no! Your girlfriend's life is still at stake," Remi replied. "Doesn't seem fair," Lulu chimed in.

"Honey, let's not argue with a man that has a bomb strapped to his bunny sack," Lars said.

For the next two hours, Lulu divulged every bit of information she could recall to Remi.

Dewey, getting his old friend to soften up, broke his steadfast rule and devoured a few freaky-deaky diamonds. Remi became fascinated by the conspiracy correlation between Zirko and what was dubbed one of the worst weeks on Wall Street, in recent memory. And why Lulu, of all people, had been sucked into this mess, a midlevel PR executive, who by his estimation was a sweet girl, but clearly posed little threat. From what he could see, the girl could not snap, whistle, or wink, so in deeper spook terms what could Lulu really offer? *Yes, she must be an unwitting cog in a bigger wheel,* he thought to himself. It made little sense to him, given his extensive experience in these types of matters.

"What's the womb temperature here? It must be like one hundred degrees," Lars joked as he sipped on an alien brew, munching on Belinda's second bag of pecan diamonds.

"Wow, these are really good. What's in here? My mom used to make these, but not as good," Lulu said, desperate to take another bite.

"Yeah, I told you guys, they're freaky-deaky," Belinda chimed in.

"Do they remind you of when you were a little girl?" D-Key jokingly asked Lulu.

"No, does it remind you of when you were a little girl?" Lulu joked back as Lars busted out a belly laugh.

"No, but it may remind Streisand over there," D-Key quipped, pointing to Lars.

"Nice one, nut farmer!" Lars shot back.

"Oh, yeah, I thought you looked familiar; I remember you now. I saw you in the *Enquirer*," Remi chimed in. "Streisand's son, right?"

"Yeah, she wants him to find a nice boy and settle down," D-Key joked.

"D-Key, *como se dice*—dickbag?"

"Okay, Lulu, let's see if there is anything floating around on this today." Remi went to his refrigerator and pulled out a child-sized cello case, opened it, brought forth a tuner, and began tuning the needles protruding from his face; matching notes to the pitchfork— he went to work.

"Not to sound ungrateful, but how in the Hamptons is this going to help me?" Lulu questioned, trying to remain composed, if nothing else. She was just buying a little time while she figured out her next move.

"Ha! Ta! How could this help you?" Dewey interjected in a sarcastic tone. "This is the help you need."

"My dear, I wouldn't expect you to understand. I just want you to witness," replied Remi in a southern preacher's voice as he stepped back into a pool of light coming from a Lekolite rigged to the vaulted, rotting, tin ceiling. He began a series of grunts and violent tremors that raced throughout his body, as if he were undergoing an exorcism. "Step back, people, I have been known to spark! Ow! Grunt! I am again it. Hey!"

"What he's doing now is considered illegal, but since we are in the confines of his home, I doubt the authorities would recognize the tag," Dewey explained to the group.

"English, please," Lulu interrupted. "Authorities . . . that's rich," Lars added.

D-Key and Belinda, still inside the tiger net, began doing downward-facing dogs and cobras, kissing each other like an undulating island of dirty debris.

From Remi's mouth, he started speaking Chinese and began shouting out some sort of military protocol in perfect Mandarin. After a moment, he shook his head, tapped his tuning fork, recalibrated two needles piercing through the folds of his outer ear and three stuck to the tip of his chin, walked over to a broken television playing a looped countdown test to the emergency broadcast system, lifted his right leg, and stuck out his left arm, still clutching the pepper spray machine gun.

"He's now fine tuning the instrument. That might have been some Chinese officer defecting, from what I could gather," Dewey explained.

Changing the position of his interactive body antenna, Remi began speaking in a perfect Russian dialect, muttering something about a nuclear submarine captain in an SOS outside of Los Angeles.

After about six hours of Hellraiser's nonsense and tripping to the bejesus on Belinda's loaded freaky-deaky diamonds, Remi had a breakthrough. He was able to pick up an encrypted message sent by two HMSS agents in the UK who were sniffing around a banking scandal. Then on his iPad, he logged into his Google Earth account, jammed the server, punched in a few strokes and a few lines of JavaScript, stealthily hacking into a spy satellite. After another two hours with Lulu anticipating his every word, she was completely hooked. She was glad as hell that she had met Pearlmutter, for by the time she left his apartment with the pranksters, Remi "the eccentric seer" had given her the information she needed.

According to Remi, the CIA, in some sort of effort to "fight a futile war on drugs," had to pay a marker on the munitions and use the market tumble to camouflage their activities. This action precipitated innocent workers to fall prey to the perverted and grotesque flagrant misuse of government leadership and funds while at the same time decimating their savings and futures. Surely Washington was behind this, not some shorted calls on some bad stocks—this was now crystal clear. And Pinhead Pearlmutter and ultimately the Dewman were to be thanked for the information. Lulu was not going to stand for this. This bigger picture represented the essence of white-collar slavery, and Lulu would have to expose it in her book.

The pranksters padded down Canal Street to Houston, still feeling freaky from the diamonds they left the Carol B. behind. As they sprang east, they made their way to Katz's Deli for a quick corned beef and pastrami fix, all before Lulu and Lars were to check into the Hotel on Rivington, out of fear that some of Skip's buddies might already be at the loft waiting to arrest Lulu.

The romantic on-the-run sex would be thrilling, which is what kept Lulu's nerves from exploding. As she glanced to her left, she saw a parked police car. As the entourage sheepishly walked past the white

NYPD car, the bubble gum machine turned on; the siren startled her, and she nearly jumped out of her skin.

"Used to freak me out, too, but I—uh—trained myself. Every time I hear a siren, I eat a piece of sour candy," Dewey explained to Lulu, noticing she was on edge.

"Oh, just like how you train a puppy," Lulu added in. "Yes, precisely," Dewey replied.

"Thought you couldn't teach an old dog new tricks," Lulu said.

"Look at D-Key; he's now going to be gainfully employed by the Hellraiser," joked Lars.

"Over my dead body," said D-Key.

"Well, that should be a cinch for him," Belinda chimed in. "Saying that we just met . . . How could you?"

"I was just kidding," replied D-Key turning to Lars. "I was doing some of Lars' shtick. For a minute, I really thought you were going to 'Boop' in your pants, Streisand."

Since flying out of La Guardia for a charity auction at the famed Breakers Palm Beach, Lars had a hard time shaking off the Boop moniker after a mind-bending ordeal that involved a warm roast beef, mushroom, and Swiss melt. In Lars' estimation it had been incubating in the easy-bake oven glass case, decomposing for about a week, before Lars embarrassingly bought it on his way down to PBI from LGA.

Immediately, as Lars tore into the first few bites, kamikaze style, the sandwich tasted a tad rank. But since the flight was delayed and he spent the duty-free price of nearly fifteen dollars on the sandwich, he was going to finish it. He was starving. He devoured the melt like it might be his last, and then crashed and burned one into the gray vinyl chair by the Jet Blue gate. Immediately knowing something was awry, he sprang to his feet, mortified to find a film of muddy residue on the chair. His eyes bugged out nearly to Brooklyn, and his heartbeat froze as he felt the back of his pants and looked down at his fingers to see the coffee-colored toxic seepage now dripping from his ring finger. As he took off his sweater in a lighting raid, he awkwardly tied it across his waist, and waddled his low-riding, wet butt straight to the men's room, where he cleaned up in the stall as best he could with some wet paper towels and retied his stinky, fresh, Fred Perry baby blue sweater and swaddled himself, duck-footing it into every store, desperately searching for something to put on, kicking himself in the ass for not packing a change of pants. But no store in the entire La Guardia airport, which caters to one of the busiest cities in the world, had at that time a pair of shorts, golf pants, sweatpants, or even a fucking kilt that a guy could put on.

After forty minutes on the hunt, Lars, now sweating profusely from every pore in his body, praying the toxins would escape, settled on a pair of fleece, baby blue, Betty Boop "Only in New York" Capri pants for the duty-free nightmare price of nearly fifty fucking dollars. He went back to the men's room, grateful he had something clean to toss on, as asinine as they looked on him. He shook his head as he saw his reflection in the huge window at gate five overlooking the tarmac and thought to himself that he looked like a stupid-ass Betty Boop cone of cotton candy, with his matching Perry sweater, and sat down on the floor, ducked behind a large fern, pathetically hoping to hide out until it was time to board.

This quickly became a fleeting thought as a seven-year-old Japanese girl sporting a brand new pair of pop wheels skated about, showing off for her family. She did her best Kristi Yamaguchi on the hard carpet. She stopped dead in her tracks as she came out of her shoot the duck. With her head tilted like a scathing critic, she cracked up, scorning Lars and his choice of travel wear. Skating to her mother, father, and two teenage brothers, nearly falling out of her new kicks, she hysterically pointed out to her eldest brother that the odd, baby blue bird behind the fern had the matching pants to her Boop wristband. Only in New York.

Lars and Lulu led the way to the southwest corner of East Houston and Ludlow. The familiar red neon sign read KATZ'S.

"This is one of my absolute favorite places in New York," Lulu said to Belinda as she tried to get her mind off of things. "Did you know that each week this place serves ten thousand pounds of pastrami?"

Lars, knowing the mantra well, finished Lulu's fun fact: "five thousand pounds of corned beef, two thousand pounds of salami, and twelve thousand hot dogs."

"If I start with that, what will you people have?" D-Key said. "Yeah, I can have that, too. Who's buying?" Dewey added.

Lars, noticing a nail salon, turned to Dewey and said, "Now there's the real conspiracy, embolden by the women in this country."

"Ohmigod, here he goes," said Lulu.

"He's right," Dewey agreed. "Those places reek so bad, women are obviously losing brain cells by the second in there with all the lacquers and acrylics. You have these ladies coming home absolutely out of their heads. It's a Korean plot, I tell you."

"Whoa," said Lars. "Dew, are you still peddling that Renoir?" "It's a Benoir, painted by Van Gogh," Dewey replied.

"What?" Lars asked.

Dewey's mother Carol passed down to him an unremarkable painting of a few Iris trees. The signature on the bottom read *Benoir*. By the looks of it, it was obviously made in the late 1960s. Dewey wanted so badly to get back at his family for what he believed to be mistreatment that he deluded himself into believing it was a painting by Renoir, mistakenly signed Benoir. Fifteen thousand dollars later, after having it X-rayed and fingerprinted using the latest in infrared technology by the world's leading forensic art expert—whose latest discovery according to Dewey was the missing Leonardo, Dewey was shaken to the core to find out it was worth only seventy-five bucks—and that was on a good day.

In the loose, wasted, shrinking gray matter of his brain, he soon invented a new way to get back at his mother and Uncle Jimmy by claiming that what she gave him was in fact an actual Van Gogh worth in the tens of millions, signed jokingly *Benoir* to make light of his rival Renoir. Spending another five thousand dollars, Dewey took a trip to Europe, where Van Gogh painted his *Irises*, and took a photo. He matched up and swore it was the same site of the Benoir painting. This would drive his well-meaning mother into a rage so severe that it could only be quelled by another stellar trip to Sri Lanka with Jeffrey "Jet Set" Oaks.

Carol, desperate for Dewey to be successful like many of the well-dressed men surrounding her, vainly attempted at every corner throughout Dewey's life to provide accomplished men as role models. She secretly hoped the very unsuccessful Dewey would get successful. For Dewey, it was the American Nightmare in reverse, a tragedy in epic proportions, because all Dewey Yates wanted to do was chase girls around Bridgehampton and take his alien brew to the stars.

Inside the delicatessen, Lulu was feeling pretty good now that she finally had some answers, but admitted to herself she wasn't out of the woods yet and in fact felt that her nightmare actually just might be beginning. As she stood back from the familiar, long glass deli counter, she remarked, "You know, during the war, which I feel like I'm in the middle of, you could send a salami to your soldier."

"Well, that works out pretty good for you, Lulu. Tell Lars so you have a reason to stay up at night," D-Key said.

"Huh?" questioned Lulu, peering around the crowded tables and looking for anything or anyone out of place. She grabbed a number from the deli counter and handed one to Belinda and stepped back to show her the infamous *When Harry Met Sally* table where Meg Ryan faked an orgasm.

"Good one, dickbag," groused Lars as he eyed up the menu.

"I'm not sure whether to go for the corned beef pastrami or the Harry Met Sally 'I'll have what she's having,'" said Lulu as she pointed to the table.

"That's the table there," she told Belinda. "And this table was the one in *Donnie Brasco*, where Johnny Depp's character met the FBI agent," she said, pointing to another table in the deli, across the crowded room.

In the time it took Dewey, D-Key, and Belinda to turn and determine which table she was referring to, Lulu vanished without a trace; unbeknownst to Lars, standing right beside her, turned away to the counter, salivating over the hand-carved pastrami station and the delicate care the deli master spent slicing the thick-cut seasoned meat.

Do Not Pass Go . . .

"Up next, more of our riveting interview with first time author Lulu Norris," FOX News reporter Craig Rivera announced. "Our very own Ben Wheatley recently sat down with the author, who is currently detained at the Metropolitan Detention Center, awaiting arraignment on a crime that, according to Ms. Norris, she did not commit. And now, our exclusive interview."

In the yard, Zeela, Lulu's one and only true friend since being wrongly detained four months ago in Club Fed, was throwing a fit, unable to get close enough to all the action. Kicking and screaming, she shoved her way through the thick crowd of the neon-orange jump suited women, making her way up to the front of the stage riser. "My baby *sha*, I got an oxtail sandwich for ya'," Zeela said as she waved the sandwich high in the air. Lulu was at her wits end with Davio and his pathetic string of excuses. "Just holla back, *sha*, if you want me to touch up your 'air. I brought me shears."

Hearing her confidante's familiar Haitian accent, Lulu motioned for the guards to let Zeela by as she addressed Wheatley, for what she was praying might precipitate some kind of resolution to this ugly, ongoing nightmare, now having a discernable and detrimental effect on her mental health. No longer was she able to block out the cries of the cell soldiers screaming their lungs out at 5:00 a.m. breaking bad for any guard or yard bird that would listen. As for the cellmate in-fighting, innuendos, mind games, and physical threats—she had had enough, and although she had met some real salt-of-the-earth women, looking back at Zeela now at the edge of the stage, she knew if she ever got out of the Grey Bar, she would certainly do everything it would take to spring her dear friend from the Big House. However, Lulu couldn't wait to get back to Lars and Kingsley, unable to see either one since the night she disappeared.

Lars was to arrive later that night for her first and last conjugal visit. She was aroused, yet at the same time appalled at the thought of making love to him for the first time in now four months in some sort of pseudo-sterile jailbird accommodations: a toilet for a wet bar and a cot the size of a Twix bar. And for all she knew there were creepy prison personnel behind a two-way mirror, taking copious notes on all of Lars' patented moves. That little dive of a motel that they were forced to stay in a few years back in Delray seemed like the presidential suite at the Plaza in comparison to this place.

As the technical director counted down from an obnoxiously fitting commercial for Life Alert to the feed, the lights, under the midday sun of the prison yard, were hellishly blinding. Feeling her stomach tighten and the back of her neck stiffen in the chilly, late April air, Lulu's lips were dry. She burned with anger for having to front herself like this before millions of people while her paid mouthpiece and college friend, Davio, was off on another fabulous cruise. But if this interview turned out to be a means to get out of Club Fed, she would rock this bitch Lizette, the firm, Zirko, and the entire rotten system into a new time zone on her own accord.

"Ben Wheatley here, for the second part of our series 'Justice Delayed,' where we profile several individuals who are wrongly incarcerated for crimes they did not commit. White collar crime has steadily been on the rise as large corporations believe they are above the law, with far too much control over their employees, becoming political machines in themselves, protecting those at the top and blaming those caught the middle. Lulu Norris has been incarcerated for crimes related to insider trading during her tenure at KAR PR. Lulu, thanks for joining us today."

"Thanks again for having me," Lulu replied stiffly.

"So for the viewers tuning in for the first time, you've been charged with five counts of extortion and insider trading, all stemming from your employment with a prestigious public relations firm—charges you flatly deny."

"Yes, clearly. That's correct," Lulu answered.

"And you have not profited monetarily in any way from the insider trading scandal you're accused of? Is that correct?"

"Precisely. As a matter of fact, the only way I have profited from this whole sordid matter, oddly enough, is from the friendships I've made in here," Lulu said, deferentially nodding to her confidantes Zeela and Ingrid, who finally now had a ringside view of the action.

"Have you really made friends at a federal detention center?" queried Ben. His broad newscaster body shifted uncomfortably in the small director's chair as he leaned forward.

"Ben, my new friends and I can't exactly go out shopping and have lunch," Lulu said, changing her tone from sarcastic to sincere. "But the friendships that I've made in here have been meaningful."

"Interesting. Bernie Madoff has been reported as saying that he's much happier in prison than he was on the outside. That he is more at ease now than he was during his last twenty years of freedom. Is that the same for you? Is that what you're trying to say here?"

"No, Ben, not at all. I desperately miss my family and my life with my loving boyfriend and puppy," Lulu said.

"So, would you say you were asked to break laws at the behest of your former employer on a daily basis, or was it more sporadic?" asked Ben, as he quickly ramped up the interview.

"Yes, whenever it was necessary and without hesitation I was asked to perform for the magicians at the upper echelons of the firm," Lulu added.

"Magicians? What kind of crimes were they asking you to do?" Ben asked, pushing for more.

"At first, it was mostly petty stuff," Lulu said with her revenge juices flowing.

"But then it escalated?" questioned Ben.

"Yes, that's the thing. At first, I had no idea," continued Lulu. "They were covert about it, you see, and I was very young. I was impressionable then, and they had the goods on me. During my seven-year tenure, my job was at stake—hourly. It was quite a lot of pressure besides the demands of the job itself."

"The unreal events depicted in your book, Lulu," Ben said, edging toward her in his seat, "seem pretty outrageous for a group of young women. So, without giving away too much of the book, what were among some of the most outrageous?"

"Home wrecking, crimes of the heart escalating into deportations and poisonings, and that's just scratching the surface, Ben," admitted Lulu ashamedly looking away in disgust over her former actions. And as she glanced into the assistant director's small Sony monitor, Lulu saw Ben's close-up from camera number one of three cameras on stage begin to break down and morph into a scaly-skinned, expandable mandible, ravenous, snorting reptile ready to devour his own soul and hers.

* * *

From the storied Palm Restaurant on Second Avenue, sitting pathetically by her fully bribed, grotesquely over-flattering caricature of herself, painted some years ago, Screwzette, with Marni and Sasha by her side, were glued to the flat screen TV above the bar playing the FOX interview, voraciously consuming every word and yelling at the monitor with loud, cursing threats. Lizette happily managed, with all that was falling down around her, to get a few double takes of her terrible cartoon from some Italian tourists, which only served to quell her repulsive narcissism.

Sporting her bloodthirsty red-and-white gabardine Chanel power suit, Lizette, with her pudgy double chin and ruddy cabernet complexion, looked like a depressed Salvation Army Santa coming up too short after combing the crowded bar for coins.

Seeing herself being dragged into the fray, unable to hold back her tears any longer, Marni began sobbing as she silently read some passages from *White Collar Slavery;* she heaved her upper body toward the table, tears pooling up on the pristine white table cloth. Sasha, not one for affection, unless of course you were up against the wall at Henrietta Hudson, tried to console Marni with her best Dr. Phil, slow, creepy, overly tactile shoulder touching.

Picking up her CrackBerry, resting on Lulu's book, Screwzette began pecking out orders. "That bitch has crossed the line. She doesn't know who she's fucking with. Federal prison is going to seem like a Parisian holiday when I get through with this stupid bitch. Poisoning, deportations . . . How about murder? Get Kline on the phone!"

"I know you're not serious. But, the case *is* still ongoing. You need to be careful," said Sasha, dialing as she glanced around the room, hoping no one was listening to their conversation, nervously fiddling over her mojito and ringlets.

Parked outside the steakhouse in the Carol B., Dewey and Lars, stepped up their field operations with what appeared to be a seventy-five-dollar listening device from Spencer Gifts and somehow managed with Hellraiser's crack help to *MacGyver* the toy into something that actually worked, faintly able to pick up the henhouse's heated reaction to Wheatley's interview from fifty yards away.

"Falcon to red sparrow . . . did you catch that? That she would fucking *kill*? Dickbag, tell me you got that on tape. You did, didn't you?" Lars shot into his iPhone, pressing D-Key, who with one decent suit had magically transformed himself from a Brooklyn burnout to a Brooks Brothers banker. Snuggled beside Belinda at a high-top table in the corner of the bar, D-Key halfheartedly tapped on his wireless Bluetooth headset in a vain attempt to hear Lars more clearly, yet actually was paying better attention to his jumbo lump Maryland crab cakes and Belinda's colossal shrimp cocktail—courtesy of Lars.

"Yes, I got it, dickbag," D-Key nonchalantly whispered into his wireless ear piece, looking down at his HD spy camera, disguised as a lighter, resting neatly atop an old pack of Marlboros, with two butts sticking out the top of the broken red box for good measure.

A businessman wearing a khaki suit, itching for a smoke, interrupted D-Key mid-chew, wasabi mayonnaise still dripping from his swollen lower lip. He motioned with his hands to borrow D-Key's lighter.

And so in his infinite wisdom, without thinking twice, D-Key hastily handed over the faux lighter like a baton in a relay race, taking the hidden camera off of Screwzette and her minions and into the hands of the impatient smoker.

"What's wrong with you? You ate all six! I didn't even have any!" cried Belinda, coiled tightly from all this spy stuff, ready to snap. "I'm talking about an inner ashram. Why won't you even do that?"

"Sounds like too much work, baby!" joked D-Key. "Even if I had an alpaca or a llama I still couldn't go the distance. That's a lot of fucking mind traveling." He tapped on the earpiece, quickly changing subjects as Lars' voice barreled in, listening to his conversation. "You took too much fucking blah blah ba-tol today? Shut the fuck up and get the shot, dickbag. No more talking. I can't hear. They can't notice you. Remember, asshole?"

"Make sure you record everything. The smallest hand gesture could be telling," Dew's voice cracked in.

D-Key, now realizing what he had done by proffering up the lighter, slithered off his barstool and charged toward the front door. Pressing on the earpiece to lower the volume, knowing full well what would soon follow, he pushed open the door, divulging to Lars his slip-up: "I—uh—gave the lighter to a guy for his cigarette . . . Getting it . . . Relax!"

"I'm going to go nuts on you! You stupid fuck! What is your malfunction?" Lars yelled as he watched the man with the khaki suit trying to light his smoke in front of the famed chophouse doors with the faux lighter.

Bursting through the double doors with a loud smack, D-Key awkwardly rushed the man who was busily shoving the Marlboro in his mouth.

Lars, listening in, jumping up in his seat, managed to hit his head on the roof of the Carol B. with a crushing blow, blurting, "Ow! Fuck! No. Don't call attention to the lighter, you fucking dunce."

* * *

Back inside the detention yard, Lulu was feeling faint from seeing Ben's image break down on the monitor into reptile form, as Dewey so aptly warned. And as Ben droned on with his questions, she envisioned herself wrestling in a death spiral with Ben's reptilian persona before a coliseum full of caged half-lizard people. The wicked Kafkaesque trial ran amuck in her mind as Ben pressed on.

"So tell me, did you ever refuse any of these requests, and how did management react?" asked Ben. His left nostril began to flare as he stared manically into Lulu's soft green eyes.

"Many times. When I absolutely refused, they began threatening my job, which ultimately led to my departure," Lulu divulged.

"And if and when you are found innocent of these five counts of insider trading, will you seek a case against your former employer?" queried Wheatley.

"No, Ben. The book is going to destroy the firm. I imagine that will be damaging enough," Lulu explained, cracking a wry smile as the lizard bout played on in her imagination. As she tightened her grip, the snarling, foreboding beast in a death lock, Ben's face melted into Screwzette's ugly mug.

* * *

D-Key, yanking the faux lighter out of the smoker's right hand, quickly tossed it into the storm drain, then jumped into the backseat of the Carol B. "You like that move? We don't know who that guy is working for," D-Key explained.

"You have got to be the dumbest fuck in the galaxy!" Lars screamed. Lulu's interview played on the miniature monitor that Lars propped up on the dashboard.

"Uh—I didn't mean to give it to him, but who knows whose side he's on?"

"Side he's on?" Lars continued screaming. "Only side that guy's on is his damn creamed spinach that he's eating now, you asshole! Side he's on? You stupid fuck! I'm going to kill you. Everything we needed was on that camera!"

Dewey unflinchingly replied in his monotone voice, "Uh, well, I've seen those guys down Sixth Avenue working the grates with some string and some gum, lifting up nickels. We can try that."

"Now listen carefully, you stupid fuck, before I drop you off at Pearlmutter's for a cyanide Pomakaze, you dumb fuck!" Lars continued screaming. "Your assignment is to stay on that bitch all day, all night, get through to her on her cell. We've already programmed her number into your phone, blocking your info, so you can't fuck this up!"

Lars stared straight into D-Key's beady, blue eyes. D-Key waited for Lars to finish his sentence, even though he'd gone over it the night before one thousand and one fucking times. Lars knew full well that after a few hits of "Herijuana" through a Granny Smith, that D-Key would forget it all. D-Key stared back at Lars with a blank page. "Forgive me, I'm a forgetful fuck."

"This is beyond stupid," Lars continued. "Dewey, have you ever seen such gross incompetence?"

"No! Never! Well, maybe from my family," Dewey replied, chuckling.

"For the millionth time, . . ." Lars maintained, "This bitch is tweaked. There is so much going on with this case and the media. If you do this right, she'll be convinced you're working for Zirko or the Feds. As long as you don't fucking say too much. Can you handle that, Chatty Cathy? Now get back in there." Lars handed D-Key their backup faux camera.

As the FOX interview cut to commercial, Lars felt proud for Lulu and how well composed she was considering the circumstance of a federal indictment looming over her and what great revenge she was missing rotting in jail. He had to get her out. He couldn't go on another second without her. Sure, he was going to see her later that night for a few racy hours for some heavy petting, but he sure needed that settlement money. Yes, that would spring his baby from the big cooler—if he could only get the *Enquirer* to settle on the Streisand mix-up, sooner rather than later, which his attorney advised that they would do any day now. This would be his way to at least bail his love out of the Grey Bar. A five-million-dollar bond was completely outrageous in Lars' mind, since Lulu was completely innocent and never profited one single cent that Screwzette had certainly blown some federal circuit judge to jack up the bail bond. And with that in mind, he hatched a plan of his own.

The revenge was sweet. During his Grey Bar booty call, he would recount every succulent minute, committing the best lines to memory for his darling Lulu, who was completely robbed of her take-this-job—and-shove-it moment in the sun, but would be happy to know she wreaked havoc on lizard lady Lizette.

Through the din of the dining room on the kiddie device, Lars, listening in could hear Hansen and the henhouse reciting passages from the book and shrieking in response. It was faint, but he could hear it clearly over his heartbeat, exhilarated by how enraged Screwzette was becoming. He wished he had a better way to record it than rigging up a Handy cam to the top of the toy.

* * *

From page 119 of *White Collar Slavery,* Lizette read a passage, her voice getting more incensed as she read aloud.

> Clad in a tattered Burberry trench coat and reeking of booze and children's Benadryl, Lizette Hansen was not the picture-perfect corporate commander of one of the most powerful public relations firms on the planet. No, rather the thought of her looking like a Magic Tree air freshener swinging from the Fifty-Ninth Street Bridge above the hordes of onlookers, journalists, and news crews taunting her to jump was more than she could handle, and she began welling up with tears.

Sasha egged her on, reading the next excerpt.

> Mr. DeLyon was unaware of the amount of control Lizette had on both Marni and Lulu. Screwzette had a maniacal, social-stabbing grip on their psyches. Like Piggy in *Lord of the Flies,* holding the conch, Screwzette held the coveted Lana Marks aqua-blue sports bag and reminded Marni and Lulu every morning that they were too poor to afford one of their own. She maintained that she treated herself to the bag, but the girls of the hatchery knew that it was a gift from Client #9, who beneath the sheets Lizette affectionately dubbed "St. Stephen" and whom Marni and Lulu nicknamed Raincoat, for the Burberry trench coat that Screwzette always kept on the back of her office door, in case a quick visit was in order.

Lars could hear screams until the high-pitched shriek of Screwzette's voice shattered his listening device like a soprano shattering a crystal glass with a high note. The toy smoked, burped, and flat lined.

Miraculously, at around 4:25 p.m. EST, D-Key landed the eagle with a quick call imploring Lizette to meet him on the Staten Island Ferry, leaving Whitehall Terminal at nine o'clock sharp—that he had some information that could absolve her from this nagging scandal. Lars knew full well that she could never resist such a tempting invitation.

Taking the reins over for Lars, who was on his way to the detention center to pay Lulu a long-awaited love visit, Dewey and Belinda went over the final details. The less-is-more philosophy would never ring more true than when D-Key intimated that the concocted information that he possessed, if Lizette was baited properly, would induce her to do just about anything—Lars stressed "anything"—to get her grubby mitts on it.

The scandal, daunting headlines together with the book release, FOX interview and Lizette's failed suicide attempt were melting down what little assemblage of socio-maniacal, wicked composure she may have left. Now with a three-ring media circus in full swing, the level of stress bent her barometric pressure, causing her to engage in a torrent of psychopathic behavior spiraling into a black hole. On paid leave for the foreseeable future and out on bail, Lizette trudged through the city streets like a designer zombie, her complexion slightly warmed over, unless she was tipping one back, which happened about every twenty minutes since she had little to do but meet with her lawyers and on occasion with Sasha and Marni. The Devil has idle hands was just about the size of it. This bitch would believe just about anything to clear her name.

Lizette wore her ill-fitting, size-fourteen, red Pucci dress so she would be unmistakable. She wondered whether the informer would be working for Zirko or the Feds, or if he was some dashing journalist wanting to save her ass. Or was it her St. Stephen sending an angel of mercy to make the tumult recede from her doorstep? The thought of a clandestine rendezvous was exciting, to say the least. Besides a bit of shoplifting, a Benadryl bender or two, and the shock and awe of Lulu's book, this was the most exciting bit of business to come her way in recent weeks.

* * *

D-Key, still dressed to the nines from the Palm, freshened up with a pristinely pressed powder blue Oxford, courtesy of Dewey, who left the shirt at his mother's for safekeeping, or worse, a family reunion. He quickly changed in the tail bed of the Carol B., and toasted himself like a fresh blueberry Pop-Tart out of the hatchback. Dewey and Belinda stared on incredulously, eyeing him up, making sure he followed all of Lars' simple instructions as he strolled the fifty yards to the entrance of the ferry terminal:

1. Say very little.
2. Say even less.
3. Be engaging and charming.
4. Divert Lizette's questions into statements.
5. Make a pass.
6. Record the entire meeting.
7. Don't be a dumb fuck.

For D-Key, it was reaching far for him to be a man of few words. Verbose at heart, it was nearly impossible. It was like asking the Pope to have a Bar Mitzvah. But he would try. Not for the old, strange bit of booty that might fall into his lap, or bribe money he was hoping to abscond with. No, he would do it for poor old Lulu, rotting away her youth in the Grey Bar hotel.

Lizette's unremarkable looks had been plastered all over the papers, so D-Key had a slight advantage. However, with his stoner-come-lately intellect it was neck and neck, having any stealthy advantage at all in terms of spook-upmanship. Furthermore, he did have a few of her photos in his cell phone. But the overly cracked pay-as-you-go could vanish at any moment and usually did, sending him into waves of panic—only to realize that the greasy Samsung ended up, mostly, in a front pocket he had thoroughly checked with a fine-tooth comb some twenty-odd times. He patted his pockets and legs down like he was being cuffed and arrested. Or by the fickle finger of fate, it might end up in his sweaty mitts out of thin air, always to his amazement and consternation.

D-Key stood by the stern of the crowded ferry, looking out towards Lady Liberty, surrounded by the huddled masses and the tired, poor workers commuting from an exhausting Friday, chained to their cubicles. D-Key's vantage point was obstructed by the passengers, but cleared as he caught a glimpse of Lizette wending her way through the jam-packed ship as scheduled.

The five-mile, twenty-five minute ride, claiming to provide breathtaking views of New York Harbor and a "no-hassle, even romantic, free ride," with the emphasis on "free ride," was the very reason Lars had picked this meeting spot, just in case dithering D-Key lost his damn wallet or something. There were to be no slipups.

Lizette, fighting against the knotty wind, checked her lipstick-stained front tooth with her tiny travel compact. Devilishly wiping the sultry red smear off with the roughened edge of her forked tongue, she noticed a debonair gentleman coming into her compact's mirror. In her estimation, he couldn't have been any more than forty. Turning around, Lizette broke a big smile. She knew this was her man, nattily dressed in a conservative, tailored navy suit and preppy pink-and-blue repp tie sporting a double Windsor knot. She quickly added up his wardrobe and pegged him right away for a messenger sent by her St. Stephen. He was too well dressed to be a journalist, too underdressed to be a banker, possibly an accountant, although with his five o'clock shadow and piercing blue eyes, he looked more like a semi-successful literary agent of some sort. She began seeing visions of movie deals dancing around in her head, with the next yet undiscovered Meryl Streep to play her role. Or maybe Kim Cattrall would do the trick. She'd seen all of the news about how to get ahead in Hollywood and sleeping your way to the top—which she actually had a lot of experience with. It would be more like method acting. Old enough to know how to defuse a man, Lizette stroked D-Key's five o'clock shadow rather softly, and as he started to coo, abruptly slapped him hard in the kisser, as if to say, "follow me."

It was clear this was to be a freak battle aboard the ferry that eve. Grabbing D-Key by his borrowed tie, Lizette led him to the covered section of the ship for a high-stakes game of bluff the magic dragon, not wanting to lose the upper hand gained by her wanton slap.

"So where's this evidence you have that's going to get me all hot and bothered, handsome?" muttered Lizette, her eyes devouring him with every bit of twisted sex appeal she could muster in the cool night breeze, as they passed the scape of lower Manhattan.

"That depends," replied D-Key quite proud of his curt answer, cracking a devious smile to prove it.

"On what?" Lizette replied hastily as the wind blew her thinning bottled-strawberry-blonde hair back into her plumped-up jowly cheeks.

"On . . . how good you look with my rod in your mouth," blurted D-Key perversely, gauging her reaction, just as the words slipped out from his still stinging, swollen lower lip. He feared immediately that Hansen might take the brazen comment out of context, like any other self-respecting woman certainly would. However, working well with the law of seedy percentages, D-Key knew exactly how to wage a love war, and always came up a winner. Still, visions of her biting his hook off and tossing it over the starboard side was definitely something he was bracing for, but it never went there. No, in fact, Lizette, the salty dog, unflinchingly responded in kind by playfully removing her three-carat Tiffany studs and led him to the back corner of the fast-moving ferry plowing through the inky night air toward Staten Island.

For a few minutes of some shadowy, muffled moaning, Screwzette did the bob of the river buoy over D-Key's fine threads, streaking her Bobbi Brown bronzer and Chanel lipstick all over her snarling face and his nutty privates, until the ripe second that he was about to wax a few pearls of wisdom directly atop her stop-sign red Pucci dress and right cheek. It was then that Lizette, choking on his totem, *chargled* out a seemingly unintelligible question.

And as "lick" would have it, D-Key, who had just earned his master's degree in "garble linguistics" at Blue University, was able to decipher it immediately, similar to the way a dentist can translate grunts and groans muttered by a patient. Or the way an anthropologist reading mud and fossils is able to discern a lost civilization.

"Rue hen gru ah ah ta ma?" chargled Screwzette, straining to show all her tricks, unbridled. Old Queen's English defines *chargle* as the best parts of choke and gargle. This was not for the novice or faint of heart, and according to D-Key should be performed only by an expert in front of a willing audience, or better, in the privacy—or not—of your own home.

"You want to know who sent me or who I am working for?" D-Key calmly deciphered, wondering if he should actually restrain himself, until he got something other than a hummer out of the inquisitive nag. However, with the precarious spot he had literally inserted himself into, he realized he needed to give her something besides a dancing candy necklace. Reaching into his breast pocket, he pushed the memo recorder on his cell and tried like hell to get something admissible to clear Lulu's good name.

"Las I uh loo!" replied Screwzette—translation: "Yes, I sure do!"

She looked up and stared directly into D-Key's midnight blues, like an orca biting through the bow of a fishing boat. Her cold black pupils devoured him whole as her jaws clamped down on the debonair gentleman without a name. Realizing it was now or never, she quickly pulled off his tiny ship, spewing from her bloody Benadryl gums: "Well?"

"*Well*," said D-Key, swinging for the bleachers, "I bring word from Theo Zirko," baiting her with some of Lars' homespun bullshit. "There's an issue with some e-mails linked to you and Zirko's assistant involving the market drop," said D-Key in such a calm, resolute, assured tone that he sent Screwzette reeling. "And it's been leaked to the prosecutor."

"What? You tell that fucker that my trades were all done through a third party. And if he's setting me up with these asshole, fake e-mails to fuck me, I will call the senator's office and freeze his fucking dick off. Tell him that!" And with that bit of business, Screwzette unwittingly divulged the bona fide confession needed to spring Lulu from the big house.

"Do you want the e-mails or not? I am fucking trying to help you 'cause I find you an attractive lady, from your picture in the paper," yelled D-Key, knowing just how to ride a heinous, fishtailing sea beast. Assuaging any doubts that he was telling her the truth, D-Key raised his eyebrows as if to say "You have been warned!"

Nearing the dock at the ferry's terminal, Screwzette wistfully went into *Free Willy* attack mode, dive-bombing back into D-Key's lap. Slack-jawed, her flippery, fat arms flailing in the balmy breeze, hiding under his sport jacket, she swallowed him whole. Lizette swirled her hairy tongue around his submersible and felt D-Key's squid shimmy loose, cannoning out, slapping her square in the face as she reared her spunk-dripping head up from his rumpled blazer.

"Well if it isn't Lizette Hansen?" said a woman's voice cutting through the final blast of the ferry's foghorn, signaling dry land. Screwzette faintly recognized the accent. Squinting through D-Key's milkish manhood, she was horrified to find Grangeway's Amy "Famy" Wallingford unabashedly staring at her; Amy's eyes burning with contempt. Clearly having already read Lulu's book, she blurted, "You know—I worried what to say to you if I ever saw you again. You're a monster! But at least now I know how to get even for ruining my twenty-fifth wedding anniversary, you nasty hooker!"

Making a blitz for her iPhone, Amy quickly snapped a compromising photo of Screwzette sneering, bent over D-Key's full frontal fishing rod, beneath his perverted dimpled grin. He was smiling proudly as if he had just reeled in a killer whale with his ugly stick to save a seaside town, all the while getting Screwzette's confession on his broken-down Samsung phone. He had, like Ishmael, been in the belly of the sea beast and came out alive.

Yes, he was no longer "Moby dickhead" because he had the goods that would set Lulu free.

Lizette leapt to her feet, her saggy left bosom bare and barreling out of her ill-fitting dress, with her face looking like it went through a love blender.

"That was all literary lies from that bitch!" Screwzette screamed. "If you publish that terrible picture, I'll have the job of everyone in your fucking family."

White Collar Slavery

This threat, quite a stretch for Screwzette, even now, at the bottom of her game. She was on the outs with KAR, Grangeway, and just about everyone imaginable, in the media and elsewhere, due to her never-ending nihilism. To say Screwzette's words were shallow threats would be akin to patting down an eighty-six-year-old grandmother for explosives at airport security. Just not a credible threat. No, there would be no orange alert for Screwzette's threat assessment, only a pornographic photo and a salacious story on the Page Six gossip column, headlined simply, "Whistle Blown!"

D-Key, away from the fray, beside the starboard rail, shrouding the Samsung from sight, slipped suddenly and watched as the phone fell like a hot potato from his hands, and bounced into the Hudson, sinking over the ship's breaking wake. When Lars and Lulu found out that he accidentally tossed the confession overboard, there might be another wake—his own. But the thought of being captured in an outdoor porn scene for posterity with a party hat on made him snicker. He made his way to Dewey and Belinda, parked nearby in the Carol B., to tell them of the sea tale, too fucking stupid to realize Belinda would slap him six ways to Sunday and make him sleep outside with her mother's one-year-old insanely aggressive Rottweiler.

* * *

Gazing out at the steel wire suspension under the first stone tower, Lars was always astonished by the feats of early American ingenuity like the iconic Brooklyn Bridge. Built in 1883, it was the first suspension bridge of its kind and was now going to be his gateway to his troubled lovebird, Lulu, whom he had not seen since she vanished four months ago from the deli counter. He had felt helpless, unable to see his love, feel her touch, and kiss her tender lips. He felt like a prisoner himself without her in his arms, and hoped this hell would soon end.

According to the rules of the Metropolitan Detention Center, all prisoners awaiting sentencing are forbidden to have any visitors who are not immediate family, so Lars felt pretty damn lucky that Lulu had arranged the visit. Due to the publicity the Detention Center received from the FOX interviews and the fact that she had been a model detainee, she was awarded what was to be a one-night-only performance of Rodgers and Hammerstein's beloved musical *Conjugal Vista.*

The Russian cabbie sported a checkered bowling shirt and had remained silent through the entirety of the fare since Manhattan. He pulled on the brakes, halting for a stop in the traffic just before the second neo-Gothic tower. He noticed Lars in his rearview mirror repeatedly checking his iPhone and uttered, "You know, living in America is like drinking a plastic suicide note!"

Unsure how to respond, Lars humored him, "What do you mean?"

"I move here from communist country thinking this land of opportunity, but now Russia is land of opportunity," said the cabbie in his thick accent. "I see no future here for me or my daughter. US is multiplex prison camp. A police state. I can't drink. I can't walk. I can't smoke! There are barricades down on Wall Street—you can't move."

"Yeah, what do you think of Occupy Wall Street?" Lars asked the cab driver, trying to take his mind off of the fact that he had not yet heard from D-Key.

"I think if you can't occupy a shower, how you occupy Wall Street—and be taken seriously? Ha!" explained the former Soviet Union military colonel, who defected in 1986 and immigrated to the United States.

"Ha! Well put—uh, Yuri," replied Lars, glancing at the cabbie's permit that was lodged between the Lexan wall divider.

"Why you go to Detention Center?" asked Yuri.

"My girlfriend has been locked up for months," Lars divulged. "See, multiplex prison camp, I tell you! For what?" Yuri questioned. "Abetting insider trading or something," explained Lars, nervously checking his phone again for an update.

White Collar Slavery

"Insider trading? She hiding billions I hope?" Yuri asked, looking back into his rear view mirror.

"She never made a dime!" screamed Lars. "You?" Yuri questioned perplexingly. "Nope. Nothing." Lars replied.

"Ha! It's the new American Way!" cried Yuri as Lars' cell phone chimed in with a call from Dewey. D-Key's high-pitched voice on the other end signaled that something had gone south. His preamble foreshadowed that he had screwed up royally, once again. And just as the yellow cab approached the security gate, Lars made a vain attempt to understand how in the world D-Key managed to sink the evidence into the Hudson. His incompetency was beyond words, beyond even Lars' imagination, but not surprising.

Inside the gates of the Metropolitan Detention Center, Lars was escorted by two burley, tattooed armed guards that looked to him like avatars straight out of Rockstar Games' *Red Dead Revolver*, with no redemption in sight. The guards, complete with buzz cuts, thick necks, blank stares, and handguns a-slingin'. Although a way station of sorts for prisoners who have either not yet been arraigned, have been denied bail, or are awaiting trial like poor Lulu, Lars immediately felt the oppressive nature that one could appreciate only by being locked inside the shrinking gray walls and bars of a federal jailhouse, among real violent offenders. Prison life was nothing like it was portrayed in the movies.

To get himself through the unnerving ordeal and to avoid a nervous breakdown before seeing his love, Lars had to imagine that prison life was like a twisted cruise ship, with all the staircases, cabins, and porthole doors of sorts, although fully realizing that instead of dining with annoying tourists from Wisconsin; Lulu was breaking bread with hardened criminals. That thought haunted Lars, filling him with remorse for not being able to do more to free her.

He noticed an almost tranquil, orderly, methodical approach to daily life. He gated down the hallway, which felt like five football fields long, bursting at the seams to see her, wondering how his dear

Lulu was surviving what had to be less than Carnival Cruise Line accommodations.

Lars recounted in his mind the hellish night when Lulu vanished from the hand-carved pastrami station. Holding ticket number 024, Lars questioned, "I'm thinking maybe you'd let me order a Reuben and steak fries. And you wanted what? The matzo ball soup. And an order of pickles?" He turned back with a half-sour look on his face, to realize that Lulu was no longer by his side. And she wasn't with D-Key, Belinda, or Dewey either. His heart immediately sank to his boots, realizing that perhaps they had come for her. After a search of the ladies' room and twenty-two unanswered calls later, Lars just knew that somebody, somewhere had her. Who or what would have the audacity to kidnap her straight from the deli line at Katz's? What kind of sadistic freaks?

Lox, stocks, and smoking barrels, someone must have absconded with his baby Lulu.

* * *

Blindfolded, gagged, and still in shock from being shuttled through the service entrance of Katz's Deli, Lulu was escorted into a vehicle just a few short blocks away with her hands zip-tied behind her back. Lulu was brought up in what seemed like a musty freight elevator, the scent of rancid trash punched her in the face. She was escorted down a long hallway that seemed to go on for miles. Finally ending up at what appeared to be the final destination, the two strong-armed men propped her up on what felt like an Italian designed hipster mod leather sofa. In the distance she faintly heard two voices speaking Spanish. Her Spanish was *más a menos*, but she could make out something about a big event that they had to prepare for. Was it a Mexican firing squad?

Panic-stricken, Lulu's mind began racing. *Perhaps this was a lot deeper than even Pearlmutter had imagined. Maybe Screwzette was behind this? The firm? Or could it be some drug lords? Or the CIA?* She had been sniffing around while writing her book. Her gut feeling told her this was Screwzette's work. She thought to herself, it couldn't be the police because she wasn't in a precinct. The blindfold and gag were not usually the NYPD's MO. Her heart pounded as her mind ran a risk analysis to determine how she would escape alive. She couldn't move from the sofa. Although her legs were numb, she could feel that her ankles were bound together. Yet with a little effort she was able to wiggle her toes.

Slowly, using the lipped edge of the sofa, Lulu slipped out of her ballet flats and with her bare feet, felt a 70's style shag wool rug under the ball of her right foot. Clinching the thick-knotted strands into the folds of her toes signaled to her that wherever she was, it certainly was baffling.

Faintly through the wall, she could hear two men arguing. Recognizing one of the voices, she ran through her mind who it might be. *Was it Zirko?* She only exchanged a few glib words with him in the rain. *Or was it a client? Somebody from Grangeway? Or someone who had lost his life savings because of the market tank and was coming after her—set up from Screwzette?* Whoever it was, she knew she only had a few moments before they would come back into the room and do God knows what to her. She tried screaming through the duct tape, as she had done for the last twenty minutes to no avail. So inching her way off the back of the sofa, she shimmied down onto the shag and rolled underneath the sofa. She hid just as she heard the door slam open, and what sounded like the men from the adjacent room burst through the doors, cocking their guns.

* * *

Hiding behind out-of-character, rock star, mirrored sunglasses, camouflaging her face, not to be recognized from the past week's Page Six story, Lizette was fawning all over Theo Zirko like a tawdry bathhouse attendant. They sat at a dimly lit banquette at Viktor and Spoils, a trendier-than-thou, late night tequila bar in the Hotel on Rivington. She propped up his midnight blue Ferragamos onto the leather ottoman. She would do anything to defray any thought he had in his mind about double-crossing her.

Provocatively dressed, she wore a white Chanel silk blouse, unbuttoned practically to her navel, exposing her naughty noir push-up Victoria's Secret 38Ds, obnoxiously *motor boating* his temples against her sagging bosoms, as she nibbled at his left ear. Her face looked more flush from her sixth Añejo smash than the red soles of her-five inch Louboutins, propping up her sawed-off cankles onto the small square ottoman beside Zirko.

"If I didn't know better, I'd think you were trying to brainwash me," Zirko said.

"That happened a while ago," Lizette replied. "Shut up before I turn you into the naughty police, Kojak."

"Who loves you, baby?" said Zirko, stroking his bald head with the palm of his right hand. "I might not get everything I need, but I need everything I get," he said, pacifying himself with a lollipop, playing into his Savalas charm.

"Are you sure they're taking care of our little problem upstairs?" Lizette questioned.

"Now tell me again why I should risk my free ride on this?" queried Zirko. "This is a little too black ops even for me."

"Listen, I can have the senator back me up on this in a fucking minute! One call and you, Skip, and his whole fucking division go up in smoke!" Lizette shot back.

* * *

Shhhh-click: the semiautomatic handgun whirred as Lulu let out a muffled scream through her bound lips.

"You wanna spill your guts under the sofa? Or do you want to come out here and tell me what you know, Norris?" said the man's deep voice.

Shaken, Lulu popped out from under the sofa, like a can of Coke into the awaiting clutches of her capture. She felt a large pair of hands against her cheeks, which made Lulu think that this might end up unfavorably. She was forcefully slammed back onto the modular sofa.

"Now, I'm gonna take the tape off, if you so much, make one sound . . . if you scream . . . it will be your last!" demanded the faintly familiar voice, taking on a deep, resonant tone. As the sleeping mask and duct tape were peeled off of Lulu's face, a macho version of her pursuer, Skip "spirit fingers" Anderson from Yoga Nation was revealed.

"This is some rain check for lunch you have here, Skip," Lulu said. "My rain check comes later!" blurted Skip as his face twitched with his dancing hairs atop his furry coffee-stained birthmark that covered his right cheek.

"You guys are trending pretty big here, this is some urban oasis," Lulu said as she quickly surveyed the floor-to-ceiling glass walls and oversized balcony with a clear view of lower Manhattan, which made her think she was on the Lower East Side. After seconds of scanning the suite, it hit her—she was at the Hotel on Rivington.

"Do you mind telling me what this is all about?" Lulu continued examining the room. The bathroom door, slightly ajar caught her eye, revealing two exterior-facing steam showers with a huge glass window facing downtown.

"You're gonna tell us everything, down to every last freakin' detail," Skip demanded, looking for any information to sell to his superiors in Virginia, who in turn, would build a case to frame her. They had a definite hard-on for this poor girl, for reasons too high up the food chain for Skip to question. The walls in Gangley, Virginia, were echoing with the name of a prominent southern senator with ties to the partners at KAR PR.

"And don't leave anything out," interrupted the other man, now standing next to Skip. He wore a drab-colored suit, had his gun cocked and pointed it at Lulu. He answered to the name of Sal.

"What are you talking about?" screamed Lulu. "Why have you been following me? What do you want with me? I've done nothing!"

"Don't play dumb, Norris," said Skip. "We've got enough on you to lock you up right now."

"For what?" Interrupted Lulu, "ordering off the kids menu at Katz's?"

"Well, don't we have ourselves our own freakin' Tina Fey, over here," said Skip turning toward Sal. "Cut the bullshit, we've got the goods on you."

"So either you cooperate with us or we do this our way, and trust me, our way ain't the way you want to do this, Lulu baby," Sal chimed in with his thick Brooklyn accent.

"Look, you've got the wrong girl," Lulu said. "I have nothing to hide. I'll cooperate with you. But you're wasting your time with me. Who you should have here, bound and gagged, is the harlot from Hackensack!"

"You were the one we caught on tape," Sal continued. "We have the calls and e-mails linking you to Theo Zirko."

"Yeah, so what does that prove?" Lulu questioned. "Of course you found correspondence between us, he's a journalist and I'm a publicist—that's my job."

"Is it your job to trade inside information on a public company, causing its stock to plummet?" Sal questioned.

"I don't mean to cut you short on your op-ed, but honestly, is this fact or opinion? I have access to a lot of sensitive information on a daily basis. Like I said, the person you need is Lizette Hansen. And, uh—can I use the bathroom? I'm gonna tell you everything you want, but I wouldn't want to rush through anything, if you know what I mean," said Lulu.

"Yeah, yeah," Sal replied.

"Well, can you untie me?" Lulu questioned. "Not likely, kid," Sal replied.

"Well, how am I suppose to . . ." Lulu asked.

"Do you need some help taking off your pants?" Sal joked.

"No. No. I got it, thanks," Lulu said. "I mean, we're at least twenty stories up, where do you think I'm gonna go?"

Sal escorted Lulu to the bathroom and stood guard outside the door with his tattooed arms folded across his chest, the Luger in his left hand.

As she locked the door, she could hear Sal and Skip arguing. If she wanted to get out alive, she had to make it quick. She kicked the toilet seat down with her foot to placate the thugs. With her hands still zip-tied behind her back, she began making animalistic grunting sounds as she used her teeth to pry open the sliding glass window.

"Honey, don't fall in. We need your testimony," Skip said crudely from across the room, hearing Lulu's grunts and moans emanating from inside the bathroom.

"That's why I don't eat deli food anymore," Sal earnestly admitted. Peering out the window, Lulu's heart did a double-gainer into her stomach as she looked down and saw a balcony directly beneath her.

Feet first, she shimmied her way out of the window, grunting and moaning to mask her escape as she leapt, free-falling onto the balcony below with a loud whack.

Twisting and ripping her ankle from the impact of the fall, she hobbled to her feet. Lulu limped across the patio, backing up against the door, she yanked on the handle of the terrace doors, only to find out it was locked. Bending down, with her still bound hands, she lifted the leg of a nearby aluminum table, swung her arms in a pendulum motion and flung the table through the thick glass window. Leaping through the shattered glass door and drawn curtains, Lulu stumbled onto the hardwood floor of the suite and hit her head on the corner of a coffee table. Moments before she blacked out, she saw the mind-bending ghastly sight of Theo Zirko and Screwzette intertwined on a king-sized bed. The revolting image was so powerful that it knocked Lulu out cold.

The chaos alerted hotel security. Skip Anderson and his partner bolted out the door, hotfooting their way down to the suite below with their guns in their belts so as not to draw any attention to themselves. This was a undercover situation. All they were told was to bring Norris into SEC custody. And before handing her over, it was their sole discretion how to fabricate the evidence to frame her.

Slowly coming back into consciousness, Lulu opened her eyes to find hazy images of hotel security, Skip Anderson, and his partner hovered over her as she lay on the floor, writhing in pain from the bloody gash on her head and her swollen ankle.

Skip leaned back to reveal Lizette, her serpent eyes full of bloodlust, whispering the words to Lulu, "This is for Page Six. And this is just the beginning."

The Fantastic Voyage

The clouds broke past the full moon as the *Pink Flamingo* slowly cruised into the port of Nassau. The weekend aboard the ship, promised to be Davio's crowning achievement, as he was hoping to make a full court press on the Senator. Finally making some real headway on Lulu's case, literally.

Davio spotted Senator X aboard the undulating lido deck full of finely manicured haircuts and tangled torsos, flitting toward the rainbow colored strobe lights. Deciding it was now or never, Davio waded through pink and green lasers cascading over his white, Marc Jacobs power suit. He darted toward the familiar Grey Flannel scent. The southern Senator's name, which had been synonymous with conservative family values and religious convictions in the community, based on the Lord's Word that the union of two people should be a holy bond between a man and a woman. However, about a year ago, once the tabloids broke with the headline "Love Guy-Angle," exposing a tryst between him, his assistant and an intern to a Senator who also served on the committee for homeland security, the Senator disassociated himself from his church and his family. He was now splitting his time between his two quarters, the coveted territory of the upper tier, the Admiral's Cove and his residence-in-waiting, the captain's prized porthole room, aboard the *Pink Flamingo*.

It was at that moment that Davio spotted Lars and his two stakeout buddies from the corner of his eye. He ascended the short flight of steps leading to the lido deck. D-Key, dressed in a pink Hawaiian shirt, puka beads, Iris Apfel signature black, milk bottle sunglasses, a yellow pleated tennis skirt, Sunday school shoes, and matching bobby socks. Dewey, donning his signature pink-and-white madras shorts with a preppy, navy blue blazer, underneath a cotton argyle vest, revealed his coveted Mr. Clean T-shirt. Peeking through the V-neck of the tight-fitting vest was Mr. Clean's bald head. Lars, sporting his lounge lizard, blue leather Diesel jeans was greeted by Davio and updated about his intended rendezvous in the Admiral's Cove at the stroke of midnight. He promised Lars that he would lay down the law and do whatever it would take to undo the congressional puppetry that Screwzette must have performed to imprison Lulu.

Davio led the group to a bank of poolside tables for a cozy view at the mouth of the water flume that stretched up practically through the clouds. The slippery slide sent the riders through a maze of twists and turns before dropping them right beside Davio's strategically handpicked table, much to the chagrin of Lars, grinning-and-bearing every last minute. He kept reminding himself that they were there on a mission to intercept the Senator.

Just as two fellas playfully shot out of the bottom of the slide, their legs interlocked, wearing matching almost nonexistent Speedo racing skivvies, Lars blurted, "Ohmigod! Look at the Speedo Gonzalez twins over here!"

"They look like they're breaking an Olympic luge record," Dewey added.

"No. No. Look at this guy," D-Key chimed in as he pointed to a giant Asian fellow impersonating Elvis, donning a cape, sunglasses, a lei of blue and pink orchids around his neck, and tiny Hawaiian lanterns hanging around his private parts. And beside him was his dwarf boyfriend, wearing an Evel Knievel getup, complete with goggles and held between his legs a rubber rocket cycle, Snake River Canyon circa 1974.

"Will you look at Mini-Knievel and Hellvis straight out of Blue Hawaii? Holy dynamic duo!" Lars said.

"Queertastic!" Davio screamed.

"This is really freaking me out. I've gotta go back to my room," Dewey said.

"Just give this five more minutes. We need to figure out what we're doing. We came all this way," Lars pleaded.

Davio, eyeing up Mini-Knievel, said, "I like the little guy, isn't he adorable?"

"So adorable!" D-Key exclaimed.

"Oooh! I want him to jump my Snake River Canyon!" Davio admittedly blurted.

"More than adorable!" D-Key replied.

"Do you think you could introduce me? I think he's an actor," Davio asked, turning toward Dewey.

Dewey cringed and blurted back, "What? Why me?"

"I dunno, I guess because you look so good,'" Davio replied.

Dewey defiantly took off his crested blazer, balled it up, hid it behind the lumbar region of his back, and used it as a rest. "That's it; you have exactly five minutes!"

"Just line up some pickup trucks across your back; he'll jump you. Mini-Knievel over there probably can't resist a challenge," D-Key said.

"He could jump my abyss of bliss anytime," Davio sang.

"Not to cut your dating off at the knees, but what exactly is your plan to get to the Senator, besides the obvious compromise?" Lars questioned.

"Don't worry, I have something on the Senator that is going to make him pay direct attention to this package," Davio replied.

"Just make sure you don't filibuster on this," Lars joked.

"No delays. But, I intend to fill-his-buster, if you know what I mean.

"Uh, that's too much information for me," Lars said.

"That's just adorable!" D-Key chimed in.

"Oh boy, so what is the plan, Spinoza? Let's get to it," said Dewey, now more uncomfortable than before.

"The plan is a round of Blue Hawaiians. Relax! And you're introducing me to Evel Knievel," Davio continued to sing, as he motioned to a tall, skinny bartender, floating around from table to table. "Hello, handsome, we'll have four Blue Hawaiians. And not a Blue Hawaii. Do you know the difference?"

"Uh, no," the waiter sheepishly admitted.

"Well, a Blue Hawaiian has rum, pineapple juice, Curaçao, and cream of coconut, not sweet and sour like the Blue Hawaii. Oh, and make that six Blue Hawaiians, the other two are for Elvis and Mini-Knievel over there."

"Oh God!" Dewey cringed.

"Focus, Spinoza. We are on a strict time table here," Lars demanded. "We're bugging out of here tomorrow at 5:00 a.m. So we need to make sure this happens tonight."

"Five in the morning? I'm ready now," Dewey said.

"Listen, we're not leaving here until the Senator sees Davio's Robert Mapplethorpe," said Lars. "I have got to get some information that will shed some light on this madness, and I know this Senator has the answers."

"Hello? There's three more days of fun in the sun!" Davio screamed. "No one's going anywhere!"

"Spinoza, we're on the first flight out of Nassau, so you better take care of this tonight," Lars demanded.

"Okay, here's the skinny," Davio started to explain. "This thing is deeper than you know. This goes beyond anything you thought. The market tumble wasn't about the war on drugs. Honey, that's what they wanted you to think. It was disinformation. And tonight at midnight in the Admiral's Cove, I will find out the 'eyes only' details, and where the information is hidden that will absolve Lulu and set her free. How deep the canyon runs, only Mini-Knievel can say."

As the clock struck midnight, the *Pink Flamingo* was mostly quiet due to some serious portside partying on the mainland of the Bahamas. Davio, dressed in his wide lapel, double-breasted, midnight purple, Oscar de la Renta zoot suit and a metallic silver swashbuckler shirt underneath, looked like a cross between Tom Jones and Prince. As Spinoza jitterbugged his hair back with his Tiffany comb, the jivers, all dressed in black fatigues, approached him at the bottom of the steps leading to the Admiral's Cove. Doing a baton girl half twirl, he asked, "So, how do I look?"

"Ha!" Dewey laughed out loud. "Simply adorable!" D-Key screamed.

"I'm digging the Purple Rain, Tom Jones look you got going on," said Lars.

"Ha!" Dewey blurted.

Lars said, "But seriously, I think I speak for everyone when I say: get us the fucking info already! I wake up in a cold sweat every night, thinking of what's happening to my poor Lulu! I mean . . . I am on a gay cruise in the Bahamas searching for evidence. Clearly, I am at my wits' end," scratching his thick, wavy hair into a faux hawk.

"You've gotta be the best boyfriend in the world," said Davio.

"You. Ha! I've got no skin in the game here. Think of me!" cried Dewey.

"Skin. Interesting choice of words!" blurted D-Key, deliberating his words carefully so as not to blow the bet with Lars that if he could use three words or less the entire cruise every time he opened his fucking mouth, he would get a free subscription to *High Times* for all eternity.

"Keep your voices down," Davio whispered.

"Now, just make sure you seal the deal," Lars said.

Just then four men dressed as members of the Village People approached the group; the Indian and construction worker had been humming *Y.M.C.A.*, complete with hand gestures.

They immediately recognized Lars from the tabloids. "Ohmigod! We love your mother's music! We saw the article in the *Enquirer*, and we feel so bad for you! We're taking you with us! We love *Funny Girl*!" each member of the group lifted Dewey, Lars, and D-Key over their shoulders, whisking them away. They started to sing, "The Way We Were."

"We're eating sushi off of a handsome Filipino boy; you are coming with us!" the construction worker said.

"Adorable!" D-Key exclaimed.

"This is my worst nightmare!" Dewey screamed.

"I'm sorry, I'm just trying to get my girlfriend out of jail," Lars mouthed to Dewey.

Davio, perched politely on the left side of the lux cabin's round queen bed with his legs perfectly crossed, was interrupted from the grand marble bathroom by a statuesque, androgynous, extremely attractive African-American woman when he heard the sound of the shower running in the other room. At first Davio thought it was Grace Jones coming out of the Senator's bathroom, with her short, cropped, purple hair and severe looking make-up. Dressed in captain's regalia, with four gold bars on each epaulet, she was carrying a sterling silver Art Nouveau butterfly-shaped serving tray. On the tray sat a colossal tin of Beluga caviar, two gaudy Liberace-style goblets, and a bottle of 1973 Château Mouton Rothschild with the coveted Pablo Picasso special edition wine label.

"You'll have to excuse the Senator; he's in the shower presently. He will be joining you shortly," the woman spoke in perfect Queen's English. "Would you care for a drink? And do please help yourself to some Almas caviar. It's some of the most sought after caviar in the world, and certainly the Senator's favorite. He just returned from Iran, as he was looking for bad boy nuclear scientists, so I think you'll enjoy."

Davio scooped a dollop of caviar with a tiny sterling silver spoon. "Girlfriend, you're too beautiful, what do you have going on for the rest of this amazing weekend? I've had more fun in these last two days with the parties and the yoga classes. Ohmigod!" Davio rambled on nervously.

"I'm the captain of this ship," the woman interrupted.

"What?" he gasped, practically spitting up his caviar. "Who's driving the boat?"

"My first mate, darling," the woman calmly replied. "She's a Dutch ex-supermodel and my first mate, of course. And you, handsome, look like Austin Powers on that round bed."

"Oh, randy baby!" Davio screamed.

"Buella, baby, is that cute ol' Randy from the SEC? He's not supposed to arrive until 2:00 a.m., with his churching best," the Senator's deep southern voice called out from the bathroom shower. "Where's my cute little Latin lawyer? I've got something for him."

"I'm on the port side of your queen side, Senator," Davio mused, chiming in.

"Oh, my darling boy, do make yourself at home!" the senator shouted back.

As Spinoza sat drinking his hearty glass of merlot, he could hear the faint sounds coming from the shower.

"If you'd like come back in an hour to make sure the Senator has a quick rinse and a rubdown," Buella said, "it would probably be quite fitting."

Realizing he was just another deli number on the Senator's salami run, he nervously replied, "I'll just come back, Captain."

* * *

Held captive by the pink mob and brought into the Peacock Room adjacent to the Admiral's Cove, Lars was completely horrified to find out that they had alerted the wild party, bragging that they invited the *Funny Girl*'s son to the bash. An Indian Chief, rallying the crowd to raise Lars, Dewey, and D-Key up in the air on three white director's chairs, carried the guys in, singing back-to-back medleys of Babs's greatest hits under the Bahamian moon.

Davio, piping aboard the Peacock Room, led down the teal green gangplank into the sea of karaoke singers. Gazing at the jivers high in the air, he moved toward them and declared, "Oh, look at you little prom queens! I never thought I'd live to see this day!"

Leaping off of the chair, twisting his ankle, Lars hobbled over to Davio and shouted, "That was quick!"

"I have to go back in an hour," Davio nervously answered.

"Are you fucking kidding me? I'm gonna have a nervous breakdown! And so is Dewey!" Lars screamed.

Dewey could only laugh off the grueling twenty minutes of the Streisand sing-along of insanity, surrounded by pitchers of caipirinhas, mojitos, and the best cold pearl sake D-Key had ever tasted. Though being warned by Lars and Dewey that perhaps it was spiked, they tried to make the best of it until a gigantic ivory tray emerged from the kitchen. Splayed out on its surface was the blond waiter from the Half King, rainbow rolls of sushi completely covering his scrawny physique. Neutralizing Dewey's uneasiness, the construction worker quickly grabbed the large Maki roll covering Hai Karate's privates and stuffed it into Dewey's already agape mouth, wide open in horror, as he spotted the most unholy of coincidences: Jeffrey "Jet Set" Oaks and Billy Sparrow, masquerading as Westminster Abbey Beefeaters. Sandwiched between them, garbed in a mesmerizing turquoise laced, finely beaded dress, complete with a full plumage of peacock feathers from her Elizabethan collar, appeared Dewey's mother—Carol Yates.

Squinting her eyes, Carol surveyed the scene. Knowing her son well, she broke out in a rapturous smile at the sight of her son's struggling soul. Finally after all these years of begging and pleading, she clasped her hands and violently shook her head up and down like she had won the lottery of the century, seeing her son in such a wonderfully compromising situation.

"Oh, Dewey, I'm more than pleased," Carol said, wiping her tears of joy dry with her Victorian velvet and lace kerchief. "I am going to back your beer project and make sure you have everything you need to be a grand success. There is so much planning to be done! We'll start with the best PR and we'll get Billy's firm to do all the marketing. We'll start with the Hamptons, Palm Beach, and Baden-Baden, and build the buzz about your beer from there. To the stars, my sweet son."

Dewey turned toward D-Key who knew ad nauseam his family plight about being left high and dry in his spirits venture. Dewey looked at D-Key with his "What should I do?" eyes.

"This is *Jeopardy!*" cried D-Key, and started to hum the familiar theme song out loud.

Dewey hopped off the chair, which was raised eight feet in the air, and ambled over beside his Victorian mum. She was perfectly seated on a sea foam green leather sofa in the shape of a puckered pair of lips. Dewey had to decide carefully how to handle the current chain of events. On one hand his family, with his Uncle Jimmy at the helm, was starving him out, forcing him little by little into a life of abject squalor. He was living in his mother's neighbor's breakwater English basement since being kicked out of his beach shack, infuriatingly with the summer rental season approaching. The Dewman had a total of $256, plus a Sears Die Hard battery worth a paltry $99 in store credit and a season ferry pass to Shelter Island—his complete nest egg at forty-six years young, not to mention his Carol B. on her last lung, wheezing and begging for a new exhaust system. On the other hand, could he ever keep up the alternative lifestyle ruse, for some unholy, godforsaken, inexplicable reason so welcomed by his society mum?

As he gazed at his mother's joyful tears rolling down her white, porcelain-painted jowls onto her ruffled silk collar, Dewey imagined himself next to Alex Trebek on the set of *Jeopardy*. Hearing D-Key in the background as he hummed the popular game-show tune, he deliberated as to what he should ultimately do about his mother's newfound support. He could hear Alex Trebek's voice in his head asking, *Who's nearly homeless and has his trust fund shackled in Houdini knots? And an alien beer business ready to ascend to the stars? Who is Dewey Yates?* He could hear the sound of the legendary host's distinct voice continue, *new category up on the board. And it's today's daily double for five thousand dollars. Could he still chase hot European tennis nannies around Southampton and at the same time convince his mother's spies around town that he was a member of the GLBT community?*

Carol Yates had spies in every corner from Manhattan to Montauk. An important figure among New York's elite society, she was inundated daily with phone calls about her son's misguided actions, "Your son, Dewey, was talking a bunch of alien reptile nonsense and knocked over an entire dessert tray at the club the other night." Or "Oh, Carol, Dewey's gallivanting around town with some god-awful garage painting of yours, claiming it to be a Van Gogh. It's so horrifying the way he was trying to convince two of Delores's sons to fund his X-ray testing of the piece. Obviously he's off his rocker, Carol."

Pulling out a folded check from her emerald-bejeweled Judith Leiber clutch, Carol broke out into another wave of tears and handed the check to Dewey. "Dewey, I have been waiting for this moment for thirty years. I just want you to be successful. You clearly had no hope of making it before. And now you have a real opportunity through this community to make something of yourself! You're just so handsome, Dewey."

"A fairy-tale ending," D-Key blurted. "How adorable!"

* * *

Lars, D-Key, Dewey, and the Senator's dear, dear, old friend Carol Yates accompanied Davio in the Senator's quarters. The group sat around drinking caipirinhas, served by Buella and her second mate, a red-haired, six-foot-three, big-breasted Korean beauty. Davio saw the shadowy figure of Senator X through the sliding glass door that led out to a starboard side balcony of the captain's perch as he began to explain the current state of our great nation while Carol attempted to push for answers for Lars' troubled girlfriend.

"Carol, what an unexpected pleasure. I haven't seen you since we had lunch with Ted Kennedy at the Everglades Club, must have been twelve years ago, going on this Easter," the Senator recounted.

"You're so right, Senator. You've got the memory of a stock boy," Carol replied.

"Oh, Carol, flattery will get you everywhere with me!" the Senator exclaimed.

"My son tells me there's some J. Edgar Hoover stuff going on, some witch hunting in connection with the innocent friend of my sweet boy, Dewey—a girl named Lulu," said Carol.

"I know all about it, Carol," the Senator interrupted. "And because you people don't have the clearance for it, I can't disclose everything there is to know. But since I'm the Senator representing the great state of discretion, I can tell you, Carol. It's about alien reptile technology concerning a big ol' cold fusion air car. It can run a million miles on a few sucks of wind, and I, Carol, know all about that."

"Adorable!" D-Key screamed.

"Now mother, what do you have to say about that?" Dewey asked.
"Oh, Dewey, pay attention," Carol replied.

"And your little Lulu, bless her sweet innocent heart, got caught up at the wrong end of the PR stick," the Senator explained. "She inadvertently passed along some information and got involved with a double-agent named Theo Bizirko—or something like that. And actually, cute little Davio here is gonna see to it that it all will work out in the wash. Davio will make a few phone calls tomorrow to Washington from the port side of my bed. Just for you Carol, I'm gonna move it up on my plate."

"So, let me get this straight. The misinformation and the market drop was to cover up sabotaging the cold fusion car, and the transportation companies and highway lobbyists stand to lose trillions if the car gets into production," Lars said.

"And would kill the electric car and solar car, I guess," said Dewey.

"There goes the bumper car!" D-Key exclaimed. "That's adorable!" Carol screamed.

"So Senator, until the elite group that controls all of our society—starting with our banking system—until that mindset is changed into some gluten-free thinking, our citizens are slaves to the stifled technology that could free us," Dewey proudly declared, as his mother, Carol, beamed at Dewey's adept and concise analysis of our troubled society.

"Exactly, my boy, I couldn't have said it better myself," the confessed. "That's why I'm sucking cock in the congressional coat room, everyday—to make a difference for the mobocracy." The silver sage light of the full Bahamian moon behind the group obstructed the Senator's face as he spoke.

"Absolutely adorable, Senator," D-Key said.

"We are on the verge of a global transformation. All we need is the right major crisis and the nations will accept the New World Order," the Senator continued.

"Gripping the world's economy, sinking it into a deep depression," Davio chimed in.

"And the big blackout where many become slaves to the few," Dewey added.

"I'm afraid that's all correct," the Senator replied. "Very astute of you, Dewey. You know, Carol, when he and his roommate from Choate were chosen for the Montauk Project, he was just a boy. I had no idea he would turn into such an agile warrior, ready to battle those big ol' reptiles in the time-transport saucer."

Dewey turned toward his mother, vindicated finally after thirty years of hell-riding ridicule. He broke into a wiser-than-thou, shit-eating grin and whispered in his mum's ear, "Mother, sorry to inform you, but I will never ever be what you want me to be," and handed her the crumpled-up check.

* * *

The redemption brothers, Tweedledee and Tweedle-Not-So-Smart marched Lars down a long hallway. After about fifty yards, they passed him off to a guard station, telling him to wait there until he could be taken to Lulu. She was awaiting his arrival in the hair salon, where the warden had promised an unfiltered and unfettered clandestine conjugal visit. The word on this came from high above and certainly was pushed to the front burner after Lulu gave such an outstanding interview for FOX, creating a friendlier atmosphere for the warden's important work.

Lulu was dressed in a neon-tangerine jumper, her hair pulled back neatly into a bun. She came through an electric locked gate, and a glass divider and locked eyes with Lars. It had been so long since they had seen each other, since they held hands, kissed, and made love.

This was the day she had been waiting for. The stacks of love letters and poems that they had written to one another over the past couple months were stuffed inside Lulu's front pocket.

Immediately seeing Lulu, Lars, misty-eyed, double-tapped his index finger to his heart and pointed at Lulu as she was cleared through the double-locked, armored bulletproof glass doors. And she replied with the same motion, which was their secret way of saying *I love you*. There was so much to say and not enough time to say it. He wasn't sure if he should grab her and throw her down right there at the guard station and make passionate love to her or be the concerned boyfriend and tell her everything he had learned from the Senator and find out how hellish her life had been for the past four months, and more importantly when he was going to be able to get her out of there. He tried to consider Lulu's feelings and what she would like to do in the precious two hours that they had with one another. Lars was still awaiting the holy call from the Senator to absolve Lulu from any wrongdoing. But as red tape would have it, the process was in a bit of a holding pattern until the Senator could free himself up to make the call to his old war room buddy, the federal circuit court judge who would then in turn issue and stamp the paperwork and send it to the warden at the good ol' detention center.

Zeela and Ingrid turned the makeshift salon into a hundred-dollar honeymoon suite, complete with cot and clean towels, courtesy of the Grey Bar Hotel. They transformed the small, steel-paneled room into a tantric temple, hoping to make Lulu feel as comfortable as possible for their long-overdue visit. Remembering a few of Lulu's poems and letters, Lars opted for the kind shoulder and some unfettered, tantric sex.

Having a considerable amount of time on her hands, Lulu expanded her yoga understanding and read several of the important literary works and criticisms on the tantric way of life to sublimate her sexual desires for Lars while locked inside the Grey Bar. She penned some of their heightened sexual proclivities and published them, so in her absence Lars could relive their sexcapades in the widely read online anonymous sex diaries column for *New York Magazine*.

Restaurant Rating Fetish
Former PR Exec, 29, Straight, NYC

Day One

10:00 a.m. A lazy Saturday morning . . . My boyfriend, quite the gourmand, languishes in bed dreaming of dancing Spanish omelets gliding across the cool, linen bedsheets that cascade softly against my naked body. To say that the two of us have an all-consuming misanthropic, devastatingly naughty food fetish would be a vain attempt to mask a deep, penetrating desire for us to maintain our lovemaking in close proximity to anything related to gastronomy. Simply put, we are food freaks. We live in Manhattan by choice, because of the number of jaw-dropping, world-class eateries within steps of every corner of the naked city. We work tirelessly to afford these bistros, which are open to anyone who can pay the price tag, and like so many of us, work a seventy-plus-hour workweek to afford the heightened pleasure of our haughty dining experiences. Manhattan offers the ultimate array of fine eateries and gastro markets, and by design, we have melded our penchant for public displays of affection with our desire for our ever-present, nagging, nihilistic food fetish, which playfully keeps our lovemaking constantly at a Zagat-rated level.

At home, I do most of the cooking, simply because my man likes to do most of the eating. And it truly gives me a perverse pleasure to watch him fawn over my fettuccini, become seduced over my sea bass, titillate himself over my tiramisu cupcakes and cinnamon lobster rolls. This balmy morning had all the makings of a raucous restaurant ratings romp. Our Saturdays meant mischief from morning to moonlight in our devout culinary quest for sexual thrill seeking. Equal opportunity sexplorers by nature, we had our eye on three spots for our exciting stay-cation. First up: dim sum on the Lower East Side.

11:00 a.m. Still exhausted from last night and walking a bit Betty Crocker-ed from my deliciously insane coconut rum cake, we roused slowly, as we did most weekends after a rough evening of edible lovemaking and night harvesting each other to no end.

That morning called for some hot and lusty dim sum and a terrific chance to support one of the city's latest underdogs: a B-rated noodle shop on the Lower East Side. It was one of our favorites because of the large, well maintained, jade green and gold, art deco designed bathroom with secure to-the-floor stall doors and well-stocked sanitizer.

11:10 a.m. After slurping and sucking down loving spoonfuls of organic carrots and freshly cut leafy spinach, I repeatedly fed my lover the effervescent, delicate broth of the coveted yin yang soup. As I tasted the house special, wise man's broth of fresh lily bulb and bean curd in a hearty chicken consommé, I removed my Sam Edelmans and playfully ran my pinky toe up the inside of his leg. And with that, I immediately arose from my seat and went to the WC on the lower level. Waiting just a few moments, my man left his sunglasses, morning paper, and painted sports jacket visible, so the waiter wouldn't think we'd dined and dashed.

11:20 a.m. A restaurant receiving a B rating, in our perverted paradigm, meant any sexual act beginning with the letter B was fair game with imagination as the only limiting factor. When my man arrived, he quietly shut the stall behind him, as I went straight for his Banana Republics.

3:00 p.m. We consider ourselves culinary crusaders of the highest order and take pride in living up to the indigenous cultures and customs of the native fare we dine on. We constantly bring this knowledge to our copious lovemaking. A yoga enthusiast of epic proportions, I recently converted my man into loving the body-bending exhilaration of the tantric way of life, so inextricably linked to the southern Bangladeshi fare that we so adore. My boyfriend did a better job at his first hot Bikram yoga experience than I would have expected. Closing my eyes, I imagined the class disappearing while I daydreamed of devouring his succulent Tandoori chicken in a wonderfully sweet coriander coconut chutney. Clearly, we are not well, and this fact drives my lover and me to awake happily every morning and fall asleep satiated every night, with our perverse secret tucked under a memory foam pillow.

3:10 p.m. We danced through the late-summer raindrops, stumbling upon a new haunt in West Chelsea where we live and operate our lust for one another. Moving fast, feeling exhilarated, we spotted a new Indian buffet. The familiar black-and-white sign plastered to the front window drew us in like moths to a flame: Grade Pending. We strolled past the buffet, taking tactical notice of the wonderful scents of organic basmati rice with saffron and coriander, chicken tikka masala, dosas, and the most wonderful samosas on this earth. Like erotic neurotics, our eyes held dominion over the endless spread. And to us it felt like twenty-five feet of spicy, sadistic, pleasure, thereby fueling our appetite and desire for each other even more.

Unabashedly, we relish a good buffet in the naked city, even more so than a free movie, concert, or museum. We love dining at all-you-can-eat Indian restaurants, so we never have to envy each other's last few bites. To be clear, we are competitive eaters, and don't willfully share our Desi secrets on the best ways to attack a Bangladeshian buffet to just anyone. This week, I will leave you with three simple tips:

1. Indulge in some strong Turkish coffee precisely two hours before eating.
2. Avoid all dishes with heavy sauce.
3. Stay away from the beguiling goat desserts.

Despite a few bits of Bollywood buzz, before visiting Club Fed, ashamedly Lulu knew very little besides curries, samosas, yoga, and the transcendental transformation of the Hindi way of life. This became somewhat of a fascination during her time spent behind bars. She imagined she was going through a metamorphosis of her own from jailbird to egalitarian writer, offering a glimpse into the literati of the future, where a public that expects better—and deservedly so—gets it, as depicted in her autobiographical, semi-fictional book, *White Collar Slavery.*

* * *

The moment they saw each other in the jailhouse salon, they felt a magnetic, polar energy that needed lusty investigation. Lulu had a tantric between-the-sheets mentality for the scheduled two-hour rendezvous with Lars. Waiting for her man to arrive, there was only one thing on her mind, and it wasn't handholding. Lulu, so pent up with frustration, rage, jealously, and defeat was fearful, given the wistful opportunity. The poems that they exchanged to keep her sanity together were fresh in her mind.

The lights magically dimmed and a wall of electric candles flickered on, lining the mirrored wall and the front part of the small institutional room. The door quietly locked behind them, giving them their first completely private moment together in four months since her abduction and incarnation. Lars embraced Lulu, looking into her weary eyes that were now a bit brighter. As Lulu passionately kissed him, he could sense she was in for a bit of mischief; by the way she playfully bit his lower lip and unzipped her jumpsuit to reveal a neon-tangerine garter belt with matching bra.

"Don't ask me how I got La Perla in prison," Lulu joked.

"I don't imagine you traded any cigarettes for it," Lars mused on.

"No, I don't imagine," Lulu replied as she hushed his lips and kissed him passionately.

"You'll be outta here by night's end," Lars said, lifting her up, placing her gently on the salon chair, while she began unbuckling his brown leather belt, tossing it against the cold tiled floor, making a dominant swatting sound as his painted pants hit the ground with a rumbled thud, looking like a Chamberlin steel sculpture of sorts.

"How can you promise that?" Lulu questioned.

"I have the best people on it. Trust me," Lars admitted.

* * *

Back at the Senator's quarters, still aboard the *Pink Flamingo*, D-Key, dressed head-to-toe in a Roman toga complete with a customary laurel wreath in his locks. D-Key was sprawled out like a young Puck plucking a soft melody on a shining chrome sitar on the starboard side of the Senator's cozy bed.

"My love can be bought in all the right places, in all the right places, for you. My love can be bought for the right price, it's true," D-Key mused, singing in his best Shakespearean tongue.

"You're so damn charming," the Senator said as both Buella and her stunning first mate served another round of drinks to the group.

"Oh, Senator, go on," D-Key sang as he stared down at his left hand at the disco ball–sized, twelve-carat diamond engagement ring that flecked and danced rainbow-colored prisms across the walls.

"Senator, tell me more about the soy conspiracy," D-Key said. "My girlfriend and I are so fascinated by that."

"Don't you just love that one?" the Senator asked. "That's my scrumptious all-time favorite."

"The Chinese are castrating our men into women by feeding us soy, which turns men into boys," Dewey chimed in, sitting uneasily on a velvet ottoman, while Lars gazed out the small round window, thinking of Lulu.

"Oh, aren't those Chinese brilliant?" the Senator continued as he sipped on his caramel-infused appletini, licking the sticky caramel from the corner of his lip.

"Adorable!" D-Key sang, as he continued playing the sitar through the dancing lights of dawn.

Lars, turning from the porthole, politely prompted the Senator, "Now, about that phone call, sir?"

* * *

"Seriously, I'm gonna get you out of here," Lars continued. "And what I have to tell you is gonna blow your mind."

"Try me," Lulu replied.

Lars divulged every salacious detail of the Senator's involvement, stopping just shy of their two-hour visit.

"The irony, that I'm a pawn of the New World Order, if that's what you're telling me, is beyond any bit of paranoia that I could have ever imagined," Lulu said.

"The endeavor to understand is the first and only basis of virtue," Lars continued.

Their tangled, naked bodies turned toward the flaming wall lined with electric candles. They softly held each other in their sweat-glistened arms.

Lulu whispered as she delicately French kissed his ear. "I was gonna sell my eggs this weekend to raise the bail money to get the hell out of here, since they suspended the profits of my book while I'm still detained."

"You're not doing that. I told you, we have the Senator on our side. He should be calling the warden any minute now," Lars said. "You have to have a little faith sometimes."

Two Months Later

With a true glimpse into the final frontier, Lars, clad in a debonair, black, double-breasted space suit, Lulu in bride white were both completely star struck as they gazed out the porthole of the spaceship at the awe-inspiring views of planet Earth and the glorious man-eating moon.

Using his settlement money from the *Enquirer* lawsuit, Lars sprung for six first-class tickets into space, and was now living out his childhood fantasy of suborbital travel, hand in hand with his love Lulu. As the tiny spaceship hurled toward the stars, the rocket blasted away from its earthy bonds into weightlessness, as the small shuttlecraft finally reached its destination altitude of 330,000 feet above the Earth.

Carol Yates, fetchingly dressed in a sherbet-green, sequined Chanel space suit, turned toward the senator, sporting a rather smart Aztec-orange, Italian-leather flight suit. He began furrowing his broad brow at the sight of D-Key and Belinda doing zero gravity yoga, perversely somersaulting into one another's downward dog, zigzagging like wayward, horny salmon through the tiny tourist space craft, thinking this may upstage his role as intergalactic envoy and space minister for Lulu and Lars' aeronautical nuptials.

Kingsley, donning a mini Alexander McQueen purple velvet Martian suit, sounded off with a succession of barks. As he played ring bearer to two classic platinum Chopard wedding couplets, spinning around in cute concentric circles of antigravity, chasing the shimmering bands tied to the end of his fluffy-tailed antennae.

"By the power vested in me, I sanction this suborbital space union, taking this young, entirely handsome couple in holy matrimony," the Senator said as he looked down at Kingsley for the rings signifying the couple's eternal commitment.

"Do you, Lars Henri Kasden, take Lulu Grace Norris to be yours, from now until the end of time?" the senator continued.

As Kingsley snapped his tail and released the couplets, the bands floated off through the hull of the spaceship and magically landed on the ring fingers of the couple's left hands. They fell into each other's gaze at the kismet moment, exchanging their vows and a tender kiss, amidst the stars.

"I have to admit, I never thought I'd see this day, Senator," D-Key said.

"You mean, loving me so hard?" asked the senator as he glanced down at the devilishly large diamond on D-Key's left hand.

"No, my buddy getting married," D-Key admitted.

"I brought freeze-dried Eskimo coconut-and-custard space cakes all the way from Earth," Belinda said in her clinched-jaw Connecticut accent, looking like a kooky cosmonaut floating through the ship doing the weightless breaststroke.

"And they're quite freaky-deaky, I might add," D-Key chimed in, as Lars kept D-Key at a safe arm's length from kissing Lulu and the Senator at the same time while going into a zero gravity swan dive.

"They're organic and gluten free. I made them from scratch. What did you get the couple?" Belinda cheekily cracked, asking Carol, her voice now higher than the 330,000 feet altitude of the craft.

"Oh, Belinda, you're so cute," Carol replied. "My big ol' gift should be waiting for them in the Presidential Suite. Oh Belinda darling, you're such a nosey, little bitch."

Looking through the top porthole, past Neptune and Uranus, Davio, strapped in beside the rugged space pilot, turned back to Lulu, winking through the cabin door to find her pointing to a fireball, hurling its way through space. They were dumbfounded to find, piloting the whirling titanium saucer was none other than Dewey

Arnold Yates, who later that year would become the talk of the tony town, saving the galaxy from the reptilian onslaught, that was scheduled to decimate our fragile universe.

Carol would get the outwardly successful son she always wanted, but clearly under his wild, paranormal terms. Her son, that once made her wince, was now the world's savior. And she was growing to accept the fact that he would never walk her walk.

Armed with a Tesla ray gun from the fifties, recovered from a crypt containing the alien saucer and cadaver from Area 51 deep inside the New Mexican desert, Dewey, in Slim Pickens, *Dr. Strangelove* style, leapt off the front lip of the saucer and landed smack dab onto his Stanley Kubricks atop the ray gun, his fall miraculously redirecting the laser beam well past planet Earth.

* * *

According to her calendar, the lecherous queen of crude was scheduled to arrive at her three o'clock dental appointment. One of the last tasks during Lulu's final weeks at the firm was to have the dental diva perform a DDS "DNR" on one Lizette Hansen.

As luck would have it, Carol Yates was introduced to Katrinka Tzeka while posing together for a photo at a fundraising event a few years back. Carol managed to convince her friend, the good dentist not to leave town for the weekend, but to instead do her a favor and deal with the eighteen-carat manic-depressive, Lizette Hansen. Walking into Tzeka's New York practice on the five hundred block of Park Avenue, Lizette was absolutely beside herself, the way Lulu had been neutered in the news and as far as she knew was rotting away in prison, waiting to be transferred to the maximum security section at Rikers—that was, if she could keep the SEC investigators at bay for a bit longer. Lizette, cock-sure she would emerge unscathed from this scandal, tickled her to no end as she wolfed down her last package of Nabisco one hundred calorie treats, salivating at the swanky address she had fallen into.

White Collar Slavery

Strutting into the grand marble office, reeking of her signature scent of Children's Benadryl and an overbearing Chanel No. 0. Lizette, a hot mess of misguided emotion, was still pathetically holding onto her glory days with St. Stephen, still wearing the ill-faded Burberry trench coat. Lizette removed the tattered coat and checked her lipstick in her tiny travel mirror that she pulled from her embarrassingly worn Lana Marks bag.

Despite canceling, skipping, and rescheduling too many appointments in her horrific lifetime, for some reason, Lizette had the maxillary misfortune of keeping the wrong periodontal appointment.

As Tzeka's hygienist warmed up the Dremel, Lizette, completely out of character, felt absolutely relaxed, clueless as to what was about to happen. Tzeka, fawning over her handbag and Pucci blouse, toyed with her prey, while she secretly prepared for her patients' permanent new look.

The sounds of Sinatra played, "Fly me to the moon, let me play above the stars, let me see what spring is like on Jupiter and Mars. In other words . . ."

And as Ol' Blue Eyes completed the iconic verse, Tzeka induced just the right amount of nitrous oxide into Lizette's noxious pie hole, knocking her out cold, as she skillfully went to work, in a medieval fashion. Treacherous Tzeka with her new industrial Dremel and vice grips, courtesy of Carol Yates went full-tilt on Lizette's well-worn crowns, moldings, bridges, and what few metal bits she had neglected to porcelain fill over the last few decades, rendering Lizette a toothless gimp in twelve short minutes.

When Screwzette awoke fifteen minutes later, comfortably numb, she sat relaxed, rousing herself by admiring her blurry reflection in the stainless spittoon. She began Novocain mumbling for the hygienist, who was nowhere to be found. Reaching over, Scewzette pulled out her travel mirror from her handbag. As she glanced down and saw her reflection, she let out a blood-curdling scream. Drop dead mortified at the very permanent sight beside her BOTOX-encrusted trout pout—an empty mouth of bleeding gums. She realized she was now absolutely damaged goods of epic proportions, like a toothless Oscar Fish, the ones that dwell on the bottom—dwellers beneath the rocks, that stick to the sides of the deep blue lakes and oceans. She cried and screamed Lulu's name at the top of her lungs to no avail, for the dentist had already skipped town. The only person left was her six-foot-five, Albanian cage-match champion fighter, brother-in-law to empty out the complaint box and pick up the broken shards strewn across the white tiled floor, smelling of charred enamel and smoldering steel bits.

* * *

In the Presidential Suite of the spaceport, with the spacecraft parked safely in the hangar, the reception for the newlyweds was in full swing, hosted by the senator, Carol Yates, Lulu, and Lars' families. Lars and Lulu ran off to their room behind the packed house of more than two hundred well-wishers of friends, neighbors, and family, all of whom had made the trek to the New Mexican desert for the couple's romantic, momentous occasion in space.

Lars and Lulu, dressed in matching leather flight jackets, checked their iPads and flopped onto the fluffy king-sized bed while the crowd cheered for a speech from the other side of locked doors. Giggling hysterically, kissing and fondling each other, they logged onto Instagram to find a photo from the dental diva, courtesy of the senator and Carol Yates. The photo clearly illustrated Screwzette's bloody, stumped gums spewing tiny cakes of clotted blood into the dental drain, reflected in the chromium covered sink stopper.

While outside, Zeela, dressed in a full-length teal chiffon halter dress, nudged up to the senator and said, "That was mighty fine of you, senator, to spring me and Ingrid, for my *pomme sha's* wedding reception. I brought a nice oxtail curry for everyone to share."

Belinda, hearing just the mention of food, chimed in, with Carol at her side. Both were sipping their flutes of Veuve Clicquot. "What kind of goat was that? Is that organically fed South African goat? Because that's the only kind D-Key and I indulge in."

"No worry, child," Zeela replied.

Looking over to D-Key, Belinda smiled with her chameleon crazy eye. D-Key, like a drunken Pepé Le Pew was dribbling on about their corner-cabin sexcapades at 330,000 feet to the elderly section of the crowd. Stinking of merlot, sounding like a French mad cosmonaut on the loose, D-Key described every lurid detail of his voyage, like a cartoon Catskills comedian trying to kiss every old lady in the house.

Carol turned toward the senator, standing beside Davio, who was staring out the huge spaceport palladium window toward the stars.

"You know Carol, one day, in the not so distant future, I hope to end my senatorial tenure with the crowning achievement of my political career in a whole new uninhabited planet," the senator smiled as he explained. "Oh Carol, just think of it—the decorating, the street naming, the space hotels . . . And it will be weightless Studio 54 for all eternity. Dancing every minute of the day. It's gonna be just marvelous!"

"We could even have a gay president to run the planet. There'd be no wars and lots of orchids," Carol added in.

"Now, Carol darling, what makes you think there hasn't already been a gay president?" queried the senator.

"I knew of course J. Edgar was a li'l light in the penny loafers, but he wasn't a president," Carol replied.

"And have you ever seen an old photograph of Martha Washington, with her wooden teeth? That's the ugliest beard that ever walked the earth," said the Senator.

Lars and Lulu, holding Kingsley, locked arm and arm, exited the double set of futuristic sliding glass doors that opened into the rest of the gigantic space-age suite and rejoined the rest of the festivities.

Filching the microphone from his best man, Lars addressed the crowd, as he gazed adoringly into Lulu's almond shaped, dreamy, green eyes.

Holding her hand and dropping to one knee, he declared, "My life has been full of violent contradictions, but marrying you in the stars, Lulu, will never be one of them, to quote the great Frank Sinatra. I love you so much, Lulu! A toast—to you, our families, our friends, and that delightful photo!"

As Lars rose to his feet, he began dancing to the discordant, drunken sounds of D-Key's screeching voice, singing a bastardized version: "Fly me to the moon, let me skid among the cars; let me see what life is like on Brutus and behind bars. In other star wars, please be true, 'cause baby, I need you."

Lars shook his head, dancing slowly with Lulu and Kingsley held tightly in his confident arms. Calmly whispering into her ear, "The more clearly you understand yourself and your emotions, the more you become a lover of what is. My whole life, all I have wanted was to become a great artist, now I realize all that's really important is to be with you and Kingsley."

The End

CPSIA information can be obtained
at www.ICGtesting.com
Printed in the USA
LVHW110158070521
686764LV00004B/56